FLAMES OF D

Desire, Oklahoma 10

Leah Brooke

MENAGE EVERLASTING

Siren Publishing, Inc.
www.SirenPublishing.com

A SIREN PUBLISHING BOOK
IMPRINT: Ménage Everlasting

FLAMES OF DESIRE
Copyright © 2016 by Leah Brooke

ISBN: 978-1-63259-868-4

First Printing: December 2016

Cover design by Les Byerley
All art and logo copyright © 2016 by Siren Publishing, Inc.

Printed in the U.S.A.

PUBLISHER
Siren Publishing, Inc.
www.SirenPublishing.com

FLAMES OF DEISRE

Desire, Oklahoma 10

LEAH BROOKE
Copyright © 2016

Chapter One

Courtney Sheldon wiped away tears that blurred the words of the letter she'd already memorized.

Her aunt's lawyer had given the letter to her only hours earlier, right after the funeral, but as she read it again, she couldn't stop crying.

My dearest Courtney,

I've been so blessed to have you with me all these years.

When your uncle was killed in Vietnam, I knew I would never marry again and knew I would never have children of my own. When my baby sister gave birth to you, it was as if I'd finally have the chance to have a child of my own.

I've loved you from the moment you were born.

When your mother left you with me, it was my pleasure to take you into my home and raise you as my own. Nothing in my life has ever given me so much pleasure.

Except for your uncle, who I've missed each and every day of my life.

You never knew this, but the house your parents lived in in Desire was our home. Mine and your Uncle Phil's. I couldn't live there after he was killed, but I couldn't bear to sell it.

I spent the happiest years of my life in that house, and now I'm leaving it to you.

I've had several offers for it, probably because oil has been found on all the surrounding properties, but I've been saving it for you.

The offers are included with this letter for you to see.

But you can't sell it. Not yet.

I want you, my darling niece, to have a chance at the kind of love that I had, so I'm asking you to live in the house for one year.

If, after that time, you want to sell it, you have my blessing.

As you can see by the offers, you'd be a financially secure woman then, and wouldn't have to worry about your future, but the love I hope you'll find there is worth more than all the money in the world.

I want nothing more than for you to be happy.

If you're reading this, I'm with your Uncle Phil. Please don't cry for me. I'm where I want to be. I've missed him so much.

I want you to find the love your mother threw away on your father.

Trust your heart, Courtney.

You've been such a joy to me—such a blessing.

I want you to find the love that I did. No one deserves it more than you do.

Love,

Aunt Sally

Looking up, she sniffed and sat back in the heavy leather chair. "I can't believe I didn't know about this. I can't believe she really wants me to go live there again."

From behind his large desk, Fred Franks, the elderly man who'd been her aunt's friend and attorney for years, smiled kindly. "Believe it. Your aunt was adamant about keeping the house for you, no matter how many offers she got—and she's gotten quite a few substantial offers. They're in the other envelope. The one on top is the most recent, and most substantial."

Her hands shook as she opened the envelope on top and scanned the single sheet of paper inside. Looking up at Mr. Franks again, she frowned, wondering if she'd read it right. "This is a lot of money for an old house."

Mr. Franks inclined his head. "It is, but not for that town. It's become a very desirable place to live, and the men who made that offer live right next door. They really want that property and can afford to pay for it. The residents become very attached to the town." Sitting forward, he smiled. "That's why your aunt wanted to be buried there, next to your uncle. You saw the town this morning at the funeral." Sitting back again, he sighed. "From what I understand, it's a very unique place to live."

Frowning, Courtney folded the paper and slid it back into the envelope. "In what way is it unique? I'm afraid I don't understand the fascination with a small town in Oklahoma—a small town that we were kicked out of when I was just a child."

Mr. Franks sighed again. "I understand that there are certain kinds of relationships that seem to be prevalent there." Raising a hand when she would have asked more, he shook his head. "No. I don't know enough about the town to help you. I *do* know that your family wasn't kicked out of Desire—just your father. Your aunt talked about it often. She's been furious with your dad ever since."

Swallowing the bile that rose in her throat at the uncomfortable memories, Courtney fisted her hands on the envelopes in her lap. "The end result was the same. We had to leave our home."

Now, she'd lost her home again.

The attorney got to his feet. "Be that as it may, you'll have to go back there. Your aunt's house here in Blackwell will have to be sold to pay off her medical bills. There should be enough left for you to live on for a while." Perching himself on the corner of his desk, he leaned toward her. "Why don't you open the flower shop you've always wanted in Desire?"

Courtney shrugged. "It seems pointless when I'm only going to live there a year."

She couldn't believe that she'd have to spend the next year living in a town that held such bad memories for her. "I can't believe Aunt Sally would do this to me."

The kindly attorney sat forward, smiling gently. "Your aunt loved you, and if she did this, she had a very good reason. You have a week to pack up your things, and then the house has to go on the market. When it sells, I'll pay off the bills and send you the difference."

"I'll have to leave my friends."

Chuckling, he went back to his chair and sat. "With your personality, you'll make new ones."

"I'll have to leave my job."

"Open your own flower shop. It'll keep you busy while you pass the time."

"I suppose I have no choice. I've saved my money for years and wanted to buy the shop I worked in but I won't buy it if I won't be here to run it."

"It's what your aunt wanted." The attorney shrugged. "Of course, you could always ignore her, but then you wouldn't get the money from the house here or the money from the house in Desire. If you don't do what she asks, you're on your own—and your father gets the money from the house in Desire."

Courtney shot to her feet. "Over my dead body."

* * * *

You're on your own.

As Courtney pulled into the driveway of the house that would be her home for the next year, the attorney's words kept playing over and over in her head.

For the first time in her life, she was truly alone, finding herself forced to live in a town she both loved and hated.

Blowing out a breath, she looked around—grimacing at the overgrown weeds.

The house looked worn and old and showed the years of neglect.

Thankful that she'd already had the electricity turned on, she pulled her key from the ignition and turned her key ring to the key Mr. Franks had given her only a week earlier, staring down at it for several long seconds before opening the car door.

It was late afternoon, and she had a lot of things to do before she could go to bed.

She was so damned tired.

The last week had been a flurry of activity. She'd had to pack up her belongings and donate her aunt's clothing.

She'd quit her job and said good-bye to her friends, promising to keep in touch with them.

Her mother had shown up just long enough for the funeral, leaving again right afterward with her husband.

Her mother's words came back to her. "Don't look for love in Desire, Courtney. There's nothing for you but heartache and loneliness here."

She had the feeling that she'd have a lot of lonely days ahead of her.

It was only a year, though, and then she could move on and do whatever she wanted to do.

* * * *

Sitting on the front porch of the house he'd grown up in, Lawton Tyler grinned at his sister-in-law. "You know, you drive my brother up the wall, don't you?"

Sipping her iced tea, Hope flashed an impish smile and leaned back in her seat again. "Of course. That's my job. Your brother was getting a little too stuffy. He needed me to shake him out of that."

Law narrowed his eyes, suspicious at the look in hers. "No. Don't look at me that way. I don't want any part of your matchmaking schemes."

Hope's look of feigned innocence didn't fool him for a second.

His sister-in-law was always up to something, and only his brother could keep her in line. Since marrying Ace, she'd made it abundantly clear that she adored both him and his brother, Zach, and considered them her brothers.

Because of that, she'd decided that meddling in their lives was her due.

Recently, she'd come to the conclusion that they'd been single long enough and had made up her mind to find the perfect woman for them.

Shrugging, she set her glass aside. "You and Zach are getting a little too stuffy yourselves. You need a woman."

Zach came through the front door with a beer in each hand. "Uh-oh. You got her started again."

Law accepted the cold beer from his brother with a sigh. "I didn't get her started. She turns every conversation into us needing to find a woman."

"Why do all women think every single man needs a woman?" Pausing to kiss Hope's hair, he lowered himself into the seat next to her. "Law and I have a very active social life."

"Bullshit." Hope leaned back and smiled at each of them. "You both go to benefits and fancy parties, each of you with a beautiful woman on your arm that means nothing to you."

Law glanced at Zach, the truth of her words depressing him. Forcing a smile, he took a sip of his beer before answering. "How do you know they mean nothing to us?"

"Because you don't ever bring them to Desire, and you don't ever share them."

Shaking his head, Law gave her what he hoped was a convincing smile. "Zach and I are very happy with our lives in Dallas."

Hope sat back and swung her foot, eyeing his steadily. "Once again—bullshit. If you're so happy with your life there, why are you so excited about building a house here? You come to Desire every chance you get. You go to the club every time you come here. You can't wait to get there, and the next day, you're both as grumpy as bears because you haven't found what you're looking for."

Law inwardly winced, not realizing that his sister-in-law saw so much. "Lack of sleep." He didn't want her to know that the nights they'd spent at the club, they spent most of their time playing cards and talking to their friends.

He and Zach had enjoyed the pleasures to be found in dominating women for years—the excitement of seeing how far they could go. How much pleasure they could give.

The excitement, though, had begun to wane a long time ago, when they both realized that sex with a stranger wasn't enough.

He wanted what the other men in Desire had.

He wanted a woman to fill the emptiness inside him.

He wanted a woman to love—and one who loved him—and Zach.

"And a pain-in-the-neck waking us up to ask us questions about the club before we've had our coffee." Zach touched his cold bottle to her foot, smiling when she yelped. "You try to get information out of us before we're awake enough to censor ourselves. Ace needs to spank your bottom more often."

To Law's amusement, Hope sighed, a small devious smile playing at her lips.

"True. True. He's been too busy with the new deputies to pay much attention to me." Lifting her drink again, she grinned, flashing her dimples. "I'm giving him a week, and then I'm going to ambush him."

Frowning, Law sat forward, amused at Hope's daring. "Ambush him *how?*"

The change in Ace convinced Law that marrying Hope had been the smartest thing his too-serious brother had ever done.

Hope was a handful, and she kept his brother on his toes.

Hope forced Ace to play and brought out the Dominant in Ace that his older brother had fought to hide for most of his adult life.

She made Ace happier than Law had ever seen him, and for that, Law would be eternally grateful.

He and Zach adored her.

Giggling, Hope rose to her feet. "I can't tell you, or you'll tell him." Picking up her empty glass, she pursed her lips. "Tell you what, I'll tell you just enough that, when you rat me out, it'll keep your brother on his toes." Leaning over him, she smiled. "I'm going to do something that he won't be able to ignore."

Zach threw his head back and laughed. "You would tempt the devil himself. You know that Ace won't put up with being manipulated."

"Yep." Hope winked at him. "That's what I'm counting on." Waving her hand in the air, she shot a warning look at both of them. "But that's not what we were talking about. We were talking about the fact that neither one of you shares women in Dallas, and you keep coming home because that's what you really want."

"We live in Dallas, honey. That's our home." Zach finished his beer and stood. "We just come here to visit you." Running a hand over her hair, he started past her, but Hope stepped in front of him.

"Don't give me that. You come here because you know neither one of you will be happy unless you share a woman, and ménage relationships aren't just accepted here. They're welcome. You want the woman you fall in love with to feel comfortable. That's why you're building a house here, and why you always leave after just a few days."

Law stiffened, understanding how Hope kept his brother sharp. He and Zach had decided they wouldn't be happy unless they shared a woman years ago, but once Hope started matchmaking, they'd done everything they could think of to stop her.

Hope, though, was a strong-willed woman, a woman gutsy enough to go after Ace with the kind of determination and single-mindedness that scared the hell out of them.

They'd tried to convince her that they'd decided to build a house in Desire to give her and Ace privacy, and that they were very happy in Dallas, but his sister-in-law wasn't buying it.

Glancing at Zach, Law sighed. "We run an oil company, Hope. We're—"

"Don't tell me you're too busy." Smiling, she moved closer and dropped onto his lap, a habit she'd recently developed that delighted him. "This is your home. Stop trying to pretend that you're happier in Dallas. You belong here." She waved a hand when Zach started to speak. "I know you have a business to run in Dallas, but you can do a lot of business from here. You're building a house here because you want to share a woman of your own, and it's obvious that you're not looking hard enough. If I help you—"

"No!" Law and Zach shook her heads simultaneously.

Zach laughed and rose to his feet. "We know what we want, honey. We'll know the right woman when we meet her. Please. I'm begging you. Don't try to find a wife for us."

Hope jumped from Law's lap and plopped back into her seat, pouting adorably. "No one around here ever lets me have any fun."

Straightening, she turned, frowning as she got to her feet. "Now, who could that be? Someone just pulled into the driveway of the house next door—the house you're trying to buy."

Law surged to his feet, stunned to see a woman get out of an older model compact car, carrying a suitcase.

Zach came up behind him. "Do you think that's the owner?"

Gripping the railing, Law leaned forward, trying to get a better look at her, but she turned her head away from him. He got a glimpse of long, dark chestnut hair, gleaming with red highlights, hair that looked like silk.

She had a body made for sin—curves that his hands itched to explore.

She moved as if resigned—defeated. Exhausted.

Intrigued and irrationally irritated, he frowned and leaned over the railing to watch her, but she disappeared into the house before he got a chance to really see her.

Hope sighed. "Either she's the owner or the owner's renting it to her."

Turning, he glanced at his sister-in-law, his eyes narrowing. "The owner's an elderly lady. She wouldn't even talk to us on the phone. She insisted on letters."

Zach straightened, crossing his arms over his chest, his eyes narrowed as he studied Hope's features. "Is this one of your ploys?"

Hope giggled. "I guess the only way you're going to find out is to go meet her."

Law had already started from the porch, determined to do just that.

Chapter Two

Courtney dropped her suitcase just inside the door, blinking to adjust to the house's dark interior. With a sigh, she dropped her purse on the floor next to her suitcase and looked around, frowning when she saw the heavy, dark drapes covering the front window.

Leaving the door open for light and air, she moved around the sheet-covered chair, cursing when she hit her leg on the corner of the coffee table. "Damn it."

Limping, she made her way to the window and tugged the edges of the heavy drapes apart, blinking against the late afternoon sun. Deciding that the first thing on her list was to get new curtains, she yanked the sheets off everything in sight, grimacing at the state of the furniture.

She knew for a fact that it was as lumpy as it looked.

Memories assailed her, making her stomach knot, and she knew that if she had to spend the next year here she would have to make a few changes.

She couldn't spend a lot of money, but she could paint and add a few touches that would make the house cheerier.

She hoped.

Taking a deep breath, she moved closer to the sofa, remembering all the times she'd waken in the morning to find her mother sleeping there.

Wrinkling her nose at the stuffy air, she turned back to open the windows, her breath catching when she looked out and saw two men approaching the house from the left.

Alarmed, she hurried toward the open door, cursing when she hit her shin in the corner of the coffee table again.

"Damn it!"

Stumbling, she grabbed the arm of the chair, rushed to get to the door before they did, but then looked up in time to see that she was too late.

The two men came up the steps to the porch and straight into the house, both frowning as their gazes raked over her.

The one who came through the door first was slightly taller than the other, but both stood well over six feet tall.

He had his dark hair cut in a short style, and even in his jeans and T-shirt, he looked sophisticated and rich, the gold watch on his wrist probably worth more than the house they stood in.

Muscles bulged from his upper and lower arms, and his chest had to be one of the widest she'd ever seen. He looked *physical*, not the type of man who spent his days sitting idle.

The other man stood about an inch shorter but had an even bigger frame, his hair, which fell past his shoulders, giving him a roguish look.

The first man stopped when she took a step back, his frown deepening. "Are you all right?" He looked a little stunned and turned to glanced at the other man, sharing a look before both men turned back to her.

"I'm fine." Lifting her chin, she shifted her gaze, looking for something to use as a weapon. "What do you want?"

His lips twitched. "Well, there's a question. The answer's a little more complicated than it was when I started over here. Let's start with introductions. I'm Law Tyler, and this is my brother Zach. We live next door."

Lawton and Zachary Tyler. Tyler Oil. The men who'd made the highest offer.

Zach stepped forward, frowning. "You're scared of us. There's no need to be." His slow smile sent an exciting, but alarming, rush of heat through her. "This house has been vacant for years, and when we saw you pull up, we wondered who you were. Did you rent this house?"

Moving around the chair to put it between her and them, she eyed both of them warily. "It's none of your business. Please get out of my house."

Law's eyes narrowed. "*Your* house?" He took a step closer, forcing her to take another back. "The owner of this house is an elderly lady. Her name is—"

"Sally Jacobs." Lifting her chin again, Courtney forced a smile. "My aunt." Unsettled at the interest and suspicion in their eyes, she sighed, anxious for them to leave. "My mother's older sister, and the woman who raised me. She passed away recently and left the house to me. Now, if you don't mind, I'm tired, and I have a lot to do."

"I'm sorry for your loss." Zach shared another look with Law. "We've been trying to buy this house. We'll make you the same offer we made her."

"Thank you, but I haven't made any decisions yet. Please go. I have things to do."

Taking another step closer, Law smiled. "What's your name?"

"Courtney. Now, will you please leave?"

Law took another step closer, holding out a hand and frowning when she took another step back. "Only if you promise to give us a chance to talk you into selling this house to us."

Shaking her head, Courtney wrapped her arms around herself, irritated that she felt herself drawn to them. The kindness and concern in their eyes eased some of her fears, but she remained alert for any sign of change in their demeanors. "I couldn't sell this house to you if I wanted to—at least not now."

Zach arched a brow. "Would you like to explain that?"

"Not now." She took a step toward the door, hoping they would take the hint, but neither man moved. "I'm tired, and I have a lot to do. I just got here. Please leave."

Law reached out to touch her arm, his eyes sharp as they raked over her face. "Have dinner with us." His voice, low and seductive, sent a shiver through her—the knowledge of his effect on her glittering in his eyes.

"I don't think so. Thanks anyway."

Zach grinned, his smile like a jolt to her system. "You have to eat, and I didn't see any bags of groceries in the car. Why don't you let us take you to an early dinner and then show you around town?"

She had a lot to do before then, and would probably be too tired to cook, and only had the ingredients for peanut butter and jelly sandwiches for dinner. "Okay."

Law inclined his head, his eyes lighting up. "We'll pick you up at five." He glanced at Zach again. "We actually live in Dallas, but we're staying with my brother and his wife next door while we're in town visiting. We can help you get settled in as much as we can before we have to leave."

"That won't be necessary. I'd like to have some time alone." The concern in their eyes had her shifting restlessly, but she didn't want to walk farther into the room, afraid they would take it as an invitation to follow.

Their sheer size made the room feel too small, the interest and speculation in their eyes making it difficult to breathe.

"We'll talk about it over dinner." Law turned and started out, pausing at the doorway. "Our brother's the sheriff, and we'll eat here in town. You can trust us."

Zach watched her steadily, a gleam in his eyes that had her struggling not to squirm. "I'd better warn you, though, that I'm going to do everything I can to get to know you better."

"I appreciate the honesty, but I have no intention of getting close to anyone here."

Leaning closer, Zach ran his fingertips up her arm, sending ribbons of electricity straight to her nipples. "I'll bet I can change your mind about that."

Once they left, she closed the door behind him, making sure to lock it before she slid to the floor, her breathing ragged and her heart racing.

Law and Zach packed quite a punch.

She'd have to be careful. Judging by the offer they'd made, they wanted her house—or at least the property—pretty badly.

Reminding herself that their attention had to be based on their desire to buy her house, she sighed, trying to pretend to herself that she didn't feel disappointed. Used.

She'd sworn off men long ago and saw no reason to change her mind.

The two men who'd been the most important in her life—her father and the young man who'd taken her virginity—had both proven to be users and worthless.

With a sigh, she got to her feet again, her spinning head a reminder that she needed to eat soon.

She had a lot of work ahead of her and didn't want to waste time thinking about what it would be like to have a man in her life—especially one of them.

Rich, sophisticated, and far too good-looking—men who'd think more of themselves than the woman they were with.

Men like her father.

* * * *

Buttoning his shirt, Zach felt a presence and looked up to see his oldest brother, Ace—still wearing his sheriff's uniform—standing in the doorway. "Rough day?"

Ace shrugged, his gaze steady. Standing over six and a half feet tall, he was a big man who had a hard look about him that intimidated most people. "Not really. Very satisfying, in fact." A rare smiled curved his lips.

Zach raised a brow, surprised that his brother had sought him out. "Oh?"

Ace inclined his head. "The new deputies are going to fit right in here, and each will be a hell of an asset to the town."

Zach nodded and turned, going to the closet for his dress shoes. "Glad to hear it. I know you, Rafe, and Linc need some time off." Coming out of his closet, he grinned at his brother. "Your wife has too much time on her hands. She keeps trying to play matchmaker. You need to distract her. She's planning something to get your attention."

Ace's lips twitched. "She usually is. I'll take her away somewhere when I can get a few days off." Lifting his hand, he gestured toward Zach's clothes. "Looks like you don't need any matchmaking help. I understand you're taking our new neighbor to the hotel for dinner. You wouldn't be trying to seduce her just to get the property, would you?"

The disapproval in his tone didn't escape Zach's notice.

Neither did the warning look in his older brother's eyes.

Understanding now why his oldest brother had sought him out, Zach shook his head and smiled faintly, still a little disconcerted by his reaction to her. "No." Shrugging, he sat on the edge of the bed to slip his shoes on. "You should know better." Pausing, he straightened and glanced toward his brother. "There's something sad and angry about her. She's distant. Aloof, but with an attitude. She looked scared, and I can't help but wonder why."

Ace's lips twitched. "And you just can't wait to close that distance and fix her problems." Straightening, Ace shook his head. "And you and Law know that attitude has passion behind it."

Zach couldn't hold back a grin. "That thought *had* crossed my mind."

"I can imagine. Just be careful." With another warning look, Ace turned away.

Zach watched his brother go, his smile fading as he thought of Courtney again. He could only imagine if his brother knew that. Although Courtney stirred him sexually, she also stirred something else inside him that he wasn't quite ready to explain.

She didn't appear to be the kind of woman who'd smiled much in her life, and he intended to change that.

Zach couldn't stand to see such a beautiful young woman look so beaten.

She looked tired. Sad.

He'd seen the grief in her eyes when she talked about her aunt, but something told him that the bitterness in her voice had little to do with that.

She'd done nothing to attract his attention but had succeeded in doing so more than any woman he'd ever met.

He rose, anticipation for the hunt ahead rushing through his veins.

He hadn't been able to stop thinking about her since leaving her house and had spent the afternoon alternately glancing at the house next door for any sign of Courtney and checking his watch.

He went to the window now, smiling at his sister-in-law as she walked past him carrying two glasses of iced tea.

Her eyes danced with amusement and happiness. "That's called stalking, you know. I'm going to have to report you."

Crossing his arms over his chest, he gave her a playful glare. "You know, I have no idea why my brother puts up with you."

Hope shrugged. "I'm adorable."

Laughing, Zach shook his head and followed her out to the front porch. "You are that. I still think Ace should spank you more often."

Turning to wink at him over her shoulder, she giggled. "I agree."

Law accepted one of the glasses from her with a smile of thanks before looking up at Zach. "I was getting ready to leave without you."

Zach checked his watch again. "It's only four thirty. You know how much women hate it when you're too early."

Law turned to stare at Courtney's house, his expression pensive. "She didn't seem to be the high-maintenance type."

Ace took the other glass of tea from his wife and snagged an arm around her waist to pull her onto his lap. "Like the women you're used to in Dallas?"

Zach sighed and glanced at his grinning sister-in-law. "Please don't get her started again. Your wife has quite a few opinions about our love life."

Law smiled. "She wants to meddle."

Hope shrugged and leaned back against Ace's shoulder, a familiar position for the two of them. "I just want you to be happy. You've both always liked sharing a woman. You want to build this huge house so you can work from here more often because you love the town and it would be a good place for you to raise a family. Your lifestyle's accepted here, and you'd want your wife to be comfortable."

Looking over her shoulder, she pouted up at Ace. "They won't let me help them find someone for them."

Ace took a sip of his tea and set his glass aside. "Then maybe you should stay out of it."

Hope's eyes narrowed. "I thought you were supposed to be on my side."

Smiling, Ace bent to kiss her hair. "I'm always on your side, love, but I think Law and Zach would prefer to find their own woman."

Zach hid a smile at Hope's snort of derision.

Eyeing her husband, she frowned. "None of you could find a woman without another woman's help. If I hadn't chased you, you'd still be coming home to an empty house every night."

Ace's brow went up. "You drove me crazy."

"Yeah, but you noticed me."

"I noticed you a long time ago. I just knew you were too young for me."

Hope grinned and wrinkled her nose at him. "I'm perfect for you, and you know it."

"Yes, you are." Running a hand over her hair, Ace smiled faintly. "Something I'm sure you're never going to let me forget."

"Not a chance."

Zach envied the closeness his brother and sister-in-law shared and loved Hope even more for bringing light to the dark spaces that had always been a major part of his brother's life.

Law smiled at Ace. "Every time I see the two of you together, she's always on your lap."

"It's a good way to keep her out of mischief." Ace stood, holding Hope close with an arm around her waist, his gaze settling on each of his brothers. "It's almost five. Get lost."

Smiling at Hope's giggle, Zach watched them go inside, the door closing behind them. Turning to Law, he moved to the chair his brother had just vacated and dropped into it. "Those two look happier every time I see them."

Law continued to watch the house next door. "Yeah, they do."

Hearing the yearning in Law's voice, Zach rose to his feet again. "Stop brooding. Let's go see if Courtney's ready."

Chapter Three

Courtney eyed her reflection in the freshly cleaned mirror above the dresser in the room she'd slept in as a child.

She didn't know where Law and Zach would be taking her but figured the turquoise, long, flowing skirt, camisole, and lightweight shirt to layer over it would be appropriate almost anywhere.

Slipping on a pair of comfortable strappy sandals in the same color, she went back to the kitchen, grimacing at the stacks of dishes on the counter.

Deciding that she might as well start on them while she waited, she crossed the peeling linoleum floor to the sink, pausing when a strange sound came from high on the wall behind her.

Giggling at the groaning sound the doorbell made, Courtney turned and went to answer the door, still smiling as she swung it open. Her smile widened at the sight of Law and Zach standing on her sagging front porch.

Both men looked gorgeous and far too sophisticated to be standing on her dilapidated porch. Their size alone took up most of it.

Opening the door wide, she shook her head. "You'd better get in here before the porch collapses."

Zach came through first, his black shirt and slacks giving him a sleek, dangerous look. Grinning, he reached for her, his brow going up when she took a step back, avoiding his touch. "Hey! I'm not fat."

"No, but both of you are huge. You've both got to be six and a half feet tall."

Zach grinned. "I'm six-four, and Law's six-five."

"Holy cow." Aware of Law's attention, she turned, heading back to the kitchen for her purse.

Their presence made the small living room feel even smaller, the sexual awareness that she'd fought earlier coming back in full force.

"What were you smiling about when we rang the bell?" Law's voice came from right behind her, and when she spun, she ran straight into him. Gripping her arms before she could back away, he smiled down at her. "You have a beautiful smile. What was so amusing?"

Leaning back against the wall next to the doorway to the kitchen, Courtney took a steadying breath, trying not to think about the fact that only a few inches separated their bodies. "The doorbell. Ask Zach to push it, and you'll see what I was smiling about."

Frowning, Zach went back outside to push the doorbell, his frown even deeper when he came back in. "That's awful."

Law's jaw clenched. "And probably dangerous. There might be a short in it. We should call Boone and ask him to come take a look at it."

Zach moved around Law and went into the kitchen, stopping abruptly at the doorway. "Jesus!"

Courtney slid along the wall and away from Law, her face burning. "I know it's a mess. I took all of the dishes out of the cabinets to wash them. I got the cabinets wiped down and then saw the time."

Over her head, Law and Zach exchanged a look, their jaws clenching.

Courtney grabbed her purse from the table and started out, her face burning. "I know it's a mess. You don't have to make a big deal out of it."

"You can't stay here."

Turning at Law's tone, Courtney smiled at both of them as they followed her from the kitchen. "I certainly can. Now, are we going to dinner, or do I need to go get groceries? I'm starving."

Zach sent a warning look in Law's direction and brushed past him to her side. Smiling, he took her arm and turned her toward the door. "Of course, we're going to dinner. We can talk later."

Once on the porch, she turned, trying to pull out of Zach's grasp to close the door behind her. "Where's Law?"

"He's right behind us. Come on. I'm hungry, too." Wrapping an arm around her, he led her to the huge, dark blue SUV parked next to her little car. "Do you know when you smile your beautiful dark eyes get these amazing flecks of gold? Fascinating."

Disappointed that he would be so transparent in his efforts to get her property, Courtney sighed and pulled away from him. "Okay, maybe this isn't such a good idea." Seeing Law's approach, she divided her attention between both of them. "I don't have gold flecks or anything in my eyes. They're brown, dull, and bloodshot from lack of sleep. I'm not falling for any lines. I'm not sleeping with you."

Irritated at their calm demeanors, she fisted her hands on her hips. "If this is about buying my property, you can get lost right now." She tried to pull away, angry at men in general and disappointed that Law and Zach were assholes just like her father. She could have sworn they'd been different.

Zach grinned and hustled her into the front seat of their SUV. "She sure has spunk, doesn't she?"

Law opened the driver's door and climbed in, turning to frown at her as he took the end of her seatbelt from her and snapped it in place. "Yeah, but I sure as hell don't appreciate that people think I would use sex to get a fucking piece of land. First Ace. Now her."

He started the engine with a quick turn of his wrist, his anger evident as he put it in reverse.

Taking in his clenched jaw, she studied him as Zach slid into the back seat behind her. "This isn't about my house?"

Shoving the SUV back into park, Law rested an arm on the steering wheel and turned to face her, his eyes hard. "I want this property, and I have every intention of having it. We'll definitely talk about it, but when I kiss you—and I will—and when I make love to you, it won't have a fucking thing to do with this property." Leaning closer, he raised a brow. "Is that clear enough?"

Swallowing heavily, she turned away from his knowing look to stare at her dirty, and slightly sagging garage door. "Crystal." Glancing at him as he started to back out of the driveway, she smiled faintly. "I don't have sex. Is that clear enough? Oh!"

When he slammed on the brakes, she grabbed for the dashboard, her breath catching when he threw an arm out and caught her before she could reach it.

Law's eyes flashed with hunger, the muscles in the arm across her breasts loosening. "Are you a virgin?"

Trembling, she pushed back against the seat, acutely aware of his forearm against her nipples. "It's none of your business."

He leaned closer, his nose almost touching hers. "I'm making it my business. Are you a virgin?"

"No, but I learned my lesson. I don't need this." She reached for the latch of her seatbelt, but Law stopped her with a hand over hers.

Zach cursed and threw his seatbelt aside. "Damn it, Law."

Law blew out a breath and released her. "I'm sorry. You're obviously upset, tired, and sad, and I've been pushing you." Sitting back in his seat, Law took his foot off the brake. "Tonight's supposed to be about getting to know you better. I promise to behave."

Stunned at his perception, Courtney looked away. "You don't know me well enough to assume that I'm any of those things."

Law glanced at her as he started down the road, his expression thoughtful. "There's something sad in your eyes that gets to me. Something about you pulls at me. You're beautiful, but that doesn't have anything to do with it. I don't know what it is, but I'm determined to find out." At her look of shock, he smiled. "I believe in honesty—especially between a man and a woman."

She laughed at that. "Yeah, that would be something if it existed. Do you often live in a dream world?"

Zach touched her shoulder, his fingers brushing over her neck. "Instead of showing you around town tonight, we'll have an early dinner and go back to your house. I want to check some things out with some friends of ours. They're in construction and know what they're doing. Before we leave you alone there, I want to make sure your house isn't a damned death trap." He pulled out his phone and began dialing.

Courtney glanced back at him and shook her head. "That's not necessary."

Law turned to frown at her. "I think it is."

"Too bad." Courtney turned to look out the side window, taking the opportunity to see the town. When she'd driven in, she'd seen some of it but couldn't look at it the way she'd wanted to because she'd been concentrating on her driving and finding the house.

The town had changed a lot from what she remembered.

It seemed much busier, with a lot more people strolling up and down the street.

She saw a lot of buildings and homes that she didn't remember from before, and some of the older buildings on Main Street seemed newly renovated.

Zach disconnected. "Boone said that he would stop by and check the house out."

Irritated at his presumptuousness, Courtney turned in her seat to look at him. "No, thank you. Call your friend back and tell him not to bother."

Zach's smile held a hint of amusement. "It's no bother."

Before she could argue with him about it, they pulled into the parking lot of the hotel. Whirling around, she faced Law. "What are we doing here? Why are you bringing me to a hotel?"

Law parked and turned off the engine. "Calm down. We're going to the restaurant. It's the best in town."

Turning in his seat, he eyed his brother. "Why the hell does everyone think we're so desperate?" Shaking his head, he leaned toward Courtney, gripping her chin. "When I take you, it's going to be with your full cooperation, baby."

Jerking out of his hold, Courtney unsnapped the seatbelt and opened the door. "That'll never happen."

Before she knew it, Zach stood at her side, gripping her arm as he led her to the front entrance. "Never is a real long time, darlin'. Come on. Being tired and hungry is making you grumpy. Let's get you fed."

Irritated that they seemed to embarrass her with no apparent effort, she tried unsuccessfully to pull away from him. "I'm not grumpy!"

Law closed in on her other side. "Of course not. I'm sure you're hungry, though. You probably haven't eaten all day."

"I ate breakfast before I left Blackwell."

Law opened the door for her. "Blackwell, huh? That's a long drive."

"I got an early start." Unable to sleep, she'd started out in the middle of the night.

Law ran a hand down her back to settle at her waist. "You lived there alone?"

"No." Courtney went through the door and headed away from the check-in desk and toward the doorway to the restaurant.

Zach took her hand in his and pulled her to his side. "Did you live with a man?"

Struck by the elegant interior of the restaurant, Courtney paused to admire the small glittering lights on the ceiling. "It's so beautiful here."

Candlelight flickered from every tabletop, every inch of the low-lit restaurant designed for romance and seduction.

"Well, hello. Who's this pretty lady?"

Courtney turned, smiling at the gorgeous man approaching. Offering her hand, she smiled back. "Hi. I'm Courtney. Is this your restaurant?"

"Sure is. Welcome, Courtney. I'm Brandon."

"Your restaurant's beautiful."

Lowering his voice, he smiled when Law and Zach closed in, each putting a possessive arm around her. "What are you doing here with these two?"

Courtney shrugged, liking him immediately. "They kinda kidnapped me. They wanted to bring me to dinner."

Brandon glanced at Law and Zach in turn and grinned. "You came to the right place. Hungry?"

"Starving."

Smiling at the good-natured grumbling coming from Law and Zach as they followed her to the table, she found herself relaxing.

They didn't get angry or try to pull her away from Brandon. No temper. No yelling. No scenes.

Once seated, Law covered her hand with his, not appearing the least bit angry. "So, who did you live with back in Blackwell?"

"Aunt Sally."

Zach rubbed her other arm, his eyes dark with concern. "How long ago did she die?"

"Two weeks tomorrow."

Closing his hand over hers, Law sighed. "You must miss her very much."

"I do." Courtney opened the menu, some of her appetite gone. "She died in her sleep. That's probably the best way to go. I just wish I'd had the chance to say good-bye."

Her cell phone rang just then, preventing her from saying more, for which she was grateful. She had to rummage through her bag for it, inwardly cursing when she saw that it was her father. She pressed the ignore button and shoved the cell phone back inside, the rest of her appetite gone.

* * * *

Law watched the light go out of her eyes and glanced at Zach to see that his brother noticed it, too.

He didn't know who would have such an effect on her, but he was determined to find out. He opened his mouth to ask about the caller, snapping it shut when her phone rang again.

She stiffened, and because he watched her, he saw past the anger to the bitterness underneath.

"Who keeps calling? It upsets you. Why?" He knew it was none of his business, but he had to know. He hated the thought of anything or anyone upsetting her.

He barely knew her and already felt too protective of her for his own peace of mind.

She turned the phone off and threw it into her purse. "It's nothing I can't handle." She picked up the menu and scanned it, pursing her lips in a way that made him desperate to taste them. "I think I'll just have the soup. The chicken vegetable sounds good."

Zach frowned and set his menu aside. "You need more than soup. Who's calling and upsetting you?"

"None of your business." She stiffened again, her eyes shooting sparks, the little gold flecks in them making his stomach tighten. "If I can't have what I want for dinner, I'm going to go somewhere else."

Law caught her before she could jump out of her chair. "Calm down, baby."

He didn't know why he'd called her that. He'd never used that endearment with any woman before, but she seemed so sweet and fragile, that it seemed appropriate.

"Stop calling me that."

Taking her hand in his, he lifted it to his lips and smiled. "I really don't think I can." Giving Zach a warning look, he sat back and picked up his menu. "I won't ask about the calls anymore." Pausing, he lowered his menu to meet her gaze. "For now." Lifting it again, he smiled. "You can have whatever you want for dinner. Tonight's about getting you fed and relaxed and getting to know you better."

Courtney glanced at him out of the corner of her eye and smiled. "So that you can try to talk me into selling my house to you."

Hoping that a glass or two of wine would help settle her and allow her to get a good night's sleep, Law ordered a bottle along with several appetizers in the hopes that she would eat something other than just soup.

Zach leaned toward Courtney and smiled. "If you thought we were going to spend the time trying to get you to sell the house to us, why did you come?"

Courtney's smile didn't reach her eyes. "I was too tired to argue with you and too tired to go to the grocery store." She sat back with a shrug and accepted the glass of wine Law held out to her. "And I was hoping that it would give me a chance to explain why I can't sell it to you, so you don't have to waste your time and mine trying to talk me into it."

Pleased that her eyes lit with interest when the waiter placed the appetizers in the center of the table, Law pushed a few of the plates closer to her. "Okay. So, why can't you sell the house?"

Courtney frowned as she watched a waiter go through the curtain to one of the privacy booths. "I'll tell you as soon as you tell me what's behind those curtains."

Zach chuckled and bent close to her, keeping his voice low. "Those are privacy booths. You can reserve them for a little privacy while you enjoy your dinner."

Law's cock stirred at the thought of taking Courtney into one of those booths. Cursing himself for thinking about the kinds of things he'd liked to do to her while she was tired and out of sorts, he reached for his own wine and let Zach carry the conversation.

Courtney nodded. "Oh. Like if it's an anniversary or someone doing business wants to talk privately."

"Not exactly." Zach grinned, clearly enjoying himself. "For example, if you were our woman, we'd take you in there and do all kinds of naughty things to you during dinner. We'd be able to touch you and have you naked if we wanted to. I'd love to see you dressed in nothing more than my shirt."

Law took another sip of wine, willing his cock to behave, the look of shock in Courtney's eyes and her flushed cheeks making him wonder just how much experience she'd had with men.

He'd bet one of his oil wells that it wasn't much at all.

"Oh." Courtney appeared slightly dazed as she turned to look back toward the curtain.

Because he watched her so intently, Law saw the exact moment that curiosity and interest took over. Turning back, she reached for her wine again and sat back, eyeing both of them thoughtfully. "So, what kinds of naughty things do you think you can do in a restaurant? I understand that sex can be very noisy, and I don't hear any noise coming from the other side of the curtains."

Zach scooped a few of the appetizers onto her plate before helping himself. "As much as I'm sure I'd enjoy the sounds of pleasure pouring from you, I wouldn't want anyone else to hear them. If you were ours, we'd make sure you were quiet."

Law's cock jumped at her impish grin. Intrigued by her playfulness, he realized that there were facets to her that he needed to explore.

Sadness. Bitterness. Playfulness. Passion.

"And just how would you keep me quiet? By gagging me?"

"If necessary. A nice ball gag would muffle a lot of it. But we'd have other ways." Law swallowed heavily and shook his head, willing his cock to behave. "It's your turn to talk. Why can't you sell the house?"

She turned her head toward him, the impact sending a jolt of desire straight to his loins. "Okay. I'll answer a question, and then you will. The reason that I can't sell the house is because my aunt made it a condition of her will that I live in it for a year before selling it." Raising a brow, she sat up, setting her glass down before picking up her fork. "Your turn. If I was in there with you, how would you keep me from making any noise?"

Pleased to see her picking at the appetizers and delighted with her playful daring, Law leaned forward, his cock twitching. "We'd teach you. Train you."

"We?"

Cursing himself for the slip of the tongue, he clenched his jaw and nodded, watching her eyes. "We. Zach and I are both interested in getting to know you a whole lot better." Her eyes went wide, the golden flecks sparkling in the candlelight. Glancing at Zach, her cheeks reddened. "That sounds dangerous." Lifting her chin, she smiled, but the hand holding her glass of wine shook. "I have no intention of getting involved with anyone. I just want to get through the year."

He didn't want to think about her leaving town. "A year is a long time to change your mind." Keeping his voice low, he smiled and looked down at her breasts, his mouth watering at the sight of her nipples pressing against her shirt. Hoping it was from desire, and not due to the air conditioning, he narrowed his eyes on her breasts. "For example, I would tell you not to make any noise and start stroking your breasts. Weigh them in my hand. Stroke my tongue over your nipples. I'd want to learn how you like to be touched."

His cock swelled as he imagined it—the sharp intake of breath when he touched her nipple.

The wonder in her eyes when he stroked her.

The pleasure of making her his.

Disconcerted by the direction his thoughts had taken, Law clenched his jaw and took her fork from her to feed her the morsel himself. "If you cried out, or made any sound, I would stop."

When he touched the food to her lips, Courtney opened her mouth without hesitation, the submissiveness in the small gesture sending his imagination soaring.

His blood pumped faster through his veins, hot and filled with an anticipation he hadn't felt in a long time—the Dominant in him reawakened.

He forked another bite of food and held it to her lips, his pleasure in feeding her surprising him. "You wouldn't like that at all. You wouldn't want me to stop, but you'd know that the only way to get me to continue would be to be as quiet as you could be. When you settled, I'd touch you again. That's why you'd stay quiet."

She swallowed the bite of food, her eyes wide. "Oh." Straightening, she reached for her wine again. "So that's what's happening behind those curtains?"

Zach shrugged, his gaze sharp as he watched both of them. "We don't know. Hence the curtain."

Law touched his fork to her lips, his cock jumping when she opened her mouth again. "Your turn to answer a question. Why did your aunt want you to live here for a year?"

Intrigued at her blush and trying not to think about sliding his cock between her full lips, Law waited for her answer.

Swallowing, she lifted her glass again and took another sip. "Because she found love here. She met my uncle here. When he went to Vietnam, she stayed. He was killed there, and she moved away. She just couldn't stay here without him, but she couldn't bear to sell the house."

Zach frowned. "That house hasn't been vacant *that* long." He glanced at Law. "Someone else lived there years ago. The asshole who owned the ice cream shop. The one who insulted Gracie and called her a whore for having three husbands."

Law frowned at Courtney's wince. "You knew them, didn't you? Wait!"

As the truth dawned on him, he realized he might have an uphill battle ahead of him. "Sheldon. They had a little girl."

Zach sat back, his eyes widening as he studied her. "They did. I remember now. Everyone suspected that the man—what was his name?"

"Edwin. Ed. His wife's name was Shirley." Law sat back, never taking his eyes from Courtney. "Everyone suspected that Ed used to beat Shirley, but she denied it."

Nodding, Zach blew out a breath. "He was jealous of everyone. He even accused Dad of having an affair with her."

Law's stomach knotted, the truth plainly visible in Courtney's eyes, along with the pain. "And when he started insulting the women in ménage marriages, we boycotted his store."

Courtney sat back and took another sip of her wine, her eyes filled with anger and misery. "Effectively chasing him out of town. Mom left with him but, within months, divorced him to move in with another man—a man who didn't treat her like dirt. A man who didn't beat on her."

The knots in Law's stomach tightened. "And you?"

Courtney shrugged. "Sent to live with my Aunt Sally. Best thing that ever happened to me."

Clearly agitated, she got to her feet and hooked her purse over her shoulder. "And the worst. I lost my mother. I hate what this town did to my family. I came here because it's what my aunt wanted, but I won't stay here one day past the year I have to spend here. You're all bossy and arrogant, and I've had enough of that from my father to last me a lifetime."

Gripping her arm, Law settled her back into the chair again. "I understand. Why don't we have a nice, quiet dinner and talk about something else."

He knew he'd never get through to her in her present mood, but he'd seen and heard enough to know that Courtney was a woman he definitely needed to know better.

Once she settled, he fed her another bite of food. "That house is dangerous. You have to understand that we would go crazy knowing that you're in a house that's dangerous. Why don't you let us pay for you to stay here at the hotel until we can find another place here in town that's for rent?"

She shook her head before he'd even finished. "If I did that, the house would be sold to the highest bidder. I have to live there. My father doesn't know it, but if I don't stay there a year, the money would go to him. My aunt knew that I would do whatever it took not to let that happen.

Law grimaced. "I agree with you. I remember your father a little, but I was too young to really know him. What do you plan to do when the year's over and you sell the house?"

Shrugging again, she toyed with the stem of her wineglass. "Leave. Go back to Blackwell. I was in the process of negotiating to buy the flower shop I worked in when my aunt died. I've saved for years to be able to buy it because the owner wants to retire. If it's not sold already, I'd probably buy it. If not, who knows?"

Law shared a look with Zach, the look of determination and interest in his brother's eyes telling him that they were on the same page.

They had to do whatever it took to keep Courtney from leaving Desire.

Chapter Four

To Courtney's relief, Law kept his promise, and they had an enjoyable dinner. She found herself relaxing more and more as they talked, and gradually became convinced that they were nothing like her father.

She'd never met men like them before.

Masculine and yet so tender, a combination she'd heard about, but had only seen in movies.

Both men seemed so interested in everything she had to say, and had been solicitous and charming throughout dinner.

Over a dessert she enjoyed, but didn't remember ordering, she started to yawn. "I think I had too much wine."

Zach smiled at her and finished his own glass. "You only had two glasses. If you spent the week packing up your things and drove all night, then spent today trying to clean the house, it's no wonder you're beat." Lifting his hand, he signaled for the waiter. "We'll get you home, and you can go to bed while we deal with Boone."

"I told you that's not necessary."

"I think it is." Law rose and held out a hand to her. "If you're going to live there a year, we're going to have to make sure it's safe. You don't want to have to leave the house and let your father get it, do you?"

Ignoring Law's outstretched hand, she gathered her purse and got to her feet, holding on to the table when her knees wobbled. "I thought we'd already established that it's not your responsibility."

The wine and her fatigue had loosened her tongue during dinner, and although she'd ended up telling them more than she'd wanted to tell them about her life, she'd also told them that she had no intention of seeing them again.

It was a decision she began to regret.

Their thoughtfulness and attentiveness intrigued her, giving her a warm feminine feeling inside that she found increasingly difficult to resist.

They didn't speak in innuendos, or pickup lines.

The conversation never faltered or became uncomfortable, and both men seemed determined to get her to relax and enjoy herself.

They asked about *her* instead of rambling on about themselves.

There was a masculinity about them that reminded her of the Westerns she loved to watch.

Law took her free hand in his and tugged, forcing her to his side. Wrapping an arm protectively around her, he ignored the curious looks from some of his friends and neighbors and led Courtney outside. "There's no way I'm going to be able to sleep tonight, worrying about you in that house. I'm sure if your aunt had known what kind of shape it was in, she never would have demanded that you live here."

Courtney had wondered about that as well. Shrugging, she allowed him to lead her across the parking lot to the SUV, leaning heavily against him as fatigue overtook her, smiling when he immediately gathered her closer. "My aunt knew that I'm perfectly capable of taking care of myself."

Zach appeared beside her and helped her into the front seat, another old-fashioned gesture that she'd thought had died out long ago. "Taking care of yourself is one thing. Taking foolish risks is another."

"I'm not foolish. If you remember, I just got here today. I still have a lot to do to settle in. I'll take care of *my* house as I see fit."

Zach climbed in beside her as Law started the engine. "Boone just texted me. He's on his way to your house."

Even tired, she found herself fighting arousal, the feel of their hard bodies pressed against hers exciting, scary, and amazingly giving her a feeling of being safe that she'd never felt before.

She yawned again, struggling to keep her eyes open. "I shouldn't have had that second glass of wine."

Zach wrapped an arm around her and pulled her close. "You're exhausted. We'll have you home in a couple of minutes, and you can go to bed."

"Hmm." Leaning against him, she let her eyes close. "Just tell your friend that I'll call him if I need him."

"Don't worry about it. We'll take care of everything."

* * * *

Zach looked down at her and smiled, wondering if she even heard him. Meeting the question in Law's eyes, he nodded, silently informing his brother that she'd fallen asleep.

Intrigued by the way Law silently watched her, and his brother's preoccupation during dinner, Zach eased Courtney onto his lap as they approached her dilapidated house.

Boone stood with his hands on his hips in the middle of the weed-choked front yard, turning at the waist as they pulled into the driveway.

When Law got out, Boone started to speak, snapping his mouth shut when Zach emerged from the truck, carrying Courtney, who slept soundly in his arms.

Zach's chest swelled with pride as he carried her across the lawn and to her front door, and he couldn't help but smile at the look of shock on Boone's face.

Law opened the door he'd evidently left unlocked, wincing at the creaking sound it made. His jaw clenched, but his eyes softened when he ran a hand over Courtney's hair as Zach carried her into the house. "Be careful not to wake her up. She'll raise hell if she sees Boone."

Zach wanted to laugh at his brother's protectiveness, but his own kept him from doing so. Nodding, he went into the house, wincing at the creaking sound his steps made on the hardwood floors as he carried her down the hallway to the bedrooms.

Pausing outside the only open door, he frowned when he saw the twin bed inside. Scanning the room, he noticed that her suitcases had been stacked neatly in the corner and that the room had been freshly cleaned and aired out.

Wondering why she would take what appeared to be her childhood room instead of the master bedroom, he turned to ease through the doorway.

She felt so good in his arms that he hated to put her down, but he wanted her to rest and wanted to get back to Boone to see what they could accomplish while she slept.

Lowering her onto the bed, he smiled when she moaned and turned to her side. When she curled her hand under her chin, he couldn't resist bending to touch his lips to her hair, gently so he didn't wake her.

Kneeling beside the bed, he stared down at her, wondering what it was about her that made him feel so protective.

Possessive.

She didn't dress provocatively or play any of the games women he dated usually played. She did absolutely nothing to attract his attention and had done her best to let both him and Law know she had no interest in them at all.

But her eyes told another story.

She was interested, but she didn't want to be.

Her fight to deny her own needs both intrigued and frustrated him, making it impossible for him to walk away from her.

He took his time removing her shoes, running a finger over her peach-painted toenails, wondering why such a small thing as tucking her into bed filled him with a possessive satisfaction that no amount of fucking ever did.

The thought of taking her had him hard in an instant, need pulsing through his veins with a strength that stunned him.

With a curse, he rose to his feet, covering her with the light blanket.

The house had no air-conditioning, but a light breeze blew in from the window, and he didn't want her to get cold.

Staring down at her, he knew he had to have her.

Her prickly nature would be a hell of a challenge—one that had his cock swelling even more.

He'd already had glimpses of her passion, her sweetness, her vulnerability, and a healthy amount of sassiness and knew that fighting his way through the hard shell she'd built around herself would be well worth the effort.

Glancing around, he noticed the faded and peeling walls, the worn floors that didn't quite look level—probably from the rain dripping down the walls from the obviously leaky windows.

Changes would have to be made.

Smiling to himself, he took one last look at her and turned, knowing that the changes had already begun.

He and Law had almost given up on finding someone so sweet. They'd almost given up on finding a woman they both were attracted to.

Something about Courtney tugged at him, and Law had already made it clear that she intrigued him just as much.

She intrigued them frustrated them drew them, and he still didn't quite understand why.

He just knew that he couldn't walk away from her, the hope of finally finding what he and Law had spent most of their lives looking for too irresistible to ignore. She was so sweet, with none of the airs of the women they usually dated. She had an adventurous streak combined with a shyness that he found absolutely adorable.

She was passionate, but didn't seem to realize it, and the excitement of showing her passions to her consumed his thoughts.

Her honesty and lack of pretentiousness was like a breath of fresh air.

She consumed his thoughts, and nothing would stop him from pursuing her.

* * * *

Law turned when Zach reappeared, understanding the smile playing at his brother's lips.

Anticipation. Satisfaction.

Wiping his brow against the heat, he gestured toward the hole Boone had made in the kitchen wall. "Boone said that the wiring's not up to code, and it's shot." He kept his voice low so as not to waken Courtney and keep her from the sleep she so obviously needed.

Shaking his head, Boone turned away from the wall, brushing his hands together. "You're damned lucky the house hasn't burned down already."

Clenching his jaw, he looked around, the concern in his eyes evident. "I can tell by the way the floor gives and its unevenness that the subflooring needs to be replaced. The kitchen needs to be gutted, and I can only imagine the bathroom does as well. The plumbing needs to be redone throughout the house."

Law listened with half an ear to Boone enumerating what needed to be done to the house, eventually following him and Zach outside.

Boone paused in the middle of the yard, turning to face the house and looking at each of them in turn. "It would make a hell of a lot more sense to tear it down. We're going to have to tear it down to build here, anyway. Doing anything to it now would be just a waste of money."

Law studied the house in the waning light, willing to spend whatever it took to keep Courtney in Desire. "We can't tear it down until we own it."

Boone frowned. "She won't sell it to you?"

"She can't." Law sighed and explained what had been in her aunt's will. "She can't sell it to anyone until she's lived in it a year."

Boone whistled softly. "That's a damned shame. I'll bet her aunt didn't realize that the house is in such bad shape."

Looking up at the small house, Zach sighed. "Probably not. The big problem is that Courtney doesn't want us to do anything. She said that she'd take care of it herself and to tell you to call you if she needs you." His lips thinned. "Judging by her car, I don't think she has a hell of a lot of money—certainly not the kind of money that needs to be poured into this place."

Law smiled, already anticipating the battles ahead. "But we do."

Nodding, Zach looked toward the front bedroom where she slept. "Yeah, but how the hell are we going to do this without pissing her off?" He met Law's gaze. "Or hurting her pride?" Frowning, he glanced toward the house again. "I don't mind tangling with her, but I sure as hell don't want to hurt her pride."

"Agreed." Law couldn't imagine hurting Courtney's pride, the vulnerability he'd seen in her eyes telling him it would be a hard blow for her to bear.

Hurting her would be like hurting himself.

Stunned at the realization, he turned away. "We'll have to figure out something. We'll keep reminding her that if something goes wrong with the house and she has to leave, her dad will get it."

Boone grinned. "We can do the same thing Chase and I did with Rachel. Your brother and Beau did the same thing when the women's club needed work after the fire."

Law nodded, remembering Ace's rage after the fire. "I heard about that. Ace and Beau had you write out fake invoices for Hope and Charity while they paid the biggest chunk of it. None of the women had a clue. They still don't know."

Zach nodded. "I like it, but we're going to have to start out easy. I don't want her overwhelmed."

Law sighed, anxious to go check on her. "Or suspicious. We'll start with the rewiring. In the meantime, Zach, why don't you go down to the hardware store and get us a couple of air-conditioning units and some extension cords? I'll sleep here tonight. I can't have her sleeping here alone if there's a chance something could happen."

Zach frowned at that. "I'll stay."

"We'll take turns until she gets used to dealing with both of us." Running a hand through his hair, Law met Boone's disapproving look. "Why are you looking at me like that? I don't want to scare her."

Boone eyed both of them. "Are you sure you want to do this? The amount of work this house needs is going to get pretty expensive. You could always go back to the lawyer and tell him that the house is in such bad shape it should be condemned."

"No." Staring at the house, he weighed his options, knowing that spending the money it would take to make the house livable would be a waste when they had it torn down.

Throwing caution to the wind—something he seldom did—Law met Zach's gaze. "If she can't stay here, she no longer has any reason to stay in Desire."

Boone's brows went up, his lips twitching. "Oh, so it's like that."

Law smiled, excitement making his heart pound faster. "Yeah. It's like that. Money's no object. Do as much as you can under the radar."

Chapter Five

Courtney woke and stretched, feeling more rested than she had in weeks.

Happy.

Opening her eyes, she stilled, momentarily disconcerted to find herself in the room she'd slept in as a child.

The events of the previous day came back in a rush.

She'd come back to Desire—a town she'd never thought to see again.

Her next thought was of Law and Zach.

Sitting up, she realized that the room seemed darker than it should have been, and a lot cooler.

She turned toward the window, frowning to see that a piece of thick cardboard had been taped over the glass at the top window, keeping out the light, and an air conditioning unit hummed from the window below.

No one except Law and Zach would have done such a thing.

She supposed it was part of making her comfortable so she would stay in Desire long enough to fulfill her aunt's wishes so that she could sell the house to them.

Mentally shrugging, she tried to ignore the pang of hurt in her stomach at the knowledge that they had selfish reasons for their kindness.

She didn't want to believe it after their kindness the night before, but since she planned to sell the house to them anyway, it hardly mattered.

Blowing out a breath, she crawled out from beneath the covers, relieved to find that, except for her shoes, she was fully dressed.

She tried to remember getting into bed but couldn't.

She could only imagine what it would have been like to wake up naked with one of them curled around her.

Hearing sounds coming from the other room, she stiffened, looking for something to use as a weapon. Seeing nothing except the small lamp on her dresser, she moved swiftly to unplug it and, holding it high, went to the door.

Easing it open, she winced at the creak of the hinges, her breath catching when she heard footsteps coming down the hall. Lifting the lamp higher, she held her breath, a soft curse escaping when Law appeared.

Blowing out her breath in a rush, she lowered the lamp and glared at him. "You scared the hell out of me. What the hell are you doing in my house?"

Law's dark brow went up. "We got air conditioners so we wouldn't have to sleep in a sweat box and went out to get coffee."

"We?"

Law inclined his head, eyes filled with amusement and something else she couldn't define. "Zach and I. You look better. How do you feel?"

"I'm fine. There was no reason for you to stay."

"We think there was. You were so tired that you fell asleep on the way home. Boone checked out the wiring, and it's too old and way too dangerous. If you'd gotten up in the middle of the night and turned on the lights, you could have burned the house down."

"So how do I have air conditioning?"

"Extension cords to Ace's house." Zach appeared, grinning as he offered her a take-out coffee. "Good morning, darlin'. I'm not sure how you take your coffee, but I have cream and sugar out in the other room."

"Why are you being so nice to me?"

Zach's brows went up. "It wouldn't be nice to beat you before you've had your morning coffee."

Law frowned. "What is it about us that makes everyone assume the worst?"

Courtney couldn't help but smile at his disgruntled tone. "Maybe people think you're being too nice to a total stranger."

"We won't be strangers for long." Law ran his fingertips down her arm, smiling at her soft moan. "There's chemistry between us, Courtney, the kind of chemistry I've never felt with a woman before. Are you going to try to tell me that you don't feel it?"

Shaking her head, Courtney eyed both of them. "No. It's there. I just don't want to play games. I have no intention of staying here. Nothing could ever come of it, and I don't want to feel obligated to you for doing things to my house."

Zach ran a hand down her back. "There's no obligation, Courtney. We don't want anything from you except to give us a chance to get to know you. Who knows what'll happen? We could all end up hating each other." Wagging his brows, he grinned. "You never know. We could end up being the loves of your life."

Courtney smiled up at him, her smile falling when she saw that, despite his teasing tone, his eyes held a sincerity that brought a lump to her throat.

Her Aunt Sally would be very disappointed in her if she ignored her attraction to Law and Zach, but she would explore it with her eyes wide open.

She didn't think she had a choice, her own curiosity and attraction to them luring her in.

Law smiled, a slow grin that made her stomach flutter. "What a pensive look so early in the morning." His gaze raked over her, sending a warm rush of heat through her system and bringing her awake more than coffee ever could. "I wish I could promise not to bite, but I don't want to lie to you."

Rubbing her eyes, she shook her head, amused at their teasing. "I need coffee and a shower before I can deal with you two. What's that noise?"

"Boone and Sloane Madison are working on the wiring and trying to be as quiet as possible so they don't wake you up. I'll tell them you're awake." Taking the coffee from her, he hooked an arm around her waist from behind and pulled her close. "The electricity's off so there's no hot water. When you finish your coffee, we'll go next door so that you can take a shower."

Courtney stiffened, her heart racing at the feel of his lips against her neck, little shivers of delight racing through her.

His hand tightened on her waist, pulling her more firmly back against him, the feel of his cock pressing against her back bringing her wide awake. "We'll go have some breakfast at the diner. I could have you for breakfast, but I don't think you're quite ready for that."

His patience and understanding just made her admire him more.

Zach moved to stand in front of her, sliding his hand into her hair with a smile. "And then you can figure out how you're going to *deal* with us."

Her stomach muscles quivered under Law's hand, her nipples tightening and aching for attention. Overwhelmed at their closeness and being surrounded by their heat, she gulped in air. "I know that you want this property, but I–I'm not going to l–let you s–seduce me to get it. Whatever happens can't have anything to do with that."

Law groaned, turning her in his arms. "The only property I'm interested in right now is right in front of me." Lifting the hem of her shirt, he cupped her breast, his eyes flaring at her soft cry. "This is what I'm interested in. I want you, and it doesn't have anything to do with this fucking house."

Running his thumb back and forth over her nipple, he stared down at her, his hooded gaze raking over her features. "I thought I'd made that clear already. Let me see if I can make it clearer. I'll have both you and this property."

He brushed his lips over hers, his touch light but with a possessiveness that gave her a tingly feeling inside. "And one has absolutely nothing to do with the other."

Courtney melted under his kiss, the heat in it so far beyond her experience that she felt a momentary surge of panic. The effect of it on her system stunned her, igniting a riot of sensations inside her that she didn't even recognize.

She wanted—more than wanted, *needed*—more, but the power of it scared her.

Her knees gave way, the unfamiliar sense of losing control of her own body not as frightening when he held her, but still overwhelming.

Swallowing her moans, he explored her mouth with a slow thoroughness that left her trembling.

Gripping his shoulders, she held him close, meeting the demand in his kiss without hesitation.

She couldn't refuse him, the sureness of his kiss and his hold too irresistible to deny.

How could she ignore the way he and Zach made her feel?

He kissed her with a confidence and hunger of a man who was used to getting what he wanted—the demand in every slide of his tongue against hers making it clear that he wanted her.

He also made it just as clear that he would be as patient and not rush her.

When he focused his attention on her nipple, she cried out at the sharp jolt of pleasure, a cry he swallowed before lifting his head to stare down at her.

His lips twitched, but his eyes had a determined glint to them that had her shaking harder. "Yes, babe. I'll have you." Lifting her chin when she would have lowered it, he brushed his lips over hers again. "Don't look so panicked. I'll give you the time you need, but if you try to deny that there's something between us, I'll just have to take it upon myself to prove you wrong."

Zach rubbed her shoulder from behind. "Come on. Let's go let Boone know you're awake."

Grateful for Law's support, she walked out to the kitchen for cream and sugar, stopping abruptly with a gasp when she saw the damage that had been done while she slept. "What the hell?"

A man stood on a ladder doing something with wires while another man stood on the other side of the room, rewiring something in her wall. Both turned when she walked into the room.

Zach slid a hand down her back. "Courtney, that's Boone Jackson on the ladder, and that's Sloane Madison. They're rewiring your house."

She couldn't believe their arrogance. "I didn't want my house rewired." She didn't even want to think about how much it would cost.

Boone pushed some wire into the open wall and came down the ladder. "I'm afraid it's my fault, and putting it off is no longer an option." Smiling, he paused in front of her. "I opened the wall to check it out, and it's not up to code and dangerous. I can't leave it. Now that I saw it, I'm obligated to fix it. If not, I could lose my license."

Law slid a hand under her hair to rub the back of her neck. "Don't worry about it, babe."

Irritated that his touch made it difficult to think, she pushed away from him. "I can't afford something like this!" Embarrassed for Boone and Sloane, she sighed, wondering if she would be able to find a job in town. "I'm sorry. I know you're trying to do what you think is best. It's just that I can't afford to put any money into this house, especially since I'll be leaving in a year. How much will it cost to rewire it?"

Boone shook his head. "It's not that much. About two hundred dollars. I already have all the supplies left over from other jobs. It'll only take us a day or two to knock this out."

Stepping farther into the room, Courtney looked around at the studs where walls used to be. "This looks like it's going to cost a hell of a lot more than two hundred dollars."

Boone shrugged. "It's just some wire, and I've got rolls of it that are just sitting in our shop. You're actually doing us a favor. We're between jobs and want to stay busy."

Sloane straightened with a smile. "Drywall's cheap. Chase and Cole are bringing it in tomorrow, and we'll have it up before you know it."

Boone nodded. "We charge less for people who live in Desire. I understand that you used to live here, but you were probably too young to remember that."

Courtney nodded. "I remember." Stirring cream and sugar into her coffee, she eyed Boone. "Are you telling me the truth about the price?" She remembered some of the bills from her aunt's house in Blackwell, and they'd been considerably higher.

"Absolutely."

Sipping her coffee, she leaned back against the refrigerator, keeping them all in view but directing her attention toward Boone. "Do you live in Desire?"

"Yes."

"Do you have a family?"

"I do." The pride on his face endeared him to her. "My brother and I have a wife and a daughter." Watching her, he stiffened, his eyes narrowing as if daring her to comment on his living arrangements.

* * * *

Law held his breath expectantly—feeling as if his entire life depended on Courtney's reaction.

Her father had been forced out of town for criticizing ménage marriages, leaving her bitter toward the town.

He just hoped she didn't have the same prejudices that he did.

If she did, he and Zach had a hell of a problem since they both wanted to share her.

Cocking her head to the side, she studied Boone. "How the hell would a woman put up with two men?"

Boone smiled, the tension leaving his body. "Well, Rachel's real good at wrapping us around her finger." Frowning, he looked at each of them in turn. "You know that's true of just about everyone we know. Women sure are powerful creatures."

Sipping her coffee, Courtney straightened. "You don't get jealous? How do you know which one of you is the baby's father?"

Boone's eyes narrowed. "We're both Theresa's father, as much as we're both Rachel's husbands. As for jealousy—yeah, it happens—but that's between Chase and I. It's not Rachel's problem."

Seeing the confusion and indecision in Courtney's eyes, Law started toward her, pausing when Zach did the same.

His brother shot him a look, his intent obvious.

Zach wanted to show Courtney that he wanted her, too.

Lifting her chin, Zach smiled down at her. "Scared, darlin'?"

To Law's delight, Courtney blushed. "I have no intention of getting married, so that isn't an issue." Turning to face Sloane, she arched into Zach's caress, probably not even realizing that she did. "Do you share your wife, too?"

Sloane reached for his own take-out coffee. "I'm not married, but yes, my brothers and I are interested in the same woman."

Zach laughed and turned her toward the doorway. "Come on. Leave Sloane alone. His love life is none of your business."

Sloane grimaced. "What love life? Sometimes I wonder if we're ever going to earn her trust."

Law sighed. "I'm starting to wonder if I'm going to have the same problem. Good luck. You know we're all pulling for you."

Leading her from the room, and into the living room, Zach held her close. "Drink your coffee. Once you have a shower and some breakfast, we'll go for a walk around town so we can show you around."

"No, thank you. I'd rather be alone for a while."

Zach frowned. "Is something wrong?"

"To be honest, I'm feeling a little overwhelmed. I haven't been here for twenty-four hours yet, and already you're making passes at me."

Smiling, he led her to the sofa and dropped into the seat next to her. "I'm not making passes. Law and I are making our intentions clear that we want to get to know you better. You're a big girl. I'm sure you can handle it."

"I only plan to be here a year, so I'm not staying, but an affair might be fun."

Frowning at that, Law sat in the chair across from her. "Fun? Just fun no longer appeals to me. I want more."

"That's all I'm willing to give." Shrugging, she sipped more coffee. "If I'm willing to give that. I need some time to think about things." After several long seconds, she sat, gesturing toward the kitchen. "I haven't been here a day and my house is being torn up, and I have a feeling there's going to be more. I came for my aunt, but I didn't want to come here. I'd hoped to buy my own flower shop. I'd hoped to escape…"

"Escape? Escape what? What's going on, Courtney?"

Courtney got to her feet and moved to the window, staring out. "My private life is my own. I hate feeling like this. I hate being pushed into things or forced to do things. I hate when people expect more from me than I'm willing to give—and I *hate* demands."

Law shared a look with Zach. They'd obviously hit a nerve, but instead of dissuading him, the anguish in her eyes made him want her more.

Getting to his feet, he inclined his head. "We'll play this your way—up to a point. We'll give you space. That's a reasonable request, especially since we've only known each other a day, but we won't disappear. Get your clothes and we'll go next door so you can take a shower, and we'll go out to breakfast. Then we'll leave you to explore the town on your own. Fair enough?"

"Thank you. You're very nice men, but—"

Standing with his hands on his hips, Law shook his head, not about to let her think they'd just walk away. "Don't make the mistake of thinking that. We can be damned ruthless when we want something—and we want you."

Chapter Six

Sitting on the front porch of his brother's house, Zach listened to the sounds of Courtney moving around, his hands fisted at his sides.

He and Law had both gone silent when the shower turned off, and he could only imagine that his brother was doing the same thing he was doing—imagining Courtney naked.

Shifting to a more comfortable position, he eyed Law, who sat across from him. "You look worried." Shrugging, he forced a smile. "As Courtney said, we haven't known her long. We'll just have to see how it goes."

"There's something there that I can't ignore. I want her, Zach." Law paused, his eyes narrowing. "Even if it means having her alone."

Shocked by his brother's admission, Zach sighed. "I'd wondered if it would ever come to that for us, but you forget that I want her, too."

"I didn't forget anything." Law's eyes narrowed. "You don't seem as interested in her as I am."

"I'm very interested in her. You and I each have a different approach, one that's always seemed to amuse you in the past. This time, though, I think it's more important than ever to take it slow." Setting his coffee cup aside, he looked toward the doorway. "So far, though, she only seems to be taking you seriously as a suitor. I need to change that."

Law's lips twitched. "I'd wondered if you'd ever make a serious move."

"She's been hurt, Law. You want to rush in and fix everything, but I think she needs some space. It's going to take her some time to trust us."

Pausing when he heard the bathroom door open, he stiffened, waiting for Courtney to appear.

When she did, he felt as if he'd been kicked in the gut.

Freshly showered, her hair still damp and hanging down her back, she came toward him, every step she took making his cock harder. The plain blue sundress she wore clung to every curve, making it appear anything but plain. Pausing in the doorway, she eyed each of them. "Thank you. I hope your brother and sister-in-law don't mind that I used their shower."

Zach grinned, the sweet, warm scent of her wrapping around him. "You didn't. You used *our* shower. We grew up in this house and still stay here when we come home—at least until we build our own house."

Courtney held tightly to her bag. "You said that you owned the property on the other side of mine. Are you going to build your house there?"

"It's too small. We need both lots for the house we're building, or we won't have any yard at all. We need a yard for the children we want."

"Why?"

"Why what?"

"Why do you want to share a wife—a family? Your brother, Ace, obviously didn't want to."

Zach shrugged, glancing at Law. "We've always known that we wanted to share a wife. Come here."

She stilled, her eyes going wide. "Why?"

Her hesitancy made his cock jump, the Dominant inside him clamoring to be set free.

Tamping down a response he hadn't had in years, he smiled so as not to scare her. "Because I want to hold you."

Courtney glanced at Law, her blush endearing, but he couldn't let her go on being embarrassed each time he gave her attention in front of Law. Wrapping her arms around her bag, she shook her head. "I don't think that's a good idea."

Not to be denied, he hardened his tone. "Too bad. I think it's a great idea. Would you rather I got up to come get you?"

"No!"

Zach hid a smile, wondering what she would think if she knew that excitement and arousal shone in her eyes, tempered with just enough trepidation to make his cock ache. "If you don't come here, I'll have to come get you."

She looked at Law, as if for support.

Reaching out, Law took her hand in his and lifted it to his lips. "We've made it clear that both of us want you."

She shifted restlessly, averting her gaze. "I don't know how to do something like this."

"I thought you were looking for a little fun. Is that how you see sex?"

Courtney shrugged, her face reddening even more, but her breathing had quickened. "To tell you the truth, I've only had sex once, and it was awful, and I don't remember the last time I had any fun."

Understanding more of what they were up against, Zach kept his tone calm and even. "Then fun it is. Come here. Don't look so apprehensive. You want fun. We'll give you fun. No strings. No ties. No talking about you selling us the house. With all the stress you've had dealing with your aunt's funeral, and now all the work that needs to be done on the house, you deserve to have some fun."

Courtney chewed at her lower lip, clearly tempted. "I don't know. I told you I need to think about it."

"You need to think about a little kiss?" Holding out his hand, Zach grinned, struggling to appear calm and relaxed when he was anything but. "Come here so I can give you something to think about."

Law took her bag from her and nudged her toward Zach. "Go on. You're looking for fun, remember? There's nothing to be scared of."

Courtney lifted her chin. "I'm not scared."

To Zach's delight, she came to him and would have plopped on his lap if he hadn't caught her in time to protect his throbbing cock. He eased her down, wrapping his arms around her and pulling her close.

The realization of how much rode on her reaction to his touch made his hands shake.

She felt so good in his arms. The slight fear in her eyes combining with arousal and curiosity stirred his blood in a way it hadn't been stirred in a very long time.

He knew he had to rein in his hunger so he didn't scare her, but going slowly had never been so difficult.

* * * *

Courtney trembled, finding it hard to believe that she'd actually sat on Zach's lap.

Blaming the flash of challenge in his eyes for her daring, she fisted her hands against her thighs to hide the fact that they shook.

His cock pressed against her bottom insistently, creating a hunger inside her she fought to ignore.

The arm around her tightened, drawing her steadily closer as he lowered his head.

She gasped at the feel of her breast pressing against his chest, her nipple aching for attention.

He took advantage of her gasp to take her mouth with his, sliding his tongue against hers in an erotic dance that sent a sharp stab of hunger to her slit.

Swallowing her moan, Zach tightened his hold, moving her against him as he deepened his kiss.

She didn't remember lifting her arm, but suddenly, her hand threaded through his hair, alternately smoothing and gripping its silkiness.

Flames of desire licked at her, making her ache everywhere.

Her breasts felt swollen and heavy, so aching and throbbing that it was a relief when her dress parted to release them, but not until a hot palm slid over her nipple did she realize what had happened.

With a cry, she arched into his hand, crying out again and again at the slide of his thumb over her nipple.

The erotic friction made her nipples tingle unbearably, each stroke of his thumb increasing the sensation.

He seemed to know just what she needed and gave it to her, cupping her breast and giving her nipple the attention she needed.

Pressing her thighs together against the throbbing in her clit, she moaned, her pussy clenching with need.

Lifting his head, Zach stared down at her and continued to stroke her nipple.

Biting her lip to hold back her cries, she saw Law out of the corner of her eye, his hooded gaze glittering with heat.

"Oh God. I can't believe this."

"Believe it." Zach bent his head, taking her nipple into his hot mouth and sucking, letting his teeth scrape lightly over it.

The pleasure stunned her, so sharp that she couldn't hold back her cries anymore. The pressure inside her continued to build until nothing mattered except release.

Law slid from the chair to kneel beside her. "She's not used to this. She needs to come." He slid his hand up her thigh, and to her shock, she parted her legs eagerly to give him access.

She needed to come so badly that she would have done anything. Hearing and feeling her panties being ripped from her only added to her excitement, and with another cry, she spread her legs as wide as the dress would allow, arching and crying out at the slide of his finger over her clit.

With Zach's attention to her nipple and Law's to her clit, she went over in a rush, the pleasure unlike anything she could have ever imagined.

She rode the finger Law pumped into her with no embarrassment at all, the hunger taking over.

Gripping Zach's hair, she held him to her as the waves of release crested, not caring about anything except the ecstasy that took over.

It held her in its powerful grip until she thought she might die of it before it released her into Zach's arms. As the pleasure subsided, embarrassment reared its head.

Mortified at what she'd done, she kept her eyes squeezed closed, waiting breathlessly for them to let her go.

Zach lifted his head, and she could feel his stare as he ran his thumb back and forth over her damp nipple. "We're not going anywhere, Courtney. There's no need to be embarrassed. Open your eyes."

Despite the fact that Law's finger remained inside her, slowly stroking in and out of her pussy, something in Zach's voice had her obeying him at once, her face burning to find both of them staring down at her.

Law's features appeared to be carved in stone. "It's taking every bit of willpower I can harness not to use my mouth on you. You're so fucking passionate that I could eat you alive."

Zach's jaw clenched. "I will see her, though. I don't want her shying away from us. Lift her dress higher.

Courtney gasped when Law slid his finger free and yanked her sundress to her waist, and Zach caught her knees with his powerful forearm, lifting them high.

Law moved, kneeling by her exposed slit, her legs preventing her from seeing his face. Sliding a finger into her again, he ran the other over her thigh. "Beautiful."

Zach turned his head to stare down at her slit, his eyes narrowing in a way that made her *feel* beautiful. "Damn, she's gorgeous. I can't wait to see her waxed."

Law slid his finger free to run it over her clit. "I can't resist. I have to have a taste. Hold on to her."

Courtney cried out at the feel of his hot tongue sliding through her slit, struggling when he slid it into her pussy. "Please. I can't take any more." Her clit had become so sensitive that even the slightest touch made her jolt, the intense pleasure too much to bear.

Zach groaned, a harsh sound that alarmed her. "Move. I want her ass."

It happened so fast that she had no defense against the powerful move.

Finding herself face down on Zach's lap, she didn't even get a chance to struggle before he slid his hands under her hips and lifted her, his tongue hot on her puckered opening.

Stunned by the foreign sensation, she froze, a cry escaping when he pushed his tongue into her.

At the same time, Law rubbed his fingers against her clit. "You're gonna come again, Courtney. Give it to me. Now."

Sensation layered over sensation, some of them too intense and primitive to absorb.

She had no chance to deny him, going over in a rush of ecstasy that left her breathless and shaking. Her cries grew weaker, her primitive response to such a primitive and decadent act alarming her.

Zach licked her bottom hole with a possessiveness that stunned her, branding her in a way that left her shaken.

Stunned.

Breathless.

When his teeth scraped over her ass cheek, she cried out again, surprised when Law moved beside her, his fingers slow on her clit as he reached under her to stroke a nipple.

"That's a good girl. See? There was nothing to be afraid of."

Zach lifted her to her feet to stand in front of him, his hands on her waist preventing her dress from falling to cover her. Leaning forward, he took her nipple into his mouth again, using his teeth to scrape lightly over it before releasing it. "Now that you know the pleasure, you won't be so nervous. You're so fucking beautiful and sweet. If you don't want to spend the day in my bed being fucked senseless, we'd better get going. My willpower's about shot."

* * * *

Aware of curious looks from his friends and neighbors, Law helped Courtney into the booth and slid in next to her. "You'll like the food here." Leaning closer when she appeared to be trying to ignore him, he slid his hand over her thigh. "It won't be as tasty as what I had a few minutes ago, though."

Delighted with her blush, he sat back to watch her, pleased to see he'd begun to learn her expressions.

Her embarrassment had eased, and she now wore a secret smile of pleasure, her movements slightly lethargic.

He felt ten feet tall.

This was what he'd always dreamed of—sharing a woman with his brother and living in the only place he really felt at home.

Suddenly, her smile wobbled and a strange sadness clouded her eyes.

"Courtney?"

She turned to him, the sadness disappearing from her eyes, but he'd seen it. "Yes?"

"Is something wrong?"

Shrugging, she closed the menu. "No. Not really. It's just a lot of changes in my life in the last few weeks, and I guess it's just getting to me."

"Would you like to talk about it?"

"No. It's just stuff jumbling around in my brain. I'm starving. Can I have the pancakes?"

From across the table, Zach glanced at his brother before smiling at her. "You can have whatever you want."

By mutual consent, he and Zach kept the conversation light during breakfast, asking about her job back in Blackwell and telling her about their offices in Dallas."

Before he knew it, she'd finished eating and pushed her plate back. "Thanks for breakfast. It was delicious."

Law smiled and sipped his coffee. "What would you like to do now?"

"If you don't mind, I want to walk around for a while."

"Good. We'll show you the town and see how much it's changed since you lived here."

Shaking her head, Courtney gathered her purse. "No. I'd like to be alone for a while. I need some time to think."

Law glanced at Zach, who watched her as he slowly lowered his cup. Not wanting to overwhelm her, Law inclined his head. "Be careful. Give me your phone so I can put our numbers in. I want you to call us if you need anything."

Shaking her head, she backed away, her smile fake and nervous. "No. Um, my battery's dead."

Clenching his jaw, Law caught her chin, forcing her to look at him. "If you feel threatened, get lost, or feel scared, just go into any store and ask them to call us."

Courtney blinked. "The entire town knows your phone number?"

Smiling, he took her hand and lifted it to his lips, not about to let her forget the intimacy between them. Getting to his feet, he helped her out of the booth. "Pretty much."

Averting her gaze again, she gave him another one of those fake smiles that irritated the hell out of him. "Thanks again for breakfast."

Because they were in the center of town, he knew she'd be safe, and that there would be little chance of her getting lost.

Watching her walk away, he let his gaze linger on her ass. "You get the feeling she's hiding something on that phone?"

Throwing several bills on the table, Zach got to his feet, watching her through the large window. "I didn't see her turn it back on after she shut it off last night, and she left her purse in the kitchen when she went to take her shower. How the hell would she know if the battery's dead—and if it was, why didn't she ask to leave it at the house to recharge it?"

Law gritted his teeth, fighting the urge to run after her. "There's a lot we don't know about her. It worries me. She's either gonna be the woman we've been looking for, or she's gonna rip our hearts out of our chests if we're not careful."

Zach started for the door. "Being careful isn't in the cards. We didn't get where we are by being careful."

Waving at the people who called out their good-byes, Law followed Zach outside, staring at Courtney as she walked down the sidewalk. "True. But only money was at stake. There's a lot more at stake with her."

Zach sighed. "I think she's worth it. Hell, I couldn't walk away from her now if I wanted to."

"Unfortunately, neither can I. Now I know why the others are so possessive. I used to think it was funny as hell." Watching her until she disappeared around the corner, he grimaced at the knots in his stomach.

Zach strode to the truck and pulled the door open. "Not laughing anymore, are we?"

"No." Law paused with his hand on the handle. "No. We're not." He yanked open the door with more force than necessary, wondering what the hell Courtney was hiding from him. "Let's go see Boone. I want to see what we can do before she gets home."

* * * *

Walking down the street, Courtney had to step aside several times for people coming the other way and make her way around those who stood window-shopping.

She didn't remember the main streets being so crowded, nor did she remember the ornate streetlights or the flowers in a riot of colors in planters and window boxes all over town.

Without thinking about her destination, she just walked, unsurprised when her footsteps led her to the building she'd walked to hundreds of times as a child.

Standing outside the vacant building that used to be her father's ice cream store, she rubbed her arms against the chill that went through her despite the hot weather.

She didn't know if she'd ever be comfortable living here, the bad memories rising up and threatening to choke her.

The fights between her parents.

Her father's temper.

The bruises and screams begging him to stop hitting her.

The soft crying afterward.

The fear.

Was she so like her mother that she would fall for the wrong kind of man?

Both Law and Zach were strong, their arrogance undeniable.

Spotting a bench not far away, she made her way to it, dropping onto it to stare at the building that had clearly seen better days.

Looking at it, she doubted that anyone had used it since her father closed its doors for the last time. She didn't even know who it belonged to.

It's a great location for a flower shop.

Calling herself a fool for even entertaining such an idea, she looked away, surprised by the number of shoppers bustling up and down the wide sidewalks.

With the intention of looking around to see if there was another flower shop in town, she got to her feet, averting her gaze from the building and making her way down the sidewalk.

Memories assailed her as she made her way down the rows of businesses. She remembered some of them, but many new ones had either sprung up or she didn't remember them.

One in particular caught her attention, a store named Indulgences. Several women walked out with pretty purple bags, and when Courtney looked in the wide ceiling-to-floor windows, she saw shelves stocked with rows and rows of bottles and tubes that appeared to hold all kinds of lotions and creams.

Deciding to pamper herself with some hand cream, she went inside.

A beautiful young women, busily restocking shelves, smiled in welcome. Slim and dressed in plain jeans and a purple blouse, she seemed to glow. "Hello. Welcome to Indulgences. I'm Brenna."

"Hello, Brenna. I'm Courtney." Drawn by the woman's friendliness, and fighting her own insecurities, she grinned. "You and I have about the same color hair and I've never worn that color before. I think I'm going to have to go buy one. It looks fantastic on you."

Brenna beamed. "Thank you. My husbands seemed to like it, too. I was almost late for work." Giggling, she put the last bottle on the shelf and turned. "Can I help you find something, Courtney?" Her smile widened. "Courtney! You're the one who owns the property next to the Tylers'."

Courtney grimaced. "Word travels fast around Desire."

Laughing again, Brenna nodded. "You bet. It's still hard for me to get used to. The way I understand it, Law and Zach wanted word passed around to look after you." Grinning, she touched Courtney's arm. "They obviously have a thing for you, so it's also a kind of warning for other men that you're already spoken for. They've already opened accounts for you all over town, including here, so shop away."

"But I just met them yesterday."

"Apparently, it doesn't take the men of Desire long to make up their minds about something."

Letting that pass, Courtney looked around to make sure there weren't any other customers. "Did you say that you have *husbands*?"

Although Law and Zach had spoken of it, Courtney had a hard time believing that anything like that could work—especially on a permanent basis.

Brenna giggled again, her eyes sparkling as she moved around to the other side of the counter. "Oh, yeah. I have two of them, King and Royce, and they're a handful. They own the men's club with Blade Royal."

"The men's club?"

Brenna nodded, propping her chin on her hand. "Yes. Club Desire. It's where Dominant men go. They talk about their need to be Dominant, play cards, and just hang out, I guess. I never get to see very much, but I do see the submissive women who go there to explore their need to submit. It's all very safe, and from what I can tell, there are a lot of rules they have to adhere to. One is that married men aren't allowed to touch any of them, which gives me a hell of a lot of peace of mind. Some of those women are gorgeous."

"Dominants?" Courtney shivered. "I can't even imagine what those poor women endure. Why do they do it?"

"Oh no!" Brenna straightened and gripped her arm, her eyes wide. "It's nothing like that. It fulfills the needs that some people have a hard time fulfilling elsewhere. Royce, King, and I have that kind of marriage, and believe me, the last thing either one of my husbands would do is hurt me."

Courtney bit back a gasp. "You're married to men who want to dominate you?" She thought of her mother and her father's need to be in charge—and all the hurt that it had caused.

Brenna smiled. "Yes, but judging by the look on your face, it's not what you think." Frowning, she paused, and then smiled again. "I'll tell you what. Why don't you come to the open house? There's one a month and women can come there and see what it's like. There's one coming up this week."

Curiosity clawed at her, but after what had happened that morning, Courtney didn't think she could work up the courage. "I couldn't."

"You'll be with me. You can sit there with me, relax, and have a drink. You can leave anytime you feel uncomfortable."

Brenna turned to the counter and wrote down a phone number on the back of a business card. "The open house is this Friday night. Let me know if you're coming. Some of the other women in town will, and I'd love to introduce you to them. I meet them at the door."

"That sounds like a lot of trouble."

"Not at all. We live for stuff like this, and love getting together, especially in the men's club. It drives our husbands nuts."

Remembering the looks on Law's and Zach's faces that morning, Courtney grimaced. "And that doesn't scare you?"

Brenna laughed softly, her cheeks turning pink. "Of course not. My husbands will be particularly amorous and *very* possessive afterward. I'm very much looking forward to it."

Picking up a jar of cream, Courtney glanced at Brenna. "What's it like to have two husbands?"

Brenna sighed, her smile falling. "I was scared, at first, but it's absolutely wonderful. I love them so much, and they love me. They're so good to me. I swear, I never knew men like King and Royce existed. The men in this town are incredible, aren't they?"

Courtney shrugged, turning her attention to the sample jars. "I don't know. I just got here yesterday. Law and Zach are arrogant. They're already telling a man named Boone to fix my house." She opened one jar, loving the lavender scent.

"Aren't they all? It can be frustrating, but I'll tell you, I've never been happier in my life. They're strong men—strong enough to make a woman feel secure. They're steady."

Courtney drew in breath and let it out slowly, knowing she had to ask. "Are Law and Zach members of this club?"

"Yes. Don't look like that. Once they've committed themselves to you, they can't touch any of the women there."

"I don't want any commitment. I'll only be here for a year." Touched by Brenna's look of disappointment, Courtney screwed the lid back on the sample jar and put it aside. "Don't your husbands ever get jealous of each other?"

"Probably, but it only makes them more possessive. Dominant. Sweet."

Thinking about her father's bad moods and tirades, Courtney seriously doubted that. "Dominant and sweet don't exactly go together."

Brenna smiled gently. "They do here—something that I'm sure you're going to find out for yourself."

Not knowing what to say to that, Courtney picked out a jar of the lavender cream from the display. "You've given me a lot to think about." Lifting the cream, she smiled. "This smells wonderful. It really smells like lavender. Do you have a flower shop in town where you buy it?"

Brenna shook her head. "Unfortunately, no. The closest flower shop is about a half-hour's drive from here, and they don't have much of a selection. We really could use a flower shop around here."

After Brenna rang up the purchase, she sighed and leaned against the counter. "I haven't been in town long, but it's been amazing. Come to the club. I'll ask Nat, Jesse, Hope, and Charity to come. Kelly's busy with her new baby, and Blade watches her like a hawk. Rachel's been spending her time with her sister, Erin, getting the nursery ready for Erin's new baby. If you have any questions, they could answer them."

Wondering if she could learn anything about her parents, and wondering what the people in town would think of her when they discovered that her father had been run out of town, Courtney hesitated. "I'll think about it. Thank you for the offer." She'd also think about the possibility of opening a flower shop in town. She could always sell it when she left, or just close it, but in the meantime she could make some money to pay for the things that needed to be done in her house. If she had to live there a year, she might as well be comfortable, and it would keep her busy.

"It'll be quite an education. I promise."

Courtney nodded, accepting the purple bag. "That's what I'm afraid of."

Chapter Seven

Thinking about what she'd learned from Brenna, Courtney continued on her way down the sidewalk, not really paying attention to or caring where she was going.

In a small town like Desire, it would be nearly impossible to get lost, and she recognized several landmarks along the way.

She remembered the police station but didn't remember the tall, imposing building situated on a side road that hadn't been there before.

Pausing, she squinted against the sunlight coming from almost directly overhead to read the sign posted in the distance.

Club Desire.

It looked so dark and imposing, even in the light of day.

She'd heard about domination and submission, of course, but she couldn't even imagine the attraction.

The thought of being at the mercy of a man scared the hell out of her.

Turning away, she crossed the street and started down the next block in the other direction, soon finding herself at the park where she used to play sometimes as a child.

Making her way across the thick grass, she found an empty bench in the shade, lowered herself onto it, and let the memories she'd been fighting back take over.

She remembered her mother sitting here, on the bench Courtney sat on now, wiping away tears after fighting with Courtney's father—more often than not wearing makeup to cover the bruises he'd given her.

Her mother had always denied that she was crying, usually telling Courtney that she had something in her eye.

But Courtney had known the truth.

Blinking back tears, she stared sightlessly toward the swing set she'd played on as a child.

She'd gone higher and higher, so high that she could almost touch the clouds—to a place where her father couldn't reach her.

"Are you all right?"

Jolting, Courtney wiped away the tears streaming down her cheeks, alarmed to find the biggest and coldest looking man she'd ever seen standing only a few yards away.

Only the fact that he wore a sheriff's uniform kept her from jumping up and running away. "I'm fine. Thank you." She slid a glance toward the man standing beside him, also in uniform—a tall, muscular, cold-looking man, his eyes like chips of ice. "Please, just leave me alone."

To her surprise, the ice in the other man's ice melted, the apology for scaring her evident as he took several steps back. "We only want to help."

Shocking her further, the man standing in front of her squatted, putting himself on her level. "What's your name?"

"Courtney. Courtney Sheldon."

His smile didn't make him appear any less dangerous. "The one who has her house plugged into mine."

At her look of surprise, he chuckled softly. "I'm Ace Tyler. Law and Zach's brother." His smile fell. "Are you hurt? Did they do something to upset you? Has anyone been bothering you?"

Amused by the rapid-fire questions and warmed by his concern, Courtney shook her head. "No, I'm not hurt. I came here to think. Yes, your brothers are a pain. They hired a man named Boone to rewire my house. He and Sloane had to tear out walls to do it, and my house is a mess."

Ace frowned. "I don't blame them. I would have been disappointed in them if my brothers hadn't seen to your safety. From what I hear, that house is in bad shape and dangerous. Why don't you sleep at our house tonight? No. Don't look like that. We have a spare bedroom, and I'm a very light sleeper."

"I appreciate that, but I can't. I have to stay in the house." Waving her hand at his frown, she sighed. "It's a long story, and I'm not up to telling it. I promise you that I'm fine. Thank you for checking."

"I already know your story." His lips twitched at her look of surprise. "I make it my business to know everything that goes on in my town." He straightened, and although he towered over her, he no longer frightened her. His size and concern in his eyes reassured her, and she found herself relaxing slightly as she accepted the card he offered. "If you need anything—day or night—just call me. If anyone bothers you, I want you to let me know about it, okay?"

Nodding, Courtney forced a smile, depression weighing heavily on her shoulders. "Okay. Thank you."

She watched them until they got into a large dark SUV, emblazoned with the sheriff's logo, before turning away. Too restless to sit still, she got to her feet and made her way toward a grove of trees that surrounded the edges of the park, walking the paths she'd seen her mother walk a thousand times before.

At one time, she'd had a lot of good memories about her childhood.

Now she seemed able to remember only the bad.

The tears. The fights. The tension.

The fear.

Living with her aunt, she'd grown stronger, but being here brought the vulnerability back. The feeling of defenseless that she'd thought she'd gotten over years earlier came back in full force as she thought about Law and Zach.

They were both overbearing men like her father, and although they hadn't displayed his temper or cruelty, she couldn't help but wonder if they had it in them.

Her mother reminisced many times about how kind and thoughtful her father had been to her before they got married.

"Baby, are you okay?"

Startled by Zach's masculine voice coming from behind her, Courtney whirled, both relieved and alarmed to see Law and Zach approaching. Both appeared dirty, as though they'd been working on something since she'd seen them last.

Wiping the dampness from her cheeks, she nodded. "I'm fine. What are you doing here?"

Law frowned. "What do you mean, what are we doing here? You said you wanted some time alone, and we get a call from Ace. He told us that you were sitting alone in the park crying. What are we supposed to do—ignore that?"

Zach moved closer, frowning when she backed away. "What's wrong, honey? Ace said you weren't hurt—at least physically. Why are you crying?"

Turning away, she stared unseeingly at the trees. "I have a lot of thinking to do. Why can't you just leave me alone?"

Law moved in on her other side, wrapping an arm around her and pulling her against him, thwarting her attempt to get away. "Because we just can't. You're sad and hurt, and we can't just walk away from that." Tilting her head back, he stared into her eyes, the tenderness in his gaze undoing her. "There's something about you that pulls at me. It's something I've searched for a long time and I'd never thought I'd find. I want to get to know you better. I want to explore this attraction between us."

Lifting a brow, he smiled faintly. "Or are you going to pretend that you didn't respond to me or to Zach earlier?"

Zach watched her steadily. "You're not going to try to deny that you're attracted to us, are you?"

"Sex isn't everything."

Zach inclined his head. "No, it's not. If I wanted sex, I could find it anywhere."

"Like at the men's club?"

Law frowned. "What do you know about the men's club?"

"Brenna told me all about it. Do you know Brenna?"

Zach grimaced. "We know Brenna. I ought to make a call to King. He needs to spank his wife more often." His grimace turned to a teasing smile. "These women are getting out of hand."

Courtney stiffened. "You think that it's okay to hit women?"

Law whipped her around to face him. "Are you out of your mind? Neither one of us would ever hit a woman—at least not the way you're talking about."

Zach smiled. "Do you realize that most of the women in this town goad their husbands into spanking them? Brenna seems to be one of them. I'll have to make that call, after all. I'm probably doing all of them a favor." Moving to stand directly in front of her, he took her hand in his. "Spankings are common in Desire. The women get the attention they love, the men get a chance to keep their women in line, and both thoroughly enjoy the pleasure."

"Pleasure? You're deluding yourself."

"No, sweetheart. We're not. Now, tell me why you were crying."

Turning, she strolled away from them, uneasy at the effect they had on her. "I came here because it's what my aunt wanted." Shrugging, she kept moving, aware that they followed. "I used to think about living here a lot, and I guess I romanticized it. I remembered coming to the park with my mother. I remembered going to the ice cream store with her when she had to work. I guess I'd tried to block out all the bad things. I couldn't block all of them, but I used to think about the good."

Zach reached out without moving closer, running a hand down her arm. "That's good, honey. It's good to remember the happy times."

Courtney brushed angrily at a fresh rush of tears. "I can't remember them now. Since I came here, everything I see reminds me of the bad. The yelling. The fights. The hitting. Always the hitting."

Law's jaw clenched, his voice dropping dangerously low. "He hit you, too, didn't he?"

Reminding herself that she didn't have to keep it a secret anymore, she nodded, taking a shaky breath. "Yes. I had to hide the marks so no one would see them."

The memory of wearing long-sleeved cardigans in the summertime made her skin crawl.

Zach reached for her, but she jerked away before he could touch her. "Is that why you went to live with your aunt?"

"Yes. Partly. My mother dropped me off there when she left my father. She just wanted a new life. She's married now. Happily. Anyway, she left me with Aunt Sally. She knew I loved her and that I would be safe there. My father argued at first, but she told him that she'd documented his abuse and would go to the police with it if he tried to take me from my aunt." She smiled at the memory. "She knew Aunt Sally was a lot stronger than she was and wouldn't let my father near me."

Law kept his steps even with hers. "So why did your aunt want you to come here?"

Courtney smiled, remembering her aunt's letter. "My aunt found the love of her life here and expected me to do the same. She was a great lady, but she did always look on the bright side of things— perhaps a little too often. She always saw the goodness in people— except for my father. He was actually scared of her."

Zach's tender smile made her want to cry again. "She sounds like an incredible woman."

Missing her aunt so much it hurt, she blinked back tears. "She was. But, in this, she was wrong. I hate it here. Desire's too full of bad memories for me to stay. I'll stay the year I promised, mostly because my aunt boxed me into a corner. If I leave, my father gets the money, and she knew I would never allow that, so I have to stay for a year." With a sigh, she turned to face them. "I could never stay here, and this is your home. I know you've never mentioned having more than an affair, but to tell you the truth, I can't do it. You're too strong. Too arrogant. Too *dominant*. The thought of being alone with you scares me."

After a long, pregnant silence, Law nodded. "I understand better now, but you have no need to fear either one of us. You want to stay, don't you?"

Shaking her head, she sniffed. "I can't. There's too many bad memories here."

Zach ran a hand over her hair. "So why don't we make some good memories?"

Courtney stiffened, her stomach clenching. "What do you mean?"

With an arm around her shoulder, he turned her back to face the park. "What do you remember about being here—in this park?"

Courtney sighed and let him lead her back toward the trees close to the swing set. "My mother crying. Feeling sad for her. Scared because there wasn't anything I could do about it. Sore from where he'd hit me. Terrified because I knew he'd do it again."

Law's eyes lit with fury. "Zach's right. Why don't we see if we can make some good memories here?"

Zach pulled her closer, his hands gentle as they moved over her back. "Your mother's happy now, right?"

Lulled by his soft tone, and soothed by his caress, she found herself leaning into him. "Yes. She's happy. She even has a new family now."

* * * *

A family that doesn't include you.
Zach wanted to hit something.

He wanted to wrap her in cashmere and lace and make sure she never got hurt again.

He'd gladly rip anyone who hurt her to shreds.

He met Law's gaze briefly over her head, unsurprised at the angry glint in his brother's eyes.

Focusing his attention on Courtney, Law lifted her chin, smiling and keeping his voice low and soothing. "There's nothing here to be unhappy about, and Law and I would never dream of hurting you." At her skeptical look, Zach smiled and bent to touch his lips to hers, unable to resist any longer. "I'll admit that we're arrogant, but we run an oil company. We can't exactly be pushovers. We get things done, though, and I have a feeling it wouldn't take you long to figure out how to get around us. God help us because I have a feeling a spitfire like you would make us as crazy as Hope makes Ace—and we'd love it as much as he does."

Law closed in from behind, nuzzling her neck. "I think you've already found it because I'd do anything to make you smile. Power in women is a dangerous thing."

Courtney smiled and leaned back against him, giving Zach a tantalizing view of the upper curve of her breasts. "That's a fantasy. Men are stronger and much more ruthless."

Law chuckled, but Zach heard the tension in it. "Have you met our sister-in-law? Hope is single-minded when it comes to getting what she wants."

Courtney's smile eased some of the knots in Zach's stomach. "She's married to Ace, right? She must be built like an Amazon to take on a man like that."

Law kissed her neck, rocking her gently. "She's even smaller than you are."

Courtney turned to look up at Law over her shoulder, blushing adorably. "You're kidding."

Zach took her hand in his and pressed her palm against his chest, loving her touch. "Nope. You can meet her at dinner."

Reddening even more, she pulled her hand away, but not before pressing her fingertips against his chest. "I, um, don't think that's a good idea."

"Hope's gonna show up at your door whether you want her to or not." With a smile, Law straightened and kissed the top of her head. "She's dying to meet you. Just take everything she says in stride. She's happy and thinks she knows what's best for everyone to make them just as happy as she is."

Zach cupped her cheek, watching her eyes as he slid a hand from his shoulder down to cover her breast. His cock jumped at her sharp intake of breath. "You like my touch. No. Don't be embarrassed. You don't know how happy it makes me."

Law wrapped his hands around her waist, a determined glint in his eyes that made Zach smile. "You feel so good. We want you so much, and need you to believe that we won't hurt you."

Watching Courtney's eyes cloud and then flutter closed, Zach double-checked to make sure no one passing would be able to see them before lifting her shirt, exposing her breast to his gaze. "You're so beautiful. I can't wait to get you naked and explore every inch of you. Before long, I'll know your body as intimately as I know my own." Closing his fingers over her nipple, he shared a look with Law and squeezed lightly.

"Oh God!"

Her cry sent a jolt of heat to his cock.

Rolling her nipple between his thumb and forefinger, Zach watched her closely for any sign of fear.

Relieved to see none, he bent to nibble at her bottom lip. "Your nipples are very sensitive. Very beautiful. I know for a fact that they're as sweet as they look. Look at me, darlin'."

* * * *

Courtney forced her eyes open, struggling to catch Zach's fleeting kisses. Moaning at the sharp stab of pleasure when the pressure at her nipple increased, she raised herself to her toes, arching her back in reaction.

The way they touched her was like a dream, every stroke of their fingers—every slide of their hands—designed to give her pleasure.

Wondering how they could know just what she needed, she stared into Zach's eyes, too overwhelmed to speak.

Smiling down at her, Zach groaned softly, a groan that seemed to ripple over her skin. "You seem to be under the impression that our need to dominate means that we get some sort of kick out of hurting women."

Lifting her chin, Courtney fisted her hands in the material of his shirt. "Doesn't it?" They didn't hurt her now. Instead, they played her body like an instrument they'd long ago mastered.

Law moved slightly, closing in on her side, his gaze steady as he slid a hand over her belly, making her stomach muscles quiver. "Not at all. We have a need to be in charge, a need to give as much pleasure as possible. Look at what happened earlier. Did that seem cruel or mean to you?"

"No. Oh God. I never thought I could feel that way."

Sliding a hand under her hair, Zach pulled her against him, dropped a hard kiss on her lips, and slid his hand into the bodice of her dress. "It can get even better. Trust us."

* * * *

Courtney gasped at the feel of a hard, warm finger slipping through her folds. "I don't trust easily."

The slide of Law's finger over her clit had her biting her lip, the rush of sensation making her dizzy.

Fisting a hand in her hair, Law bent to brush his lips over hers. "Which is going to make your trust even more precious to us."

Zach bent to touch his lips to her nipple, running his tongue over it before lifting his head again. "Damn, you're sweet. Those soft little cries have my cock throbbing to take you."

Finding it nearly impossible to concentrate on anything except the slow slide of Law's finger over her clit, Courtney moaned. "Yes!"

"No." Zach smiled. "The first time we take you, it sure as hell isn't going to be in the park. We will show you, though, how a little pain can bring a great deal of pleasure."

Stiffening, Courtney pressed her hands against his chest, her knees weakening as flames of need licked at her. "P–pain can never b–bring pleasure. Pain hurts. That's it."

Zach nuzzled her neck on the other side, the combination of their lips and hands on her making it difficult to stand. "I'm going to change your mind about that."

Courtney cried out, a cry Law muffled with his own mouth, when Zach tightened his fingers on her nipple, the sharp jolt of pain sending a rush of the most incredible pleasure to her clit.

She trembled everywhere, the pleasure seeming stronger each time they touched her.

More familiar. More exciting.

Each touch became more intimate, more assertive.

Dominant.

The word came to her just as Zach tightened his fingers, the pressure on her nipple sending another rush of pleasure to her slit.

Law swallowed her cries, his fingers moving relentlessly against her clit and sending her over. "See, babe? Only for pleasure. God, I love how you feel in my arms. I love those little cries of pleasure. Christ, you get to me."

Zach released her nipple and watched her eyes as he bent to lick it, the low, slow stroke of his tongue like little sparks of electricity on her sensitized flesh. "See, darlin'? There's nothing to fear. We wouldn't hurt you for the world. We want to learn your body and your needs. We want to learn every inch of you."

* * * *

Straightening, Zach righted her dress, pressing soft kisses against her shoulder. Smiling at the shiver that went through her, and loving the feel of her soft skin beneath his lips, he straightened and gathered her close. "Easy, darlin'. Just hold on to me."

Zach wanted to throw his head back and yell, the primitive rush of possessiveness making him want to shout his pleasure at finding his woman to the world.

The sexual dominance he'd experienced in the past didn't even compare to the need to dominate now.

This was different. Special. All-consuming.

He wanted more than sex. He wanted the right to hold her. Dress her. Take care of her in the thousands of ways a man cared for his woman.

Meeting Law's gaze over her head, he watched his brother move behind her again.

With a slow grin that Courtney couldn't see, Law kissed her temple, his eyes filled with satisfaction. "Knowing you're not wearing panties because I tore them off you excites the hell out of me."

Courtney jolted upright, her cheeks a fiery red. "I can't go around without panties. I feel naked."

Zach hid a smile, enjoying himself more than he had in years. "Looks like you're not going to have any choice. Don't worry. I'll go by Rachel and Erin's shop in a little while and buy you some new ones."

"You can't buy panties for me!"

Zach smiled again, wondering if there'd ever been a woman so adorable. "We can make you come, but we can't buy panties for you because it's too intimate? God, you're sweet."

Law smiled and turned her to face the park again, leading her slowly out of the grove of trees, obviously in deference to her wobbly legs. "It's going to be a lot of fun picking out lingerie for you."

Zach smiled at the sight of his brother holding her close and running a hand up and down her back to help settle her.

As they made their way across the park, Zach touched her arm, urging her to stop next to him. Wrapping an arm around her, he turned her to face the grove of trees, lifting her chin until her gaze met his. "I hope when you look at the park now, it's a good memory. Law and I want you very much, Courtney. Maybe replacing those bad memories with good ones will convince you to stay."

He sure as hell hoped so. Every minute he spent with her made him want her more.

A year could be a long time, but not if he had to replace years' worth of childhood memories.

They had to make every minute count.

Chapter Eight

Courtney shifted restlessly as she listened to Cole Madison explain that they'd finished the wiring and would be back the next day to fix the drywall. She didn't hear most of it, distracted by the sight of bare studs all over her house and the knowledge that she wore no panties.

Her slit still hummed with an awareness that she'd never known before, making it difficult to stand still. Her knees still shook, and the intimate looks Law and Zach gave her made it even more impossible to stay focused.

She wanted them—badly—and struggled to understand why they hadn't taken her yet.

If it was because they didn't want her that way, she'd been a fool, something she didn't want to think about until she was alone.

Redoubling her efforts, she turned her back to Law and Zach and focused on Cole. "You broke my house."

His expression went from cool and businesslike to indulgent and mild amusement. "I know. Some of the plaster practically fell apart in our hands. We also had to put some new insulation in. What you had was almost nonexistent. We'll have it all fixed up for you tomorrow."

With her hands on her hips, Courtney looked around, purposely avoiding Law and Zach. "This is going to cost a whole lot more than two hundred dollars."

Shaking his head, Cole held up a hand. "No. We stand behind our estimates. We knew we would have to replace some drywall and paint. We left the paint samples on the coffee table over there. I'm afraid we're going to have to paint every room."

"*Every room?*"

"The paint's old, and probably contains lead. I'm sure this house hasn't been painted in a long time. We'd never be able to match anything."

Aware that Law and Zach moved in closer, she moved farther into the kitchen. "I don't care if it matches or not. I'm leaving in a year. I can deal with mismatched walls until then."

Cole frowned. "We don't leave a job half-finished."

"That's a lot of work for two hundred dollars."

"This is Desire, not Dallas or Houston. Don't you worry about a thing." Chuckling softly, he gestured toward Law and Zach. "Your men are watching out for you. If I tried to cheat you, I'd have to deal with them."

"Do I at least have hot water? Can I turn on my lights?"

"Yep. All taken care of."

Courtney shot a grin at Law and Zach. "Good. Then I won't have to bother your brother and sister-in-law again for a shower."

Zach frowned. "It's not a bother—and you used *our* shower."

Cole gathered his things, looking slightly preoccupied. "I'll see you tomorrow." He met Law's and Zach's searching looks. "Sloane took Marissa to the doctor today. Brett left a little while ago to go see her."

Law's eyes sharpened. "Is she all right?"

Cole sighed. "She's pale and listless, and when Sloane showed up at the shop and strong-armed her into going to the doctor, he found out she had a fever."

Turning to face Courtney, he smiled, a smile tight with worry. "Marissa works in the lingerie store in town. Rachel Jackson and Erin Preston are sisters, and they own the store. They made Marissa the manager and hired several women for her to train. You met Sloane. He and Brett are my brothers."

Zach nodded. "With Rachel overworked and Erin about to give birth, Rachel and Erin need the help."

Cole smiled. "Marissa loves being trusted with the responsibility. She thrives on it, but after sleepless nights taking care of a sick little boy, she ended up sick. She's worn out but won't let us help."

Law looked meaningfully at Courtney. "Frustrating, isn't it?"

Cole sighed. "Yeah, but now she has no choice. She's down with a fever and needs help, whether she wants it or not." He started out, pausing at the doorway to turn. "By the way, I forgot to tell you that we checked out the plumbing, and it's fine. Surprisingly."

Hiding a grimace, Courtney nodded, knowing that she'd have to do something about finding a job in order to fix up the house a little. She didn't want to touch the money she'd set aside for her flower shop. "Thank you."

Courtney watched him go, surprised that Law followed him out. When the door closed behind them, she went to sit on the sofa and met Zach's searching gaze, her face burning at the memory of what they'd done in the park. "I had a nice day. Thank you."

Zach came into the room to sit in the chair across from her. Raising a brow, he leaned back, stretching his long legs out in front of him. "I don't want platitudes from you. I think we're a little past that now, aren't we?"

"Are we?"

"Why don't you get showered while we run next door and do the same? I'm covered in drywall dust, and it's itchy as hell. I don't know how they do it all day."

"You're used to sitting in an office, aren't you?"

"For the most part. We can talk about it over—" The ringing of his cell phone cut off whatever he'd been about to say, and with a muttered curse, he dug it out of his pocket and answered it. "Zach Tyler."

While he spoke on the phone, she took the time to study him.

Even angry and dirty, he looked sexy as hell. With his shoulder-length hair tied back, he had a bad-boy look about him, emphasized by the jeans and dirty T-shirt that he wore like a model.

His jeans, although not tight, encased a perfectly formed ass that she itched to touch, and as he paced her small living room, she couldn't help but admire it.

Wide shoulders and firm muscle bunched and shifted as he gestured angrily.

His voice, like fire encased in ice, sent a chill through her, and she knew that if he ever used that voice with her, she'd be running for the door.

His strength, both in body and character, was like nothing she'd ever known before.

He and Law were like rock—solid and inflexible once they'd made up their minds—but both had shown a tenderness she'd never before seen in a man.

She couldn't afford to make any mistakes, and with her background, she couldn't help but wonder how deep that tenderness went, or if it was all a show to lure her in.

With a curse, he disconnected, his features hard as he shoved the phone back into his pocket and turned to his brother, who'd just come back inside. "We've got a problem in Dallas."

He turned to her, surprising her by moving closer and kneeling in front of her. "This is just a short trip. Believe me, we're going to get back as soon as we can. I want your cell phone number, and I want you to have ours. You can call either one of us anytime." He dug out his phone again and punched in the number as she rattled it off.

Wrapping his arms around her, he pressed his lips against her thigh, her breast, her neck, and, finally, her lips. Lifting his head, he pushed her hair back from her face and smiled down at her. "You're so sweet." Rising to his feet, he braced a hand on the back of the sofa on either side of her and leaned over her. "Think about me while I'm gone."

He touched his lips to hers, nibbling lightly. "I'll call you later."

Law took Zach's place. "Call Trevor and have him get the plane ready. I'm just gonna say good-bye to Courtney."

Firm hands pulled her closer, and with a groan, Law pressed his lips against her belly. "Ace and the others will watch over you." Lifting his head, he cupped her jaw, his eyes glittering with something that stole her breath. "Behave yourself. You'd better miss me because I'm sure as hell gonna miss you."

* * * *

Lying in bed, she rolled to her side, wrapping her arms around the pillow she held against her.

She was tired—pleasantly so—but thoughts of Law and Zach kept her awake.

Her body still hummed with awareness, but it was the memory of the way they'd looked at her before they'd left that kept playing over and over again in her mind.

They'd looked torn, as if leaving her cost them dearly, something she hadn't expected.

They hadn't known each other long enough for that kind of closeness.

Then why am I lying here missing them so much?

Her phone rang, startling her. With a gasp, she sat up and checked the display, her heart pounding at the thought of her father calling again.

Seeing a strange number, she pressed a hand to her chest, hoping it was Law or Zach. "Hello?"

"Hey, babe. How are you?" Blowing out a breath at the sound of Law's voice, Courtney took the pillow she'd been cuddling and pushed it against the headboard to lean back against it. "I'm fine. How are you? The way you raced out of here, it must have been some emergency. Or did you have your secretary call so you had an excuse to leave?"

"I hated leaving you, and no, if I wanted to go, I would have gone. I don't need a damned excuse." His voice lowered. "You get real brave when we're not there, huh? I guess I'm going to have to do something about that."

The deep chuckle told her that Zach was also on the line. "We'll have to see if we can give her the confidence to be that brave in person. Courtney, how are you, honey? Ace said that you only picked at your food at dinner. Is something wrong, or are you just missing us?"

"He and Hope picked me up. Neither one of them would take no for an answer. It must run in the family."

Law laughed softly. "See? You're beginning to understand us already."

Scooting down in the bed, she pulled the covers higher and yawned. "I met Hope. I like her."

"She likes you, too." The amusement in Law's voice made her smile.

Curling onto her side, she let her eyes drift closed. "She wants to take me shopping."

"Good. You should go and have a good time." Zach paused. "Baby, your words are slurring. Are you in bed?"

With the phone braced, she wrapped her arm around the pillow again, listening to their voices in the darkness. "Yes."

"Hmm. I wish I was with you."

Law groaned. "So do I, but that damned bed's too small. We need to get you a new one so there's room for all of us."

Courtney had been imagining them curled next to her for hours. "Don't you think it's a little soon for that?"

"The sooner the better. You feel it, too. It happened fast between us. Why waste time?"

Courtney frowned, promising herself that she wouldn't fall for any of their lines. "Because I'm not sure."

Law sighed. "I understand that you're nervous. You've been hurt in the past and are afraid of being vulnerable."

Uneasy with his perceptiveness, she tried to turn the table on him. "How many lovers have you had?"

Law sighed at that, and for the first time, she recognized the fatigue in his voice. "Enough to be a good lover to you and give you everything you need. That's the only important thing. I'm clean, and so is Zach. You have nothing to worry about in that aspect."

She let her eyes close and smiled. "That's good. I'm healthy, too. I can't believe you actually brought that up. I know I should have, but I didn't know how."

"I believe in honesty and demand it from my lover."

"Do you believe in being just as honest?"

"Of course. You can ask me anything, but first, I want an answer from you. What happened when you lost your virginity? What made it so bad that you didn't take another lover?"

Rolling to her back, Courtney sighed. "It was awful. It hurt and then was over so fast that I ended up feeling used and ugly."

She frowned, opening her eyes. "I can't believe I just told you that."

"I'm honored that you did. Having two lovers is going to be a big adjustment for you. You're going to feel even more vulnerable, and Zach and I need to earn your trust. You're starting to trust us already, aren't you, baby?"

Courtney sat up, wrapping her arms around herself. "How much do you have to trust someone to have an affair with them?"

The tense silence that followed filled her with apprehension, but the calmness and weariness in Law's voice eased some of her nerves. "Probably more than you think. It looks like we're going to be here for a few days. Will you miss me?"

"Maybe."

His voice lowered seductively. "I just might make you pay for that."

Feeling braver on the phone, surrounded by darkness, Courtney found herself lured by the intimacy. "Is that part of that dominance that you crave?"

Law chuckled. "Absolutely." His voice lowered. "I want to make sure you're thinking about me all the time and to understand that I have a need to take care of you."

Courtney smiled at that, running a hand over her beaded nipple. "I can take care of myself."

Zach's voice sounded deeper than ever. "We know that. That doesn't mean that you can't let us take care of you, too. I'm wishing right now that I was there holding you instead of here, having a drink in the hopes that it'll let me sleep."

Touched, Courtney smiled. "Do you miss me?"

"Like hell." Zach groaned, and she heard the tinkling of ice against glass. "I keep thinking about how it would be to be falling asleep cupping your breast instead of sitting her holding a cold glass."

Struggling to understand their needs, and what they expected from her, Courtney chewed at her lip. "I don't understand this dominance thing. You talk about taking care of me, but my father was domineering and never took care of my mother. I just don't understand what you expect from me."

Law sighed. "It's complicated to explain, but it is whatever we make of it. There's no set limits. It's a work in progress. You'll understand what we want from you soon enough."

Pulling the sheet higher against the air conditioning, Courtney dropped back against the pillows. "That's what I'm afraid of."

Zach chuckled. "It'll be the most exciting adventure of our lives. Are you okay? I know you must be a little uneasy sleeping in a new place alone. I'm sorry we had to leave. Would you like me to send the plane for you?"

"No. You know I have to stay here. Besides, I need some time alone."

The ice clinked before Zach spoke again. "I don't like leaving you alone. I think I'm going to have to make a call to that attorney. I'd like to bring you to Dallas, and it shouldn't violate the terms of your aunt's will."

"I can't let my father have this property."

"He won't."

Not wanting to think about her father, Courtney changed the subject. "I closed my bedroom door. I have no walls, but I closed the door. Stupid, huh?"

Law chuckled. "Not stupid at all. Cute as hell. I talked to Chase, and he assured me that you'll have your walls back tomorrow. Did you pick out paint colors?"

"I'm just going to paint everything white. It doesn't really matter since you're going to tear it down in a year."

Another pregnant silence followed before Zach spoke again. "When we get home, we'll show you the plans for the house we want to build."

Stiffening, Courtney rose and made her way to the kitchen, too restless to sleep. "I know you're in a hurry to build your house, but you're going to have to wait until I leave."

Zach made a growling sound, a sound filled with frustration. "I'm not in a hurry for you to leave, damn it!"

She turned on the light, grimacing at the mess in her kitchen. "But you're in a hurry to build your house. I'm afraid the two go hand in hand." She could practically feel her heart breaking and could only imagine the pain she'd have to endure if she allowed herself to get involved with them any further. "Look, I appreciate your help, but I think it would be better if we didn't get involved."

Zach growled again. "We *are* involved."

Moving carefully across the floor, she made her way to the window, looking out into the darkness, wishing she'd met them under other circumstances. "We haven't made love so—"

"Something I'm going to take care of as soon as I get home."

"We." She heard the creak of leather and could almost see Law sit forward. "I don't like that you're trying to brush us off as soon as we leave town. Next time, you're coming with us."

"And I don't like the reminder that you're only interested in me because you want my property."

Law cursed. "I already told you that wanting you and buying that piece of property have nothing to do with each other."

"Law, be serious. I'm not stupid. A small-town girl with practically no sexual experience couldn't even begin to hold a sophisticated man like you, and certainly couldn't hold two of you. You talk about honesty? Okay. Let's be honest. You want the property, and I want to learn how to trust again."

Biting back a sob, she shrugged. "I'm lonely. I'm scared about the future. I'll have an affair with you, but I don't want any delusions. I need to go into this with my eyes wide open. If you want to have an affair, fine. I'll have an affair with you and then sell the house to you in a year. Just don't pretend that it's more than it is. I've been hurt enough, and I'll be damned if I let anyone hurt me again."

A long silence followed before Law spoke again. "Those are your terms?"

Taking a shaky breath, she pressed her hand against her rolling stomach. "Yes. Take it or leave it."

What would she do if they left it?

"Fine." Law's voice sounded colder than ever. "Then you'll have an affair with both of us, but if you want to learn to trust again, we're going to go all the way. Those are my terms."

Courtney gulped. "What does that mean?"

"You know what that means. It means that you're going to learn to trust us enough to submit to us. Everything. All the way, baby."

Courtney gasped.

Zach groaned. "We'll take it slow, but it's all or nothing. I can't do this half-assed with you."

Shaking with lust and nerves, she wrapped her arm around herself. "What if I don't like something?"

Law cursed again. "Too bad."

Zach blew out a breath. "You have to give it a chance, but if you don't like it, we'll know. You'll also have a safe word that you can use, but you'll use it only if you're really in distress."

Courtney gulped again, shocked at the rush of moisture that dampened her panties. "In distress? What the hell do you plan to do to me?"

"Everything." Law's growl sent a surge of heat straight to her slit.

Zach sighed again, his voice calm and soothing. "Nothing that you can't handle. Trust, remember? You're not always going to know what we're going to do to you, but you'll always know what we expect of you. We'll have a nice talk about that when we get home."

Excitement and apprehension waged a war inside her, but the chance to be with Law and Zach would be worth it.

The chance to feel wanted proved too irresistible to ignore.

Grateful that they couldn't see her burning cheeks, she retrieved a bottle of water from the refrigerator. "Just sex, right?"

"Not a chance. An affair isn't just about sex, and what we have between us is more than that. For the next year, you'll essentially belong to us."

"I don't like the sound of that."

What would they think if they knew that she did?

"Take it or leave it." The tension in Law's voice was unmistakable.

Courtney took a sip of her water, but it did nothing to cool her. "I'll take it on two conditions."

She thought she heard a sigh of relief but decided she must have been mistaken.

"What are your conditions?" Zach's voice held a wariness that made her smile.

"One, that you don't see anyone else while we're having an affair."

"Done. Next."

Surprised at how easily Zach had agreed, she took the time to take another sip of water before continuing. "That you don't try to pretend it's something that it's not."

"Agreed. Since we're all clear on the terms, I guess you're ours for the next year."

Not quite sure how their conversation had come to this, Courtney paused. "Um, maybe we should take some time to think about this."

"We've already agreed to your terms. There's no point in wasting time. Go back to bed." The authority in Law's voice both stirred her and settled something inside her, filling her with a warm rush of arousal and emotion.

Confused, she set the bottle on the table. "How did you know I'm not in bed?"

Law chuckled. "I heard the refrigerator open. Get some sleep. We'll call you tomorrow."

Chapter Nine

After a restless night, a night filled with erotic dreams about Law and Zach, Courtney woke aroused and irritable. The sun had just started to peek over the horizon, and knowing that Boone and his men wouldn't appear for a few hours, she took her coffee out to the back yard and, dressed in only her nightgown and robe, watched the sunrise.

It didn't occur to her until after she'd had her second cup of coffee that she hadn't thought about her father or had a bad dream all night.

Uneasy at how much Law and Zach had affected her in such a short time, she went to take a shower, thankful that most of the walls in the bathroom still stood.

She'd take advantage of the beautiful morning and walk around town. Hopefully, she'd find a help-wanted sign and would be able to get a job.

Dressed in jeans and a green, sleeveless cotton shirt, she came out of the bathroom just as her cell phone started ringing.

Stopping abruptly, she swallowed heavily, nervous about talking to Law or Zach again. Their conversation had played over and over in her mind, and each time, she tried to imagine exactly what they expected of her.

Smoothing her damp palms over her thighs, she made her way to the nightstand and picked up the phone, not even bothering to look at the display. "Hello?"

"Don't you dare hang up on me again!"

She didn't bother to hide her wince at her father's angry tone, knowing he couldn't see her. She'd become adept at hiding her feelings over the years and adopted a bored tone that she knew he hated. "Oh. It's you. What do you want?"

"Watch your tone, little missy."

He used the tone he'd used when she'd been a child, and it irritated her that it still had the ability to send a chill down her spine.

Dropping to the side of her bed, she blew out a breath in an effort to loosen the knots in her stomach. "What do you want?"

"I want to know when you're leaving."

"I'm not."

"You don't really plan to stay in that godforsaken town, do you?"

"That's none of your business."

"You're my daughter."

"To my everlasting shame."

"You think you're so smart, don't you, little girl? You sound more like your aunt every day. Fucking busybody. Well, I'm smarter. You won't last in that town, and when you leave, I'm gonna make those bastards pay for what they did to me! I finally have the chance to get back at them and get what I want at the same time, and I'm taking it. They ruined everything."

"*You* ruined everything—or don't you remember the beatings?" She broke out in a cold sweat as memories came rushing back again.

"I can't let you stay there."

Courtney surged to her feet. "You don't have any choice."

"Yes, I do. Once you're out of there, the property's mine! Then, they'll have to come crawlin' to me."

Courtney struggled to keep her tone calm and even as she made her way to the living room. She knew that her father thrived on fear and anger, and she wouldn't give him the satisfaction of showing either. "What are you talking about?"

"You know damned well what I'm talking about—or did you think I wouldn't find out? It'll all be mine." *He knew.*

"I won't let that happen."

"You won't have any choice. I'm going to get even with them if it's the last thing I do. And you. By the time I'm through, everyone's gonna have to respect me. Even you."

"What are you going to do?

With a laugh, he hung up, leaving Courtney feeling chilled. "Damn it!" She threw her phone across the room, gratified when it hit one of the studs and broke into several pieces.

Her father would cause all the trouble he could, and judging by his anger, would be capable of anything.

* * * *

Zach's jaw clenched tighter with every ring. Pacing back and forth in front of his desk, he met his brother's gaze. "She's still not answering. Something must be wrong. Do you think we pushed her too hard last night?"

Law glanced up from the contract he'd been reading. "If something was wrong, Ace would have called, and no. I don't think we pushed too hard. She's got a hell of a backbone, and we just have to prove it to her."

Zach wasn't convinced, but he did the only thing he could. He started dialing again. "I'm calling Ace."

Zach gripped the phone and waited, relieved when Ace answered on the second ring.

"Sheriff Tyler."

"Ace, it's Zach. Courtney's not answering her cell phone. Is something wrong?"

"Not that I know of. Hope went over there earlier and took her to show her around the town. She was going to introduce her around. I'll call her and check."

"No. I'll call Hope myself. Thanks."

"Is everything okay there?"

"Yes. Costly, but okay. Luckily the spill was caught before it got too bad. A lot of damage control because one of the workers was drunk. We're trying to get home as fast as we can, but it looks like it might take us a couple more days."

Anxious to talk to Courtney, Zach paced. "Watch out for Courtney for us until we get back."

"How many more times are you gonna tell me that? You think I don't know my job?"

"She's special to us, Ace."

"And you think I don't know that, too? Why don't you and Law take care of the company and let me deal with my town?"

Zach raked a hand through his hair. "It's times like this that I wish you ran the company with Law and I was the sheriff."

"Too late. I don't want to deal with the business. I like being sheriff. You don't want to run it anymore—sell it."

"I'd be bored out of my mind."

"That's what I thought. Call Hope."

Zach chuckled when Ace disconnected abruptly and glanced at Law, hurriedly punching in his sister-in-law's cell number. "Courtney's with Hope. I'm calling her now."

Law sat back and blew out a breath. "That's a relief. Hell I hate being away from her."

Zach nodded, pacing impatiently until his sister-in-law answered.

"Hello, dear brother-in-law. What a pleasant surprise."

Smiling at the sarcasm in her tone, Zach shook his head, moving away from Law when his brother's cell phone rang. "You always were a smartass. My brother should turn you over his knee every day."

"I agree." Hope giggled. "What can I do for you?"

"I'm looking for Courtney. I've called her cell phone several times, but she doesn't answer. I'm getting worried."

"She's here with me. Here. You talk to her."

After a short whispered conversation, he heard Courtney's voice. "Hello?"

"Hello yourself. Why aren't you answering your cell phone? We've been calling all morning and were getting worried."

"It broke. Sorry."

Something in her voice had him stiffening. Inwardly cursing that he didn't know her as intimately as he'd like, Zach moved to stare out the window, taking in the view of downtown Dallas. "What's wrong?"

"Nothing."

"You're lying to me."

Courtney's voice lowered. "I don't have to tell you everything."

Frustrated, he willed his cock to settle, the challenge of taming her sending his need to dominate soaring. "When I get home, darlin', you're going to understand just how wrong you are about that."

Law jumped to his feet. "What? Thanks." Disconnecting, he strode toward Zach. "Give me the phone."

* * * *

Courtney wrapped her arm around herself, surprised at the warm surge of desire that accompanied her apprehension at his steely tone.

Threats from her father chilled her, but for some reason, threats from Zach and Law didn't.

Her stomach clenched when she heard Law ask for the phone and actually jolted when he spoke into it.

"Courtney?"

Swallowing heavily, she turned away from Hope, pressing a hand to her stomach against the fluttering inside. "Yes, Law?"

"Why the hell is your phone in pieces on the floor of your living room?"

Courtney stiffened. "How the hell did you know that?"

"Chase called. He said they found your phone in pieces on the floor. They got worried and called us. What the hell's going on?"

"I got mad and threw it. No big deal. When Hope got there, I forgot to clean it up."

"What made you so angry?" She didn't want to talk to them about her father. She didn't even want to think about her father. "None of your business."

His voice lowered and deepened. "Do you know that every time you say that to me, my hand itches to connect with that delectable backside?"

Aware that Hope shamelessly eavesdropped, grinning the entire time, Courtney kept her voice cool. "You wouldn't dare."

"The itching's getting stronger. The other night, you took a call that pissed you off and turned off your phone. Now, you destroy it. Who's been calling you? You got another boyfriend out there that I'm gonna have to deal with?"

Stunned by the jealousy in his voice, Courtney rushed to reassure him. "Of course not. I already told you—"

"Then who the hell is harassing you? So help me, Courtney, if you don't tell me right now, I'm flying up there and beating your ass until you tell me!"

Alarmed, Courtney blurted out the truth. "It's my father! Okay? I can handle him. He thinks that because my aunt's gone that he can intimidate me the way he did when I was a little girl. I'm not that child anymore. The people in this town turned their backs on me then, and I sure as hell don't need help from them now!"

She jabbed the disconnect button and held the phone out to Hope. "Your brother-in-law is too damned arrogant for words. Now that I think about it, both of them are."

Hope nodded. "Yep. I think you could pretty much say that about most of the men in town. As a matter of fact, I can't think of any that aren't arrogant. It's one of the most frustrating, but comforting, things about them."

Courtney blinked. "Comforting?"

Hope grinned and shrugged. "They're strong enough to do what needs to be done, and there's not much they can't handle. They're also very protective of their families but also of the other women who live here. They all watch out for us." As they started down the sidewalk again, Hope sighed. "Law and Zach have been denying themselves for a long time."

Frowning, Courtney glanced at Hope as she navigated the busy foot traffic. "Denying themselves how?"

Hope sighed. "They used to go to the club every chance they got. They date in Dallas but always with sophisticated women who wouldn't dream of being shared, and certainly wouldn't be happy living in a small town."

Courtney pushed back the jealousy that reared its ugly head at the thought that either one of them could be with one of those women right now. "Then what do they see in me? I can't compete with that kind of woman."

"You've got it wrong." Hope grinned and shook her head. "They can't compete with you."

"That's ridiculous."

"Is it? I've seen Law and Zach try to deny their need to share for years. I've seen them pretend that the women in Dallas mean something to them, but you know something? They never call anyone when they're here. They've never brought anyone home with them. Very telling, don't you think?"

Courtney shrugged, trying not to get her hopes up.

Hope continued to her car, pausing alongside of it. "They used to go to the club and dominate a woman together, but they haven't done that for years. Their need to share and need to dominate has been denied because it's only with strangers. They've outgrown that. They want a woman—a real woman—one who isn't interested in their bank accounts. They need a woman who wouldn't turn their nose up at living in a small town like Desire. They need a woman who wants them, not for their money and not for just a night of mind-blowing sex."

Hope smiled, the concern in her eyes proving just how much Law and Zach meant to her. "They want a woman they can take care of. They want a woman who would belong to them in every way a woman can belong to a man."

Giggling, she unlocked the car and got in, not continuing until Courtney got into the passenger seat. "They're very old-fashioned. They believe that it's a man's job to take care of their woman. Ace is the same way. Dominant. Yes, it can be frustrating at times, but there's nothing he wouldn't do for me. We argue—of course. Who doesn't? But you know what? I feel safe every minute of my life. I know I'm loved. I know my husband would lay down his life in a heartbeat for me. He would do anything in his power to protect me—and I would do anything for him. He'd do anything to make me happy. We're closer than most couples. We don't hide anything from each other. I can tell him anything. Secrets. Fantasies. He teases me out of my bad moods and holds me when I cry."

Hope started her little car and turned the air conditioner on high. "Ace *knows* me, and I know him. Honesty is very important in this lifestyle, and you get out of it what you put into it."

She laid a hand on Courtney's. "Law and Zach don't want to overwhelm you. They just want your love and to know that you trust them to take care of you. They want to know that you'll come to them with your problems. They want to know that they can give you more pleasure than you've ever imagined and trust them enough to be vulnerable with them."

Sitting back, she sighed. "Believe me, when you give them what they need, you get the kind of life most people only dream of."

Courtney stared out the window. "I wish it was so easy. It's different for me."

"Why?"

"Because the town scorned me once."

Shaking her head, Hope put the car in gear. "They scorned your father. The way I understand it, they practically begged your mother to stay here with you. She went with your father instead."

"She was scared. My father was a very intimidating man."

Hope started driving, heading out of town. "I heard what you said to Law. It seems your father's still trying to intimidate you. Where's your mother?"

"Remarried. Happy. Somewhere in Oregon." Courtney swallowed a lump in her throat and wondered if her mother ever missed her at all.

Hope glanced at her and smiled. "Good for her. Now you just have to get on with your life."

"I can't stay here."

Hope glanced at her and frowned. "Why not?"

Looking straight ahead, Courtney couldn't help but wonder what would happen if she let herself fall in love with Law and Zach, something she feared had already begun to happen. "Too many bad memories."

With a shrug, Hope turned onto the road out of town. "Make new ones. If you run, you're letting your father win again."

Sitting back, Courtney admired the scenery. Trees and flowers as far as she could see. "I don't know if I can be what Law and Zach want."

Hope glanced at her again, her eyes searching. "Are they what you want?"

Courtney smiled and glanced at her new friend. "I'm beginning to think they're even more than I ever imagined. I never knew men like them existed."

Hope laughed at that, speeding down the highway and checking her rearview mirror. "Yeah. The men in Desire have surprised a lot of women. They tend to be a little overwhelming."

"Hope, can I be honest with you?"

"Of course. Our conversation is confidential."

"My father was a dominant man, and—"

"Whoa!" Hope lifted a hand. "Your father was nothing like the kind of men Law and Zach are."

"They threatened to spank me!"

Hope laughed again, dividing her attention between the road and the rearview mirror. "They will, and you'll love it. Can you imagine men so intent on giving you pleasure that they'll do anything to do it? Can you imagine being tied up while they tease you? They'll make you face your own needs and force more pleasure on you than you think you can stand. Why the hell do you think I'm speeding? If I get another ticket, Ace is going to spank me good!"

Courtney couldn't believe what she was hearing. "You'd actually provoke him into that?"

"You bet. He's getting pretty tame lately, especially with worrying about getting new deputies. Once he gets them trained, I'm going to have to take him in hand."

Courtney had the feeling she was missing something. "Ace is even bigger than Law and Zach. He doesn't hurt you?"

"Not in the way you're talking about. The only way to understand it is to experience it. You're coming to the club with us this week, aren't you?"

Courtney shrugged, wondering if she'd have the courage to walk into a place like that. "I don't know. I guess. I have to admit I am a little curious. Scared, but curious."

"Good. It won't cost a thing. The women in Desire get in for free, and the men who come to watch out for us will buy us drinks all night. Don't worry about getting drunk. Someone will make sure you get home. We generally walk there if the weather's nice."

Courtney shook her head, excited now. "Okay. I'll go. What do I wear?"

Hope laughed again. "What the hell do you think we're going shopping for?"

The unmistakable sound of a siren had Hope looking into the rearview mirror again. Whooping, she slowed and pulled over, grinning from ear to ear. "Linc caught me. Guess I'm gonna get that ticket!"

Chapter Ten

The knock on the door startled Courtney, and with a groan, she started to sit up. Boone, who was in the process of cleaning up painting supplies, popped his head over the back of the sofa, grinning down at her. "You look worn out. Do you want me to get it?"

"Would you? It's probably for you anyway."

She let her eyes flutter closed again, surprisingly comforted by the sounds of the men clearing their things away.

"Courtney?"

Opening her eyes again, she smiled at the sight of Boone standing at the edge of the sofa next to a deliveryman holding a box. "What is it?"

Boone gestured toward the box. "This was just delivered for you. It looks like it's from Law and Zach. You have to sign for it."

Groaning, she sat up and signed the clipboard, waiting for the deliveryman to leave before opening it. "I wonder what they could have sent."

Surprised to find a cell phone inside, she jumped when it rang.

Ignoring Boone's laugh, she watched him walk away before answering. "Hello?"

"Now you have a cell phone, and only Zach and I have the number. If you want to give it to Hope and any of your other friends, go right ahead, but don't you dare give it to your father."

Mentally struggling to clear the cobwebs in her brain away, she dropped back against the cushion. "You bought me a phone?"

"How the hell else am I going to be able to talk to you? Don't throw this one against the wall. "

She heard the creak of leather and could picture him leaning back in his chair with his feet on his desk. "I won't. How is everything? Hope told me what happened."

She didn't mention that she'd have rather heard it from them.

"Hope said you caught it fast. Was the oil spill bad?"

"Bad enough. What really pisses me off is that it was caused by someone who decided to get drunk on the job."

Warmed that he'd told her something that he probably wouldn't have admitted to the press, she settled back. "Wow. I can only imagine what happened to him. You and Zach are pretty tough."

"We have to be. He won't work around here anymore. I don't want it to get out that he was drunk. I don't want to talk about him. Thankfully, one of my foremen caught it before it could get too bad, and the cleanup is well under way. It should only take another day or two, and then we'll be home. How are you?"

Waving good-bye to Boone as he passed, she waited until the door closed behind him before dropping back again, lifting her feet onto one of the new pillows she'd bought. "My feet are killing me."

"Why?"

Courtney groaned and adjusted the pillows to a more comfortable position. "Hope took me shopping."

Law chuckled. "That'll do it. What did you buy?"

Wondering what his reaction would be if he ever saw her in it, Courtney shrugged. "Just a dress and a pair of shoes."

"Good. You need some clothes. We'll go to the lingerie shop when we get home."

Courtney smiled at that. "Why bother? You said that you wouldn't let me wear my nightgowns to bed when I'm with you, and you keep ripping my panties. I guess I could use a few new bras, but I'll go and get them myself."

Law chuckled. "What makes you think I won't rip them, too?" After a long pause, Law sighed. "Are you okay now?"

"I'm fine." Touched by the tenderness in his voice, Courtney smiled and wiggled her sore feet.

"Would you like to tell me what happened now?"

Stiffening, she sat up. "I can handle it."

Law's voice firmed. "Do you remember the terms of our agreement?"

"Yes. But that—"

"How the hell can I take care of you if you don't let me know what's wrong?"

"Law, I need to take care of this on my own. I understand that you want to give me pleasure, but you certainly don't need to handle my problems."

"That's for me to decide. I want to know what's upsetting you." His voice lowered seductively. "You're my lover, aren't you?"

When he used that tone, something inside her melted.

"Yes, but—"

"Then it's only natural for you to tell me what's wrong. When you asked me what was going on here, I told you, even though the public has no idea that one of my workers was drunk. News channels would love that kind of story. I trust you to keep it to yourself, but you won't tell me what your father said to upset you. That's a little one-sided, don't you think?"

Blowing out a breath, Courtney dropped back again. "You're right. Do you always have to be right?"

"It's part of my charm. Spill it."

Rolling to her side, she reached down to push aside the lid of the shoebox, idly playing with the straps of her new shoes. "My father's just being a jerk. He somehow found out that, if I leave Desire before the year's up, he's going to get the house. Then he's going to soak you for as much money as he can. It's his way of getting revenge on the town for kicking him out. He's failed at everything he's ever tried to do—"

"And blames everything on the townspeople of Desire."

"Exactly." She had to admit that it felt good to finally be able to talk about her father. "He's always broke and never even paid child support. He sounded furious. Determined. Who knows what he'll do?"

"What exactly did he say?"

"That he was going to make you pay for what the town did to him. He was going to make me pay. Even if it was the last thing he did. He said that he's going to make everyone respect him. Even me."

"I don't like the sound of that, Courtney."

She didn't either, especially when her father had sounded so desperate.

Trying to calm Law, Courtney adopted a nonchalant tone. "What can he do? He can't force me to leave."

"I don't like it." Although his voice remained calm, the ice in it came through.

"I don't want to talk about it anymore." Thinking about it made her head hurt, and she didn't want Law to know how much she still feared her father.

Law sighed, but something told her that she hadn't heard the end of it. "Fine. For now. Did they finish the drywall?"

Courtney rolled to her back again and looked around the room. "And the spackling and painting. Four people were here. Boone, Chase, Cole, and Brett. They were flying through the rooms. I have the windows open because of the paint smell. It's still wet."

"Why are you there then? Damn it, Courtney! Why don't you go out to get something to eat? I'll call Ace."

Just the thought of moving again made her groan. "No. Hope and I ate something in the mall. I'm not moving. My feet hurt too damned bad. I might just sleep here on the sofa tonight."

Law chuckled softly. "Poor baby. If I was there, I would rub them for you. Will you take a rain check until I get back?"

Confused, Courtney lifted her head again. "Why would you rub my feet for me? I thought you would be expecting me to rub yours. I'm supposed to submit to you, aren't I?"

Law chuckled. "Some Masters would expect that. I don't. Oh, baby. You have so much to learn about what I want from you."

Inwardly wincing, Courtney smoothed a hand over the pillow. "You make me feel stupid."

"You shouldn't feel stupid. You would have no way of knowing what to expect. Zach and I don't know what to expect."

"You don't?"

Laughing at that, Law must have dropped into his seat because she heard the leather creak. "Honey, no two of any kind of relationship is the same. It is what it is and evolves into something more—or less. That's up to us. It changes, and when it does, we'll change with it. Honestly, baby, I wish you would just relax and we'll all see what happens."

Bending, she lifted a show out of its box, staring at the high heel. "I talked to Hope some today."

"Did you?"

Smiling at the uncertainty in his voice, Courtney sat back, setting the shoe on her lap and running her finger over the smooth leather. "She explained things. Did you know that Ace dominates her?"

"Of course. That's why we're always telling her that Ace needs to spank her more often. She agrees, by the way."

"So she said. She even went out of her way to get a ticket so he would spank her for it. I swear I don't understand any of this. What if I can't give you what you need?"

"You already do."

"You're just saying that."

"No, baby. I'm not."

Unsure of what to say to that, she sighed and changed the subject. "How's Zach?"

Law laughed softly. "He's good. He's going to call you tonight. He's busy chewing someone out right now. It's sounds as if he's enjoying it."

"You're both scary."

"Baby, of all the people in the world, you're the one who should fear us the least. Keep the cell phone charged. Zach's gonna call you tonight, but I won't make you wait to get an answer from him. He feels the same way I do."

After hanging up, she stared at the phone, smiling. Telling them about her father hadn't been as hard as she'd thought, and it didn't sound as if Law would cause any trouble at all.

* * * *

Law disconnected from Courtney and started punching in numbers again, this time calling his brother Ace.

Afterward, he felt a little better but knew he wouldn't settle down again until he was back in Desire.

He'd have to keep a sharp eye on Courtney.

Whether she knew it or not, she was his and under his protection.

Smiling to himself, he leaned back in his chair, filled with a sense of satisfaction that he'd been searching for his entire life.

It felt better than he'd expected.

Grinning, he called Hope again.

"Wow. Two phone calls in one day! It's not even my birthday."

"You really are a smartass."

"Yeah, but you love me." The happiness in her voice made him even more determined to hear the same happiness in Courtney's.

"That I do, despite the fact that you're a pain in the ass. Heard you got a ticket today."

"Did Courtney tell you?"

"She did. Wasn't she supposed to?"

"Yep. Now, if you want to do me a favor and tattletale to your brother…"

Shaking his head at her daring, he reached for a piece of paper. "She said that the two of you went shopping today. I need her sizes. Give them to me, and I'll rat you out so fast your head'll swim."

Hope giggled. "Deal."

Chapter Eleven

Smoothing a hand down her black, curve-hugging dress, Courtney glanced at Hope as they made their way up the steps to the front entrance of the men's club. "I can't believe I let you talk me into this. Are you sure Ace doesn't mind you coming here while he's working?"

Giggling, Hope shared a look with her sister, Charity, before smiling up at her. "He trusts me. Besides, Charity's husband, Beau, will show up, and he'll give Ace a full report." She hurried up the steps, her tight, red leather dress and stiletto heels not slowing her down at all. "That's one of the reasons I opened Lady Desire. This is their turf, but they aren't allowed in the women's club."

Courtney smiled at that. "It might be fun to join while I'm here." At least she could meet some of the other women while she was in town.

From the other side of Hope, Charity smiled. "You'll love it. We can talk about the men and not be overheard."

Courtney grabbed onto the railing. "I can't believe I let you talk me into these shoes."

Hope looked down at the strappy sandals she'd talked Courtney into buying. "You look great in them, and you know it. Besides, you're not going to be on your feet. Hell, half the time I have these babies on my feet are up in the air. I hope Ace pops in. These shoes drive him crazy." She winked at Courtney. "I'd love to see the men's faces when they see you in that dress and those heels."

Her dress, made of a stretchy lace, proved more comfortable than Courtney could have imagined. A wide band of solid material covered her just enough to be legal while the thinner elastic on both sides left the rest of her skin bare and made it obvious to anyone looking that she wore no bra or panties.

Jesse Tyler and Nat Langley, owners of the store where Brenna worked, burst out laughing. Nat shook her head, smoothing a hand over her more demure black dress. "Jesus, Hope, you're going to scare the hell out of Courtney before she even walks through the door."

"Bullshit." She paused at the top of the stairs and turned to face Courtney. "In here, you're safer than in your mother's arms. The reason we come here for the open houses—besides the chance to get dressed up and get together for a drink—is to drive our husbands crazy. You can't do that if you aren't dressed the part. Hell, they enjoy it as much as we do. Call it foreplay, honey."

"Yeah, but Law and Zach aren't here to see me in it."

Depressed that she didn't feel the excitement that the other women felt, she forced a smile. She couldn't help the jealousy that knotted her stomach because she didn't have a man who would be jealous or protective while she was at the open house.

She didn't have a man who would see her dressed in the sexiest dress she'd ever worn and would want to strip her out of it at the end of the night.

Besides, she missed them.

Waiting for Hope's knock to be answered, Courtney looked around, stunned to see how many cars filled the parking lot and the number of women crossing the large lot toward them. "I've never been in a club like this in my life. No one's going to expect me to do anything, are they?"

Jesse patted her arm. "Honey, you're going to have a great time. And don't worry about a thing. Like Hope said, you'll be safer in there than you can imagine. As the only single one at our table, I'm sure you're going to get a lot of attention, though. Just sit and drink with us, and you'll be fine."

The huge door opened, and to Courtney's surprise, a butler appeared.

Courtney didn't know what she'd expected—perhaps a half-dressed man in leather—but she hadn't expected the stone-faced butler dressed in a conservative tuxedo.

"Good evening, ladies."

Brenna appeared at his side, looking slightly flushed as if she'd been rushing around. Dressed in a black leather cat suit with zippers strategically placed over her breasts, she gripped the butler's forearm and flashed a smile. "Thanks, Sebastian. I've got this."

Hope grinned. "I love that outfit!" Leaning forward, she kept her voice low, sending a warning look at the butler. "Logan's making one for me, but I don't want Ace to know. I want to surprise him on his birthday."

Laughing, Brenna stepped back to let them inside. "Logan made mine. Royce and King gave it to me earlier to wear tonight." Lowering her voice conspiratorially, she glanced back at Sebastian. "For some reason, these open houses seem to rile my husbands up."

Sebastian's lips twitched. "Only when you attend. Your table is waiting."

To Courtney's amusement, Brenna gripped Sebastian's lapel and pulled him down to plant a quick kiss on his cheek.

"Thank you, Sebastian." Releasing him, she grinned up at him as he straightened. "You're a sweetie."

Sebastian ran a hand over his lapel as if to brush away any creases, his look of superiority tempered by a playful glint in his eyes. "That's a nasty, false rumor, one that I wish you would stop spreading."

Amused and intrigued when the straight-faced butler addressed each of them by name as they entered, Courtney paused in front of him. "You and I have never met before. How do you know my name?"

Sebastian smiled, the aura of superiority surrounding him. "I make it my business to know everyone who comes into the club. It's my job to keep track, especially since your men are members here. It's important to know who belongs to whom."

Irritated at Law and Zach for not being here, and at herself for missing them, Courtney snapped, "I don't belong to anyone."

Sebastian inclined his head, his eyes twinkling. "As you wish."

Courtney opened her mouth to snap back at him, and just as quickly snapped it shut again when she realized that she had no idea what she could say. Turning away from his knowing look, she followed the others down the wide hall to a huge double door on the left that stood wide open.

Music and voices came from inside, mingling with the occasional feminine laughter, and Courtney found herself getting more nervous with every step.

Fisting her hands on her small purse that she held in front of her, she continued down the hall behind her new friends.

As she started through the doorway, Courtney finally got a look at the room inside. She gasped and stumbled, coming to an abrupt halt. Her mouth dropped, and stunned, she scanned the most incredible room she'd ever seen.

She'd spent the last several days imagining what the club would be like, but nothing could have prepared her for the impact it would have on her senses.

Letting her eyes adjust to the darkened interior, she found her gaze drawn to the large stage on the far wall, the spotlights evidently intended to draw attention there.

Heavy red drapes framed both sides of the wooden stage, but it was the restraints dangling from the ceiling that made her breath catch.

Gulping again at the mental image of being restrained there—naked—with Law and Zach on either side of her, she shifted restlessly and hurriedly turned away. The discreet lighting at the bar drew her attention, and turning her head toward it, she couldn't hold back another gasp at the sight of a man sitting at one of the small tables there with a naked woman on his lap.

He ran his hand down her back, his head bent low to whisper something to her while his other hand slid up her body to cup her breast.

The woman on his lap arched her back, pushing her breasts out and biting her lip when he tugged at her nipple.

Courtney moaned in response to the rush of heat to her own nipples and the sharp tug of awareness to her clit.

Stunned and embarrassed at her arousal, she turned away, her gaze going back to the stage again.

"That's where they hold the auctions. They're *extremely* popular here."

Courtney jumped at the sound of Brenna's voice, whipping around to face her. "*Auctions?*"

Brenna nodded, a strange smile curving her lips, and even in the semi-lit room, Courtney could see that her cheeks were flushed. "I know it's a little hard to believe. I couldn't believe it when Royce and King first told me about them."

Wrapping an arm through Courtney's, she led her past the table where the other women sat and closer to the stage. "A lot—and I mean, *a lot*—of women come here to be auctioned off. There's a huge waiting list."

Courtney gaped, trying hard not to stare at the stage. "Why? Why would anyone want to be auctioned off?"

Brenna smiled faintly. "I know what you're thinking. I thought the same thing, but the more I learned, the more I understood it." Shrugging, she led Courtney closer to the stage. "Some women come because they want to live out a fantasy. They've come to the open houses and dipped their toe in the water, so to speak, and want to go further. Some of them know that they want to be dominated but can't work up the courage to ask the men they're dating to fulfill that kind of need."

Turning, Courtney sighed and leaned back against the stage. "Some either don't have—or don't want—a steady Dominant. It actually fits a lot of needs in women who want somewhere safe to go. All of the playrooms are monitored—"

"Do you mean that someone *watches* them?"

Nodding, Brenna straightened again. "Absolutely. The men are diligent about making sure that the women here are safe. That part is not negotiable. Women know that they're safe here, so they come in droves. Any man mistreating a woman gets kicked out and is never allowed back."

Courtney grimaced. "Kinda like they do with the men in town."

Brenna touched her arm, her smile falling. "You know, I never thought I'd find a town where men are so obsessed with keeping women safe. I really didn't believe it at first, but it's true. You don't know how important it is to me. You don't know this, but the reason I came here was to confront a stalker."

"No!"

Nodding again, Brenna led back toward the table. "He was a member here, a man who Blade, Royce, and King watched closely. They continued to talk to him even after they kicked him out, hoping to get him to change his ways. He was fixated on me, and I came here to chew them a new asshole for encouraging him, when in reality, they were doing the exact opposite."

Courtney shook her head, her mind spinning. "I just can't wrap my head around all of this. Is there a book of rules somewhere?"

"No. It's between you and your Master. Dominance and submission are a lot of things to a lot of people. I learned from Royce and King—hell, I'm still learning—that it is what you make it." Giggling, she paused, her breath catching. "We're always experimenting. Here's my darling husband and Master, Royce, now."

Courtney followed Brenna's gaze, her jaw dropping.

The man Brenna introduced as Royce had to be one of the most beautiful men Courtney had ever seen. He was dark everywhere, his olive skin, black hair that fell around his face in curls, and deep brown eyes giving him a wildly sexual look—a look emphasized by his black leather pants, black shirt, and devilish smile. His gaze lingered on his wife's features, his eyes glittering with emotion before settling on Courtney. "It's a pleasure to finally meet you, Courtney. I've heard a lot about you." His hand closed over Brenna's waist. "I'm glad you accepted my wife's invitation."

Courtney gulped and nodded, trying not to gape at the man who embodied what she'd imagined a Dominant would look like. "Thank you. It's nice to meet you, too."

Brenna grinned. "And this is King."

A barrel-chested man, all hard lines and muscles, appeared next to her, his large hand skimming over Brenna's hair. He wore his blond hair in a short military cut and moved with a kind of powerful grace that both Law and Zach had in abundance, making her miss them even more.

King's smile held a gentleness and reassurance that Courtney hadn't expected. "Hello, Courtney. You're safe here." He laughed softly when she blinked. "No. I'm not a mind-reader. I'm just observant. You have that deer-in-the-headlights kind of look in your eyes. No one will bother you here."

Turning to frown down at Brenna, he pulled her closer. "You didn't introduce me as your husband *or* your Master, of which I'm both. Would you like to explain yourself?"

Brenna stunned Courtney by winking at her before lifting her face to King's. "Maybe I was bad."

King's brow went up, giving him a dangerous look. "There's no maybe about it." The gleam of hunger in his eyes, and in Royce's, screamed possession.

King's gaze raked over Brenna from head to toe before meeting hers again. "When this is over, you and I have an appointment in the playroom."

Giggling, Brenna went to her toes to kiss his chin. "I was counting on it."

King slapped her bottom as he turned to face Courtney. "Do Law and Zach know that you're here?"

Stunned by the faraway look in Brenna's eyes, Courtney swallowed heavily before lifting her chin. "No. They're still in Dallas." She'd purposely avoided having a conversation about tonight with Law and Zach, hoping that she could learn a little more about their lifestyle before seeing them again.

King's brow went up again. "I see."

Shrugging, and aware of Royce's searching look, she shifted her feet. "Besides, what I do is none of their business."

Royce's eyes danced with amusement. "Then tonight should be very interesting. They just walked through the door, and by the looks on their faces and the way they're staring at you, I think they consider it very much their business."

* * * *

Courtney barely breathed as Zach closed in on her side. Wrapping an arm around her waist, he talked with Royce and King a minute or two before both men made their excuses and walked away, but not before smiling in her direction.

King nodded. "I like her."

Zach's hold tightened on her waist. "So do I."

Soon, Courtney found herself alone with Zach, watching the others walk away until she found her attention once again drawn to the couple sitting at a small table close to the bar.

"Nice dress, darlin'." Moving to stand behind her, Zach closed his hands on her waist. "You like watching them, don't you? It arouses you. Your nipples are poking at the front of your dress, and I'd bet every dollar in my wallet that your inner thighs are soaked. I'd also bet that your nipples are just aching for as much attention as your clit is."

Closing her eyes, Courtney fought the need clawing at her. "You're wrong." Shivering at the feel of his warm breath against her ear, she crossed her arms across her chest, pressing them against her aching nipples. Opening her eyes again, she shrugged, finding it difficult to keep her face averted from the couple. "I'm not aroused. Just curious."

The hands at her waist tightened. "Do you really think you're going to get away with lying to me, or do you really believe that I'm so oblivious to the signs of your arousal?"

Courtney opened her mouth to speak, but another rush of moisture escaped to coat her thighs. "I, um…"

"Don't make it any worse for yourself. Look at them."

"I don't want to stare."

"If he didn't want anyone to see his submissive naked, he wouldn't have brought her here and removed her clothes. If she didn't want to be on display, she wouldn't be. They're regulars here and come to show perspective subs what may be expected of them. There are several others here as well."

God, she couldn't imagine doing such a thing, but the thought of being naked on Zach's lap and having him touch her the way the other man touched his submissive had her close to coming. "Zach, I know you expect this kind of thing with me—I mean, while we're having an affair—but I have to tell you I would never be able to sit in public naked like she is."

"And you wouldn't be expected to. Or permitted to." Lifted his head when she turned to look up at him over her shoulder, Zach cupped her jaw, holding her firmly for his light kiss. "Law and I are too selfish to share you that way with anyone. No one else will be allowed to see your naked body."

Courtney stiffened, licking her lips where they tingled. "What w– would you expect of me?"

Brushing his lips over hers again, he branded her as his in front of the entire club. "Your trust. Your honesty. As long as we have those, the rest will come. We'll take it step by step."

He lifted his head to stare down at her, his eyes unreadable. "Exploring you and your boundaries is giving both Law and me a great deal of pleasure."

"We've already started?"

Releasing her jaw, he wrapped his arms around her from behind, his lips warm against her ear. "Hmm. Yes. We've started, which is why you're going to explain why you came here without telling us and why you're showing off what belongs to us in this dress."

Bristling against his arrogance, she fought to hide the rush of heat his possessive tone sent through her. "Was I supposed to tell you that I was coming here?" She'd wondered about her need for a reaction from them for days and chosen the dress she wore now in an attempt to make sure they heard about it. Uneasy at what that said about her, she waited expectantly for his answer. When it came, she realized that she'd gotten more of a reaction than she'd bargained for.

Sucking in a breath at the sharp slap to her bottom, she tried to rub it, but Zach caught both of her wrists in his with a speed that made her wonder if she'd underestimated him.

"You know damned well we wanted to know what you were doing and asked you about your plans many times. We knew you were coming here and waited for you to tell us." Running his hand over her bottom, he spread the heat. "Are you going to try to tell me that you didn't wear this dress to defy us?"

"You never told me that you had to approve my clothing." Realizing that she taunted him—and enjoyed it—Courtney snapped her mouth shut.

She didn't fully understand why she needed him to react this way or why she got a thrill at the possessiveness— the demand in his tone and in his touch—but she did, and she struggled to come to terms with it.

"Well, now you know. You'll be allowed freedom in bits and pieces, based on your behavior."

"I'm not a child."

"No. You're not. You're a woman, one who needs this as much as I do. Now, behave yourself and watch them."

Courtney couldn't take her eyes from the other couple, unable to stop imagining what it would feel like to be in the woman's position. Noticing that the other man looked away to speak to someone else, Courtney shook her head. "He's not even paying attention to her."

Zach chuckled softly against her ear. "Oh, yes. He is. She's the center of his focus. She's the most important thing in the world to him right now. It's his right, his responsibility, and his honor to take care of her. He keeps her safe and makes sure she has everything she needs from him."

"What is it, exactly, that she needs from him?"

What is it that I need from you? Why am I so drawn to this?

"It's different for everyone, but I can imagine one of the things she needs from him is the security of knowing that she's cared for. I'm sure she needs to know that he wants her, cares for her, and gets pleasure from her."

He nipped at her earlobe, his hands firming when she shivered. "He needs to know that she trusts him enough to let him fulfill his own needs while satisfying hers. He needs to know that she gets pleasure from him and that she feels confident enough to turn herself over to him. He needs her to know that he wouldn't do anything that she couldn't recover from."

Courtney stilled, her heart racing. "That sounds scary."

"A little bit of fear will make things more exciting, but when you realize that Law and I are concerned for your well-being above all else, you won't be so nervous." Scraping his teeth down her neck, he groaned, the hunger in his touch stirring her own. "Of course, a little apprehension adds spice, like what you're going to feel when you learn that some sort of punishment is involved because of your defiance."

"What defiance?"

"Hiding the fact that you were coming here tonight and going out without us wearing a dress that barely covers your great assets. You did it to test us. You don't expect me to ignore that, do you?"

She didn't want to admit it to him but had to admit to herself that she would have been disappointed if he'd let it go.

Trying to hide the excitement bubbling through her veins, Courtney shrugged. "I didn't tell you that I was coming because I didn't know how you'd react and I didn't want to argue about it. It was something I needed to do for myself."

"I have no problem with you coming here. Next time, though, I want to hear about it from you." Gathering her close again, he pressed a hand to her belly to hold her back against him, his fingertips dangerously close to her mound. "I want you—more than I've ever wanted another woman. You've reignited a hunger in me that I thought I'd lost forever. The thought of earning your submission—your surrender—excites me more than you can imagine."

Struggling to control her breathing while the heat from his hand traveled lower, Courtney glanced at the women waiting at the table for her, shaking her head at Hope's grin. "How did you know I was here?"

"Ace. He knows that you belong to us now and that we want to know things like this. Law and I keep tabs on you. You've given yourself to us. You belong to us now."

"I belong to you—just because we're having an affair?"

"It was the kind of affair you agreed to that makes you ours. Now, stop trying to renegotiate our agreement." Straightening, he ran a hand over her ass, the threat in the gesture unmistakable. "Go join the other women and have fun. We'll be close by."

Chapter Twelve

Courtney reached for her drink, her hand shaking as she watched the mock auction, an auction unlike any other.

Several men had joined in the fun, and even though Nat had assured Courtney that the auction was fake, Courtney found herself drawn into the excitement like everyone else.

Jesse's husbands, Clay and Rio, played poker at the table next to theirs with Nat's husbands Jake and Holt, along with Law and Zach. All six men kept a close watch on the women's table, a sharp look from any one of them enough to discourage the few men who'd tried to approach.

The others had taken their seats before she'd arrived at the table, leaving a seat for her that both faced the stage and allowed her to see Law and Zach.

It also allowed Law and Zach to watch her.

Jesse patted her hand. "Don't worry. No one else will come to the table. Every once in a while a few of the Doms from out of town, the ones looking for someone, come and sniff around the women who come to the open house. It's a nice, safe way to meet people who are in the same lifestyle."

Brenna nodded, setting her drink down. "Royce said that business almost doubled since they started doing the open houses. A lot of people come because there's no pressure." Picking up her drink again, she grinned, raising her voice to be heard over the large crowd. "They couldn't do anything of a sexual nature, even if they wanted to. Only the Doms and submissives already signed up are allowed to do that kind of thing." She gestured toward the stage where the mock auction took place.

Nat sighed and leaned back, a small smile curving her lips. "The men are always all riled up after the open houses."

With a smile, Jesse reached for her glass. "It's not just them. We're all riled up after the open houses."

A cry had all of them turning back to the auction—a feminine cry of pleasure that inspired shouts of encouragement and demand from the men who'd crowded closer to the stage.

Courtney found herself drawn to the activity on the stage, and the excitement surrounding it, uncomfortably aware that Law and Zach watched her from the next table.

Although she couldn't hear what the man said, Courtney watched, mesmerized, as he spoke to the woman while securing her wrists in the cuffs above her head, leaving the woman totally exposed.

Courtney couldn't help but wonder what he said to the woman, but the woman smiled trustingly at him as if he was her entire world.

She couldn't imagine what it would feel like to be in the woman's position but couldn't deny that seeing the events playing out on the stage created a hunger inside her.

She mentally replaced the woman's face with her own and the crowd of men with only two—Law and Zach.

Her phone vibrated, startling her, and she looked down to see that she had a message. Wondering who could have sent it to her, she checked it, surprised to see that it came from Zach.

You'll be explored by Law and me the same way. We want to inspect our property.

Courtney's face burned, and without looking toward the next table, she quickly deleted the message.

Property!

She felt their gazes as if one of them had traced a finger down her cheek, urging her to look their way.

She could almost feel it.

Uneasy, but unable to deny the excitement at the growing connection between them, Courtney concentrated on watching the action on the stage, fighting her growing arousal.

"Oh my God. Hunter and Remington are here." Jesse grinned. "They tend to really get into these fake auctions. Their demands are legendary."

Nat blew out a breath. "I can't wait for them to meet someone. Something tells me that, when those two fall, they're gonna fall hard enough to shake the whole town."

Curious, Courtney followed their gazes, fascinated by the stunningly masculine men near the front of the stage.

They had an angry look about them, their features all hard lines and angles as they strode front and center. Their voices, deep baritones, carried through all the noise. The one on the right raised his voice to be heard above the others. "I want to see how she takes nipple clips."

Grateful for the noise that drowned out her gasp, Courtney shifted restlessly in her seat, her heart pounding when her phone vibrated again.

This time, the message was from Law.

I can't wait to see your nipples adorned with the clips I bought for you.

The rush of heat to her clit had her shifting again, the sharp awareness in her nipples driving her crazy.

She couldn't resist sneaking a glance at him, unsurprised that he watched her steadily.

His gaze lowered to her breasts, making them feel swollen and achy, before lifting to hers again, the hard glint of possessiveness in his eyes alarming. Exciting.

Turning away, she looked toward the stage again, her breath catching.

The woman appeared to struggle against her bonds, inciting the crowd.

Her Master teased her nipple with the tip of a small leather whip, increasing her struggles, much to the amusement of the men in front.

"Use the whip."

The crowd quieted slightly as the tip of the small whip came down on the woman's nipple, the cry from the woman carrying easily across the room.

The man said something to her that had the woman thrusting her breasts out again, her eyes on his as he attached a clip to the nipple he'd struck.

"Let's see that pussy."

The dark side in the two men that Jesse and Nat had spoken about, Hunter and Remington, sent a chill through Courtney, and she found her gaze sliding to Law and Zach.

She'd already seen glimpses of dark desires in *them*.

She saw it now.

It was as if a veil had been whipped away, revealing a hunger and possessiveness that she hadn't seen before.

Dazed and aroused beyond belief, she turned toward the stage, her stomach filled with butterflies.

Her clit burned as the man on the stage parted the woman's folds to expose her to the men watching.

Courtney swallowed heavily, feeling it as if it was happening to her.

Her heart pounded furiously when the woman's Master slid his hand into the pocket of his jacket and pulled out a dildo.

He wouldn't!

Reaching for her glass, Courtney took a huge gulp and then set the glass back down with hands that shook even harder. Unsteady now, she glanced toward the next table.

Looking from Law to Zach, she took several deep breaths, tightening her hand on her phone until the dizziness passed.

Fascinated by the demonstration on the stage, and stunned at her overwhelming reaction to it, Courtney turned back to watch more.

The woman writhed, crying out the word no over and over, but the man ignored her and ordered her to spread her legs wide.

Nat must have seen Courtney's discomfort because she reached over and patted her hand, smiling in understanding. "No is not her safe word. She's using it as part of the fantasy. If she really wanted her Master to stop, she'd use her safe word."

Courtney leaned close to Nat to be heard over the noise. "Safe word?"

Nodding, Nat also leaned closer. "We all have safe words to use if we want the scene to stop, or if we have trouble struggling to adjust. Being forced to do something, and accepting pleasure you don't think you want, can make it even more exciting. You have to understand that that kind of relationship is based on trust. They're closer than most couples. You can't believe the level of intimacy it takes to be in a long-term relationship like that."

Her eyes clouded, a small smile playing at her lips. "It's like nothing else in the world. It's like you're a part of each other. Jake knows what I'm thinking and feeling, almost before I do. There's nothing he wouldn't do for me, or I wouldn't do for him. Hoyt and I are getting closer than we've ever been because of that kind of trust. I can put myself in their hands completely."

Still leaning close to Nat, Courtney eyed the woman on the stage, shocked to see her spreading her thighs wider. "So, she really wants this?"

Nat laughed and patted her hand. "Oh, yeah. She does. Damned right she does. Hell, I'm going to attack Jake when I get home. Watch her face."

From the other side of her, Brenna leaned close. "And his. He's watching her closely. She's really into it, and he's backed off a couple of times to give her a chance to settle. See how he's talking to her while he's running the dildo over her breasts. He's giving her a chance to settle so she doesn't come before he wants her to. Damn, I can't wait to get to the playroom tonight."

Nat nodded. "He still has to put the other nipple clip on her. Oh, hell. This is getting me all riled up."

Courtney turned back to the stage, watching the couple in a different way.

She could see the woman's excitement and, now that she looked for it, saw the way the submissive looked at her Master for guidance.

He lifted the dildo away from her body and attached the other clip, bending close to whisper something to his submissive.

Courtney leaned toward Brenna. "What's he saying to her?"

Brenna smiled, her gaze glued to the stage. "Probably something soothing. He needs her to get used to the pain. It'll ease in a few seconds. There. See? She got past it."

"How do you know?"

"He's moving on. He's getting ready to fuck her with the dildo."

"In front of everyone?"

"Of course. That's what this is all about. She loves being on display. She loves being exposed that way. She's got a hell of a lot more guts than I do."

The noise died down, and Courtney finally got to hear the man's voice.

"Look at how well she takes the clips. Look how eagerly she spreads her thighs. She also takes the whip well. Be still, slave."

Reaching up, he released her hands. "Show everyone that clit."

Courtney couldn't believe it when the woman lowered her hands, spreading herself wide. When the man brought the small leather whip down on the woman's clit, Courtney actually jumped in her seat, almost coming on the spot.

Fighting not to look in Law and Zach's direction, she watched the man insert the dildo into the other woman's pussy and begin fucking her with it.

The woman's cries filled the air, but it was the man's face that caught Courtney's attention.

Pride. Love. Adoration. Hunger.

Gulping, Courtney continued to watch them, hardly able to believe what she was seeing.

At the demands of the crowd to see the submissive's ass, the Master inclined his head and turned her around. "Bend over and keep those legs straight."

With a cry, the woman obeyed him.

Courtney couldn't hold back a moan when the man on the stage demanded that she reach back and spread her ass cheeks.

Trembling, Courtney turned her head to see both Law and Zach staring at her, the sharp hunger in their eyes both terrifying and satisfying.

She looked back at the stage just in time to see the Master generously lube the dildo and place the tip of it directly against the woman's puckered opening.

Courtney could feel it as well as she felt Law's and Zach's intense gazes.

She felt the other woman's vulnerability. Her excitement. Her arousal.

The woman cried out as the dildo started to push into her, the sight of it sending Courtney's senses reeling.

It suddenly became too much for her, and with a cry of her own, she jumped up and turned, racing for the exit.

* * * *

Law had seen enough of the demonstrations to know exactly what was going on the entire time, so instead of watching the stage, he watched Courtney.

Imagining doing to her what Nico, the Master on stage, did to his submissive, Susan, kept him rock hard.

Over the years he'd become bored with the lifestyle, unable to get the satisfaction he needed. He wanted something more permanent, and a hell of a lot more fulfilling.

The anticipation flooding his veins now renewed his excitement, the idea of having Courtney to explore almost more than he could stand.

Her own excitement, and the hint of fear in her eyes as she watched the stage, only made him want her even more.

The shock on her face when Nico focused his attention on Susan's ass had Law stiffening and poised to go to Courtney, and he was on his feet as soon as she jumped to hers.

Brenna and Nat both started after her, stopping when Law waved them back into their seat. "I've got her."

With Zach on his heels, he ran after the woman destined to turn his life upside down, catching her before she reached the end of the hall.

Whipping an arm out, he snagged her waist, yanking her close, alarmed at how badly she trembled. "Hey, baby." Desperate to see her eyes, he lifted her chin, stunned to see tears sparkling in her eyes. "What's wrong, honey? Talk to me."

Shaking her head, she closed her eyes, letting the tears fall. "I can't do that. Oh God. This is crazy. I'm so aroused I can't even stand it, imagining doing something that I know I could never do. Let go of me. I need to get out of here."

Zach came up to her other side and grinned, but Law saw the concern in his brother's eyes. "I saw that you were drinking a Margarita. Jake taught me how to make his, and they're legendary. I have all the ingredients at the house. I'll make a pitcher and bring it over, and we can all sit down and talk."

Law bit back a smile when Courtney whirled on them.

"I don't want to talk!" She raced down the hall to the front door, yanking it open and rushing outside.

Following closely behind her and prepared to catch her if she fell, Law slid a hand to her waist, led her down the steps and steered her toward their SUV. "Then we won't talk."

He knew she was struggling to come to terms to her reaction to the evening's festivities, and it was important to him to be there for her while she did.

They only managed to go about another twenty feet before she whirled on him again, her eyes flashing as she gestured toward the club. "I can't do that!"

Law kept his voice cool and even, hoping to calm her. "No, you can't—and you won't be required, or permitted, to show your body to anyone except Zach and me."

"Permitted? Property?" Glaring up at him, she poked him in the chest, her daring reigniting passions he'd almost forgotten and needs he'd pushed aside, thinking he'd never fulfill them. "In Zach's text, he said that you would want to inspect your *property*!"

Standing in the middle of the well-lit parking lot, Courtney stamped her foot, her eyes flashing. "I have no intention of becoming anyone's *property*!"

The Master inside him roared to life as his fantasy played out in a way that gave him hope that he hadn't felt in a long time.

With her chin lifted in defiance, and her audacity at poking him in the chest, Law couldn't contain a smile, adrenaline and anticipation coursing through his veins.

He studied her features, his chest tight when he noticed the glimmer of tears in her eyes.

Sorrow. Regret. Apology.

Arousal.

She wanted him, but the emotion in her eyes told him it was much more than sexual hunger.

It was something far more dangerous.

His chest swelled, his mouth going dry.

She was the one he'd been waiting for—the woman he'd never thought he'd find.

Threading his hands into her hair, he bent to brush her lips with his, his stomach clenching with an overwhelming combination of possessiveness and emotion that stunned him. "You, my darling, are my most treasured possession."

Her lips trembled, inviting him to taste them again. "But, Law, I can't. Oh God. I'm in over my head. Watching them excited me, but I know I could never be—"

Law cuddled her close, running his hands up and down her back. "Neither one of us wants you to be anything except what you are."

Zach moved in behind her, a look of disbelief in his eyes as they met Law's. "Baby, Dominance and submission is what we make it. Everyone is different. It has to satisfy all of us."

Courtney lifted her head, looking up at Zach over her shoulder. "It's all too confusing. I thought an affair—"

Law's cock throbbed with need, the feel of her body against his threatening his control. "You thought we would just have an affair, and Zach and I threw a monkey wrench in your plans. We're sorry for that. We made demands that you aren't ready for." Pressing his lips against her hair, he sighed. "We lost our heads with you. We wanted to be honest with you, not scare you. Just settle down, baby, and we'll have the most wonderful affair you can imagine."

Courtney shook her head, sending a chill of alarm down his spine. "I can't be what you need."

Zach growled and lifted her high against his chest, hugging her close. "You're exactly what we need. Just settle down and let's enjoy our affair."

Law followed them across the parking lot, smiling when Zach's teasing and kisses against Courtney's neck earned a feminine giggle that loosened some of the knots in Law's stomach.

He slid into the seat next to Courtney and slid the key into the ignition, pausing when her small hand settled on his forearm.

"Is there really such a thing as a safe word?"

Struggling to hide his excitement, Law inclined his head. "Yes." Waiting while she pondered that, he met Zach's gaze briefly over her head.

Looking up at him through her lashes, she shifted in her seat. "What would mine be?"

His heart tripped, but Law kept his voice calm and controlled. "Whatever you'd like it to be."

"Could we go slowly?"

"In what way?" He wanted to be sure she spelled everything out for him.

Averting her gaze, she shrugged. "I'd like to try. Even though I'd never have the courage to do what they did in front of an entire room full of people, watching them aroused me."

"You're honest. I like that." Law studied her features. "So what would you like to do slowly? Spell it out, Courtney. I want no misunderstandings between us."

"I'd like to try to submit, but I'm scared."

Zach ran a hand over her hair. "Scared of what?"

"Scared of not being able to do it without panicking."

Law took her hand in his, unsurprised that it shook. He wondered if she knew the strength of the passions inside her. "You'll have a safe word, and we're not going to attack you. We'll push your boundaries and experiment. Some things you'll like, and others you won't. Some will make you uncomfortable, but it's important to take you out of your comfort zone at times. You won't always know what we're going to do to you, and that's where trust comes in—trust we'll have to earn."

Zach smiled. "Baby steps, honey. We won't rush you. If you're not comfortable with that kind of lifestyle, it's okay."

"No. It's not. I saw your faces. You need that."

Law gripped her chin. "We saw your face, baby. You need it, too."

Chapter Thirteen

Trembling with nerves and arousal, Courtney unlocked the front door and stepped inside, shivering with need at the feel of Law's warm hand at her back.

To her surprise, instead of heading straight to the bedroom, he led her to the worn sofa while Zach dropped into the equally worn chair across from them.

Leaning back, Law patted his thigh. "Put your feet up here, and let's get you out of those shoes."

Courtney tossed her purse aside and bent to unbuckle the ridiculously high, but gorgeous, black stilettos. "I can do it. Would you like some coffee?"

"No." Law moved fast, bending to grip her ankles in one large hand and lifting them onto his lap.

Off balanced, Courtney fell back against the arm of the sofa. "Hey!"

"Hey yourself." Law frowned and began unbuckling a shoe. "I've told you—repeatedly—how important it is for us to take care of you. Is allowing me to take off your shoes such a big deal?"

"Of course not, but I can take them off myself."

"I know you can." Smiling, he shook his head. Dropping one shoe to the floor, he reached for the other. "That's not the point. You're our lover now. Besides, I'm sure a foot rub would feel good, and I still owe you one, don't I?"

She glanced at Zach to see him watching her, his eyes hooded and unreadable. "It's really not necessary."

She turned back to watch Law's firm, warm hands make quick work of the buckle. "I mean it. I know you want to have sex, so why don't we—"

Law shook his head again. "Oh, Courtney. I have no idea what I'm going to do with you."

"Several options come to mind." Zach's deep voice and the glint of erotic intent glittering in his eyes added to the waves of heat bombarding her system.

Law massaged her feet, the combination of his firm touch and gentle caresses easing the soreness and reigniting the arousal that had been simmering since they'd left the club.

Currents of electricity raced from Law's hands up her legs to center at her slit, making it increasingly difficult to sit still.

Law smiled, sliding his hands higher to massage her calves. "I know you're aroused, baby. Why would you try to hide it?"

Biting her lip to hold back a moan, Courtney fought the urge to rock her hips when his hands slid higher. "I must seem so naïve to you."

Law smiled, sliding his hands under her tight dress, closing his fingers over her hips and raising her stretchy dress to her waist. "Not naïve. Delightfully innocent. Enticingly sweet."

Squeezing her thighs closed against the throbbing in her clit, she swallowed a moan, her breath coming in short pants. "I don't know how you do this to me."

Sliding his hands under her bottom, Law lowered his head, his eyes dark as they held hers. "We've barely begun, honey."

Courtney cried out at the slide of his hot tongue over her slit, and she tried to jerk away from the too intense sensation.

Law's hands firmed, not allowing her to escape. His tongue flicked in and out of her pussy, the sensation so intense that she kicked at him.

Sitting up, Zach smiled. "He won't stop. He keeps talking about the way you taste. He's hungry for you, darlin'. It's your job to make sure he has what he wants."

Thrashing on the sofa, Courtney cried out at the heat, the pleasure so extreme that it alarmed her. Her clit burned under his tongue, feeling swollen and heavy as he focused his attention there. "I can't. I can't."

Zach smiled again. "Of course you can. You really don't have much of a choice, do you? That's it. Let it take you."

Courtney cried out again as the pleasure slammed into her, pressing her feet against Law's back, her body bowing. Gripping the sofa cushions, she called out Law's name in a voice she barely recognized.

When the pleasure crested, she expected him to release her and lift his head, but although he slowed the quick flicks of his tongue, Law didn't stop.

"Law. Oh God. Please. I can't take anymore."

Wondering if he hadn't realized she'd come, she kicked her feet again. "Law, I came. Please. I came."

Still gripping her tightly, Law lifted his head, his eyes glittering like onyx. "Do you think I don't know that you came? This is for me, Courtney, or would you deny me the pleasure of tasting my woman?"

She couldn't deny him anything, especially when he looked at her as if she was the most beautiful woman in the world. Still trembling from her orgasm, Courtney couldn't stop rocking her hips, her clit so sensitive that even having her legs parted proved nearly unbearable. "It's too sensitive."

"It's for my pleasure. Not yours. This is mine, and I want it."

Suddenly, she understood. She glanced at Zach before looking at Law again, surprised to see the tension and apprehension from both of them. "This is part of submitting, isn't it?"

Law inclined his head. "It is. Now, can I get back to *my* pleasure?"

Courtney nodded, her breath catching. "Yes."

The smooth swipe of his tongue on her sensitive clit had her struggling to close her thighs, but his wide shoulders prevented it.

The sense of vulnerability excited her more than she'd expected, the knowledge that she could stop him at any time giving her the confidence to surrender to him.

She knew that stopping him would also disappoint him, and she wouldn't do that for the world. She wanted to be everything to him. To them.

To her surprise, he slowed, adjusting his hold to lift her hips higher.

His groan vibrated against her slit, his tongue moving continuously over her heated flesh, the sensation strong and creating the most pleasurable torture she could imagine.

Writhing on the sofa, Courtney couldn't hold back her cries, her breath catching at the feel of another pair of hands on her body.

Opening her eyes on a moan, she looked up at Zach, stunned by the tenderness and possessiveness in his eyes. A whimper escaped when Law focused his attention on her clit again, his slow caresses building her arousal to a fevered pitch.

"It's too intense. Oh God. I can't take it." Shaking uncontrollably, she gripped Zach's forearms, her toes curled against the pleasure as Zach cupped her breast through her dress.

Zach worked her out of the dress, tossing the material aside. "Yes, you can." His gaze settled on her breasts, making them feel swollen and heavy. "You'll be surprised at how much pleasure you're capable of handling. Let us show you." Bending to touch his lips to her aching nipple, Zach smiled. "Let us guide you while we explore this thing between us."

Courtney couldn't focus, the pleasure spiraling out of control. Caught up in sensation, she closed her eyes, her body stiffening as she went over again.

Her orgasm seemed to go on and on, the pleasure rippling through her in waves even after Law lifted his head.

On his knees between her thighs, Law unfastened his trousers, his features tight with hunger.

Stiffening, she braced herself for rough handling, surprised when he stilled.

Smiling faintly, his eyes filled with concern, he bent over her, gathering her close. "Trust will take some time, baby, but we'll get there." Rubbing her back, he nuzzled her neck, the tender gesture calming her. "You're the most precious thing in the world to me. I'm hungry for you, but you don't need to be afraid of that hunger." Lifting his head, he stared down at her, pushing her damp hair back from her face. "You don't need to be afraid of me."

Lifting her, he rose, kissing her hair when she wrapped her legs around his waist. "I love the feel of you naked against me. I have to warn you. I'm going to get you naked every chance I get."

Zach appeared beside them. "I want to kiss her goodnight." Sliding a hand down her back, he kissed her shoulder before touching his lips to hers. "I'll see you in the morning, darlin'."

Surprised, and more than a little embarrassed, Courtney hid her face against Law's neck. "I'm sorry. I thought Zach...Is he going home now?"

Law patted her bottom, the arm at her back tightening as he carried her down the hallway. "You think that Zach doesn't want you? You couldn't be more wrong. You're scared, and he doesn't want to overwhelm you. There'll be times when we take you together, but both of us are going to want time alone with you."

Lifting her head again, she saw Zach standing where they'd left him, watching them, his eyes filled with longing.

When Law started to the left, Courtney stiffened, her stomach clenching. "No. I want to go to my room."

Pausing, Law leaned back, searching her features. "Why don't you want to go into the master bedroom?"

She'd opened the door to the room shortly after she'd arrived, slamming it closed again at the memory of her father's angry voice coming from inside. "My father slept there. I can't sleep in his bed. I can still smell him."

* * * *

"He's not here." The steel in Law's voice drew her attention back to him, her eyes going wide. "It's just us, and I want your attention focused on me." With a hand at the nape of her neck, he bent her back over his arm and took a beaded nipple into his mouth, the Dominant inside him wanting her attention focused entirely on him.

The man, already half in love with her, wanted to shield her from the memory of her father's rages. He wanted to surround her with comfort.

With passion.

With the kind of love she could trust.

He strode to her twin bed and lifted his head, smiling down at her. "I haven't made love in a twin bed since college. I'm going to have to keep a firm hold on you to make sure you don't fall out."

Determined to wipe away the lingering sadness in her eyes, he lowered her to the bed, guided by the moonlight streaming in through the window. Stripping off his clothes, he took in the sight of her slender body, bathed in moonlight, and reined in his more primitive urges.

Rolling on a condom, he knelt on the bed and stared down at her. Noticing that she still trembled, he covered her body with his, pushing her thighs wide with his own. "You're trembling." Running his thumb over her nipple, he smiled. "And aroused."

Unable to hold himself back any longer, he thrust into her, groaning at the tight, warm feeling of her pussy clenching on his cock. Holding himself still, both to let her get used to the feel of him and to make it last longer, he stared down at her, his heart clenching at her beauty.

Touching his lips to hers, he breathed in the scent of her, wondering what it was about her that made him so desperate for her. "You feel so good."

"Law, oh God!" Thrusting her hips, she moaned again and again, clenching on his cock until he fought for control.

Gritting his teeth, he clenched his hands in the pillow beneath her head and began to move, slow, angled strokes designed to send her over quickly.

"Law! Yes. Please. More. More. I can't...I need—"

Law growled against her ear, a rumbling from his chest that he hadn't made in years. "I know what you need. You're mine, Courtney. Mine. Say it. Say it, damn you!"

Instead of scaring her as he'd feared, his demand seemed to thrill her, something he looked forward to exploring further.

"Yes. I'm yours. Yes. Please, Law. Please, make me yours."

When he lifted his head to look down at her, she tried to hide her face, something he couldn't allow. Wrapping both hands in her hair, he kept his thrusts quick and shallow, working the head of his cock against a spot inside her that he knew would give her the most pleasure. "No. Look at me." He nipped her bottom lip, delighted with her sharp intake of breath and the clench of her pussy on his cock. "You are mine. Very soon, love, you won't have any doubts about that."

Still holding her face, he pumped into her, fighting back his orgasm until she stiffened, her cry of release like music to his ears.

She responded to him like no other woman, making it nearly impossible to keep his hands off of her.

His own orgasm ripped through him, the strength of it astounding him. A groan escaped, a deep groan that seemed to come from his soul.

His thighs trembled under the pressure, his cock jerking as he spilled his seed.

It went on and on, his cock pulsing at the feel of her pussy clamping down on him, her inner walls rippling around him with a strength that wouldn't let go.

"Jesus!" Gathering her close, he buried his face against her neck, letting her soft cries wash over him.

Nothing had ever given him so much satisfaction. No woman had ever filled him with the sense of destiny, as if he'd come home.

As if he'd found what he'd spent most of his life looking for.

The need to possess grew stronger—a hunger for something that had always been part of his life but had lacked an elusive quality he hadn't understood.

He understood now.

Emotion had never been part of it before—and the permanence that he'd never wanted before had become all important.

Although his body was spent, his mind worked overtime.

Needs that he'd suppressed and then become bored with now demanded satisfaction.

But only with Courtney.

He would make her his—in every way.

Chapter Fourteen

Stretched out on the worn, lumpy sofa, Zach listened to the news with half an ear while listening for Courtney with the other.

Pleased to see that they praised the efforts of Tyler Oil for their immediate and thorough response to the oil spill, Zach smiled and sipped his coffee. Turning his head when the door opened, Zach smiled at the sight of Law coming through the doorway, his arms laden with groceries. "Did you get bacon and eggs?"

Law used his shoulder to close the door behind him, glancing toward the hallway. "She still sleeping?"

"Yes. I checked on her a little while ago. She's bundled under the covers, sleeping soundly. I assume you're the one who turned the air conditioner on high?"

Law grinned. "And she cuddled against me all night. I turned it down when I got up. She's a burrower."

Jealous that Law knew something so intimate about Courtney, Zach nodded and grabbed a bag, his smile falling. "Did you call the attorney?"

Law followed Zach into the kitchen, setting the bags onto the scarred, wooden table. "Yes. I got his voice mail and had to wait for him to call me back. He said that visiting Dallas doesn't violate the will as long as she doesn't spend more than a week there before coming back here. She can only be gone one week out of the month. I got one of our attorneys to get that in writing."

Gathering the bacon, eggs, and bread, Zach nodded. "Good. We need to get her out of here so Boone and the others can fix this mess.

Do you realize that only one burner on this stove works? Did you pick up a toaster?"

"They were out." He opened the refrigerator to place the milk, juice, and butter he'd bought inside, cursing when he realized what Zach had learned earlier.

The refrigerator had stopped working.

Zach grinned. "The hot water heater gets the water warm, at least."

"Yeah, but for how long?"

"I've already told Trevor to get the plane ready."

Zach lined bacon into a skillet that had seen better days. "This place is clean. That's about all I can say about it. We'll take her shopping in Dallas for things she needs in the house." Half turning, he smiled. "You're nervous about taking her to Dallas."

"And you're not?"

Zach turned his attention back to turning the bacon, wondering how long it would take the scent of bacon to wake Courtney. "I'm excited to get her away from here and spoil her a little. I can't wait to see the look on her face when she gets back and sees what we've done to the house."

Law sighed and dropped into one of the wobbly chairs. "She's gonna be pissed, but how the hell are we going to let her live like this?"

"I agree." Zach grinned at the thought of how much better she'd live with the renovations they'd already planned. "Once it's done, though, there isn't much she can do but accept it."

"Well, I'm still not looking forward to it." Law sighed. "Everything's still too new, and I sure as hell don't want to scare her off."

Zach shrugged and started plating the bacon. "It's all part of taking care of her. You go on ahead, and we'll meet up with you for dinner. She has an appointment this morning at the spa. After that, we'll head to the airport."

Law nodded and glanced toward the hall. "This is harder than I thought it would be."

Zach turned again. "Too bad. You know damned well that we both need time with her. I had to pace the damn living room last night listening to you make love to her." Shrugging, he poured himself a glass of orange juice. "Look at it this way. Tonight, we both get to be with her."

* * * *

Shuffling down the hallway, Courtney followed the smell of bacon, trying to hide her disappointment.

She hadn't expected to wake up alone and hoped Law hadn't left her because he'd changed his mind about her.

The memory of his lovemaking and his warm tenderness afterward made her smile but also left her feeling a little vulnerable.

Turning the corner to the kitchen, she blinked at the sight of Zach standing at the stove.

"Good morning, darlin'. Law sends his apologies for not being here when you woke up. He went to buy some groceries and then had some things to do." Grinning, he reached out a hand to her. "I heard you get up, so I started your eggs. Juice, coffee, and bacon are on the table. Sorry, there's no toast."

"Yeah." She pushed her hair back, knowing she must look a mess. "I was going to buy a toaster when I was out shopping this week, but I forgot it."

Smiling, he placed the plate of eggs on the table and reached out a hand to her. "Did you? So what did you buy?"

Surprised that he sat and pulled her down to his lap, Courtney shrugged, but the memory of the man in the club holding his submissive on his lap had her pussy clenching. "That dress and shoes that Hope talked me into and then just some things for the house."

Zach scooped up a forkful of eggs, feeding them to her while running a hand up and down her back, reminding her of the night before. "I saw the new pillows in the living room and the welcome mat. What else did you buy?"

Surprised that he not only held her but also seemed determined to feed her breakfast, Courtney reached for the fork, too aroused to sit there any longer. She couldn't stop thinking about the way the man at the club had held his submissive, and the memory had the power to arouse her even now. "I can feed myself, Zach." She attempted to stand, only to find herself pulled more firmly against him.

Slipping the fork between her lips, Zach nodded and set the fork aside, his eyes hardening. "I know you can. That's not the point. Law and I have already told you that we want to take care of you."

Courtney swallowed the mouthful of scrambled eggs, her breath catching when Zach slid his hand inside her robe to caress her breast. "But, Zach! I can feed myself. I don't need—"

"I do!" His gaze held hers, disappointment making his eyes flat and cold. "Does it really bother you so much to be taken care of? Do you really mind being fed?"

"You don't have to." She didn't want to admit how much she liked it, scared of sounding like a child.

"It means more to me than you can imagine." His thumb worked back and forth over her nipple, the possessiveness in the gesture making her heart beat faster.

Seeing the truth in his eyes, Courtney nodded and leaned into her caress. "Okay. But I feel silly."

Zach pushed the edge of her robe aside and bent to touch his lips to her nipple. "There's no reason to feel silly." Lifting his head, he smiled, leaving her breast exposed as he reached for the fork again. "Now, tell me about your shopping trip."

Courtney giggled, still embarrassed at being fed. "You really don't want to hear about my shopping trip."

Zach's brow went up, his jaw clenching. "I wouldn't have asked if I wasn't interested." Touching her lips with a slice of bacon, he met her gaze squarely. "You'll find that I'm interested in just about everything you do. Now, tell me what else you bought." The ice in his tone sent a wave of hunger through her, as did the possessive way he caressed her breast.

Swallowing heavily, she struggled to concentrate and bit into the bacon, almost choking on it when he began to toy with her nipple. "N–new curtains. I hated those heavy, dark ones. I took them down the first day."

* * * *

"I noticed that they'd disappeared." Zach waited until she finished the bacon before loosening her robe completely, allowing it to fall open. He wanted her to get used to being exposed and touched, and he couldn't resist having her naked as often as he could. He couldn't stop caressing her, the desire to explore every inch of her keeping him awake all night. As he scooped more of the scrambled eggs, he slid his hand under the robe to rest on her firm bottom, trying to appear as nonchalant as possible when his insides were wrapped tighter than a drum.

He wanted to get her used to his touch, but the feel of her against him made him want more.

She was precious to him already.

She fit him, like a puzzle piece he'd been missing his entire life but could never find.

She picked up her juice and took a sip, staring at the far wall. "You know, I just remembered how the people in town used to visit. The Prestons used to come by. So did Gracie and at least one of her husbands. My father used to yell at them to go away."

Glancing at him, she blinked back tears. "I used to be afraid of them. My father called them evil and said they wouldn't stop meddling in his business. He said it was because Mrs. Preston and Gracie each had three husbands, and they were sinful."

She took a deep breath and blew it out, her body trembling against his. "Momma used to hide behind those damned curtains. Bruised. Crying. I wanted to run outside, but my father would have hit me if I'd tried."

Zach's stomach clenched, fury threatening to choke him. He couldn't imagine a man beating on his wife and young daughter. Protecting women had been ingrained in him his entire life. He pulled her close, rubbing her back, a surge of male satisfaction making his chest swell when she laid her head on his shoulder. "I would very much like to meet up with your father one day."

He didn't want to upset her by telling her that Ace had already found her father and that he was being watched very closely. "They were checking on your mother. I remember everyone talking about how your father beat your mother and how they tried to get her away from him. She wanted to stay with him. She wouldn't leave him."

"She was scared to be alone. She couldn't handle my father. My aunt is the one who finally talked her into leaving him. My mom knew he would follow her to get me. He always used me to threaten her. So, my aunt talked her into leaving me with her."

Lifting her head, she smiled. "My father was always afraid of my Aunt Sally and wouldn't come near us. It left my mom free to make a new life." She smiled again, her smile not reaching her eyes. "I haven't hung them yet. I also forgot to buy a ladder."

Gritting his teeth at the thought that Courtney had been uprooted and left by her mother after being beaten by her father, Zach scooped another forkful of eggs, determined to spoil her rotten. He'd make sure that she never needed for anything ever again. "When we get back, Law and I will hang the new curtains for you."

"Get back?" Her disappointment made him smile. "Where are you going?"

Pleased that he'd already made plans for her, Zach grinned and fed her another forkful of eggs. "Where are *we* going? You're going, too."

"But I can't—"

"Yes. You can. Law already talked to your attorney and had our attorneys talk to your attorney. You can go out of town one week a month and not violate the terms of your aunt's will."

She stiffened against him, eyeing him warily. "Are you sure?"

"Positive." Zach sighed and fed her another bite of scrambled eggs. "Courtney, I know trust is hard for you, but neither Law nor I would do anything to sabotage you. We want you to get the house, remember?"

Averting her gaze, she reached for her coffee. "How could I forget?"

Zach sighed inwardly, knowing that nothing he could say would convince her that their interest in her had nothing to do with the property she'd inherit when the year had passed.

Only time and trust would take care of that, and the three of them had a long way to go. "You've got a busy day ahead of you. Come on and finish your breakfast."

Setting her coffee aside, Courtney reached for the bacon, pulling her hand back at the last second. "Where am I going?"

Pleased that she'd accepted that he wanted to feed her himself, Zach smiled and fed her another slice of bacon. "We're making progress. You accept that you're coming with us."

Courtney looked a little unsettled by that, so Zach pressed on before she could object. "Our first stop is the spa. You have an appointment in a little less than an hour."

"The spa?"

"Yes. There's a magnificent spa on the other side of town."

"I can't afford—"

"We're paying, and they already have instructions—another errand Law took care of this morning."

"But I don't need to go to the spa."

"Yes, you do." Setting the fork aside, Zach slid his hand up her back while cupping her breast, delighted with her sharp intake of breath and the look of shocked pleasure in her eyes. "You're stressed and tired, so it should relax you."

Lifting her chin, he stared into her eyes, not wanting to miss her reaction. "Your body is ours now. Remember?"

Her eyes went wide, the shock and arousal in them unmistakable. "Yes."

Sliding a hand down her body, he ran the tips of his fingers over the soft curls covering her mound. "You're going to be waxed."

"Waxed?"

"Yes." He purposely hardened his tone, easing her into the world of submission. "I want to be able to see your pussy and clit when you're spread, without anything blocking my view. It's also going to heighten your awareness there, something that Law and I are going to do often."

Not about to give her a chance to make herself nervous, he finished feeding her. "We're flying to Dallas and doing some shopping for you. Law and I want to pick out some clothing and other items for you so you don't need to pack a thing. We'll provide everything you need."

"I don't need any clothes."

"Part of caring for you is dressing you—something Law and I are very much looking forward to." He stood, setting her on his feet, staring down at her as he pushed both sides of her robe aside and cupped her firm breasts. "I don't know why that should scare you. It's just clothes. Now, go get ready while I clean up the kitchen so we can get going."

Turning her, he grinned and slapped her bottom, urging her along. "Get going. I'm anxious to get to the lingerie store and shop for you while you're at the spa."

Meeting her look of shock, he smiled at the flash of excitement and apprehension in her eyes. "There's not a damned thing to be scared of, and you know it. We'll play a little—explore a little—and by the time we get back from Dallas, you won't have any doubt that you belong to us."

Chapter Fifteen

Wearing the short sundress that had been waiting for her to put on when she'd finished her spa treatments, Courtney stepped off the plane and into a waiting limo, her breath catching at the feel of air against her naked slit.

Keeping her hand in his, Zach lifted it to his lips. "Bernard, this is Courtney. She's ours. She's not to go out unescorted while we're in Dallas. Thomas has been assigned to her." His smile sent little shivers through her, his jeans and pullover shirt doing nothing to hide his city sophistication while his bad-boy grin screamed country boy.

It was a dangerous combination, one so overwhelming that she found her breath catching when he focused that smile on her.

With his long legs stretched out in front of him, he adopted a relaxed pose, but she sensed a raw energy in him, as if he remained poised to spring at any moment.

The smiling chauffer inclined his head. "Very good, Mr. Tyler."

Zach closed the partition between them and Bernard, releasing her hand as he sat back. "We had to leave so fast I didn't even get the chance to inspect you. How did you like being waxed?"

Courtney hid a smile, her face burning. "I cursed at you quite a bit. Didn't your ears burn?"

To her delight—and relief—Zach threw his head back and laughed. "Cursed me, did you? Poor baby. I promise to make it up to you." His grin, fill of sin and promise, sent a fresh rush of warmth through her. "It feels good, doesn't it?"

Disconcerted at how important he and his brother were becoming to her, Courtney shrugged and tried to feign nonchalance. "It feels bare. Naked. Sensitive."

She turned away to stare out the window, not seeing much except the airport parking lot. Turning back to him, she studied his features, surprised that he regarded her steadily, obviously waiting for something.

Unsettled that he seemed to know her better than she would have imagined, she asked him a question that had been bugging her for hours. "It makes me feel vulnerable. Exposed. You and Law did that on purpose, didn't you? You want me to feel vulnerable. Why?"

She'd spent years building walls to hide behind—walls that kept her feelings hidden and kept her parents from hurting her any further.

Smiling, she raised a brow in challenge. "Are you and Law afraid of a strong woman?"

Zach's expression became unreadable, his gaze sharp and steady on hers. "Do you realize that it takes a strong woman to submit? Only a strong woman could allow herself to become vulnerable enough to let someone else get as close as Law and I want to get to you."

Wrapping an arm around her waist, he lifted her onto his lap. "I don't want any walls between us." With one hand flattened on her back, he ran the other under her dress to caress her thigh. "There's no room for them."

Cupping his jaw, Courtney nodded. "I know. I just don't know if I can do that."

"I know." Sliding his hand to her hair, he pulled her close, his lips warm and firm against hers. "Trust takes time, darlin'. One day I hope you realize that Law and I are the only walls you need."

Puzzled, she pushed against him to look into his eyes. "What does that mean?"

"It means, honey, that part of taking care of you is standing between you and anything that may hurt you."

"I can take care of myself."

"I know you can, and I'm very proud of what you've done. You had a lot of hard issues to deal with, and you're still sweet."

Giggling, Courtney slapped at his chest before laying her head on his shoulder, a moan escaping at the feel of his hand sliding higher to her ass. "I'm not sweet, damn it!"

"Well, I guess I'm going to have to find that out for myself." Without warning, he lifted and turned her in a show of strength that impressed the hell out of her, laying her onto the seat next to him. "I want to see how well they waxed you. Show me."

The dare in his eyes had her biting her lip and glancing toward the partition. "Bernard can't see us?"

"No. If I thought he could, I wouldn't be doing this now. It's also the reason we took the limo instead of the helicopter. I wanted to spend some time alone with you before we get to the penthouse. Now, show me."

Courtney took a shaky breath when he lifted her left thigh onto his right one, leaving one leg dangling, her new sandals sliding on the thick carpeted floor.

She hesitated, the knowledge that what she did now with Zach would change the dynamics of their relationship forever—or at least as long as it lasted.

Both Law and Zach would be her lovers, and separately and together, they would lead her into the world of Dominance and submission.

Zach eyed her steadily, lifting a brow at her hesitation. He said nothing, but the tension in his body and the yearning in his eyes spoke volumes.

Courtney drew another breath and blew it out slowly in an effort to slow her breathing and, with shaking hands, lifted the hem of her skirt.

Instead of looking down as she'd expected, Zach continued to stare into her eyes, his own glittering with something breathtaking. "You are so precious to me."

He blinked, a slow smile playing at his lips. Lowering his gaze, he ran a finger over her now bare mound. "Beautiful." He looked up again at her gasp. "I know it's sensitive, darlin'. It feels good, though, doesn't it? Hmm, much more sensitive." His fingers moved slowly over her mound before dipping lower. "Spread your legs, Courtney. Lift your knees to your chest."

Biting her lip again, Courtney obeyed him, stunned at the feeling of being so completely exposed.

Bracing a hand next to her head, he leaned over her, his fingertips light on her folds. "We're going to keep you this way, you know? I like having you smooth and bare. Exposed."

Courtney gasped, her breathing harsh and ragged. Every inch of her body trembled with need, her hips rocking in an effort to get friction against her clit. "Zach. Oh God. Please." The feeling of being exposed proved more arousing than she could have imagined. "I didn't know it would be like this!"

Zach smiled and bent to touch his lips to hers. "I did. You're going to have to trust me, darlin'. See what a little daring will get you. Now, keep your legs up." Running a hand down her side, he slid lower. "I plan to enjoy myself, and I don't want anything in my way."

Tightening her hands on her thighs, Courtney threw her head back and cried out in anticipation, her clit swollen and throbbing with every beat of her heart.

"Quiet!"

The slap to her thigh added a heat she hadn't expected.

"I don't want Bernard to hear your cries of pleasure. Not a sound."

Courtney bit her lip at the feel of Zach's warm breath on her slit, focusing on remaining quiet when the tip of his tongue slid into her pussy. Shaking everywhere, she kept her eyes squeezed tight against the need clawing at her.

Her breath caught at the feel of his hot tongue running over her slit, the sensation so extreme she lost her grip on her thighs.

Zach lifted them again, his eyes glittering with something so powerful it took her breath away as he slapped her sensitive inner thigh. "I told you to keep them up. I can see that we're going to have to use restraints to keep you in place when we explore you."

The thought of it sparked her imagination and had her gripping her thighs again and writhing for relief. Her clit burned, her pussy clenching with need. Her breathing became even harsher, the whimpers of need pouring out of her so intense, she pushed her face against the back of the seat to muffle them.

"That's better. Don't lose your grip again. I want to explore you with my mouth before we get to the office. I think Law's gonna want to see you before I take you upstairs."

Courtney whimpered again, the need so overwhelming she started to beg. "Please, Zach. Please. I can't take it." Shuddering when he ran his tongue from her clit to her puckered opening, Courtney cried out again at the sharp awareness in a place she'd never thought of as sexual. "You can't." Her ass clenched, the need he'd created there causing little ripples of release to overtake her. "God. Oh God. What? How? Oh, Zach! I'm coming!"

She lost her grip on her thighs again, crying out again when they dropped and cut off her orgasm just as it began. Groaning with frustration, she tried to raise them again, but Zach wouldn't allow it.

Sitting up, Zach pulled her back onto his lap. "You didn't do what I told you to do, did you, darlin'?"

"I couldn't." She couldn't stop trembling, the waves of pleasure and need still racing through her. Pressing her face against his neck, she held him close. "I'm so sorry. I know I'm a disappointment."

"You could do it—if you tried harder. We're going to have to work on that. You didn't get the orgasm I'd intended for you because you didn't obey me." He pushed her thighs apart when she attempted to rub them together. "No. Now you're just going to have to suffer. The building's on the next block."

Rocking against his thigh, she buried her face against his neck, not even caring that he chuckled. "Please, Zach. I can't stand it."

Fisting a hand in her hair, he lifted her face to his, smiling down at her. "Then you should have obeyed me. Remember that the next time I tell you to do something." Taking her hand in his, he kissed her fingers. "And don't even think about trying to pleasure yourself. That pussy and clit are mine, and if you touch them without my permission, you'll pay for it."

To her surprise, he took a comb out of his pocket and fixed her hair. "There. You look beautiful—all flushed and slightly dazed. Law's gonna come in his pants when he sees you."

When the limo stopped in front of a huge skyscraper, Zach took her hand in his and helped her out. "By the way, darlin', you really *are* sweet."

"And you're mean for keeping me this way. Why don't we get back into the limo and you tell Bernard to drive us around the block a few times?"

Laughing, he wrapped an arm around her waist and guided her past two guards and into the building. He addressed each guard by name, smiling at each of them as he led her through the thick glass door and into a lobby. "Nope. You're going to have to wait now. It's gonna be even worse after Law gets his hands on you."

He hustled her into an elevator, gesturing toward a keypad. "Only those with the code can get to our offices." He gave her the code, nuzzling her neck as he tapped it in. "I'll show you how to get up to the penthouse after we go see Law. He's anxious to see you."

"Does he know about the spa?"

"Of course. He's the one who went out to make your appointment. He's looking forward to seeing the results."

As they exited the elevator, several pairs of eyes followed their progress, but a glance from Zach had them all turning back to their work again.

Zach led her through a thick, wooden door and into a huge office, the presence of two desks telling her that it belonged to both of them.

Gleaming hardwood floors reflected the light from the floor-to-ceiling windows, bathing the room in a warm, glowing light. Two heavy looking desks faced each other at an angle, both desks facing a plush cream-colored sofa.

Law looked up immediately, his intimate smile bombarding her with memories of the previous night.

Her pussy clenched, the hunger Zach had created growing stronger. Glancing at Zach, she moved closer to Law, determined to seduce him into relieving the aching hunger.

He got to his feet at once and came around the desk, holding out a hand to her. "Hello, baby. Come here. I've been thinking about you all day."

* * * *

Thinking about her had kept him from getting much work done, but he couldn't remember spending a more satisfying day.

After waking up under her that morning, he'd spent several minutes just holding her close, breathing in the scent of warm woman.

No cloying perfume—just Courtney.

He'd made her appointment at the spa and put his credit card on file for many more, surprised at the satisfaction he got in the small gesture.

She belonged to them now, and he was determined to spoil her rotten.

He hadn't anticipated how much pleasure it would give him. Once he got started, he hadn't been able to stop.

He hadn't known how she would consume his thoughts or how important she would become to him.

Having her in his life had already begun to fulfill a need inside him that he barely recognized but one that he felt he'd been waiting for all of his adult life.

Seeing her now, something settled inside him while excitement made his heart race.

Reaching for her, he smiled. "You've got me all twisted up inside. Did you have a nice day?"

Courtney shrugged, taking his offered hand and allowing him to lead her around his desk and onto his lap. "It was nice, but Zach's been mean to me." Her sideways glance in his brother's direction met Zach's amused one.

"Oh?" Delighted by the feel of her on his lap, Law ran a hand over her hair and down her back, sliding the other over her smooth thigh. "What did he do to you?"

Looking up at him through her lashes, she pouted, looking absolutely adorable in her effort to play him against his brother. "He got me all worked up and then left me that way. *In the limo*! I was sitting there admiring the scenery, and he started touching me and then stopped."

Law shared a look with his obviously amused brother as Zach stretched out on the long sofa. The closeness between them had become even more pronounced since Courtney came into their lives— just another way she'd improved their lives for the better.

Adjusting her on his lap, Law bit back a groan when she wiggled against his cock. "Really? That doesn't sound like Zach. He's usually a very generous lover. There must have been a reason that he left you unsatisfied. Stop wiggling."

He got harder each time she moved, and the idea of bending her over his desk and taking her from behind became more and more appealing. "Tell me what happened." He tapped her bottom when she hesitated, his cock twitching. "Zach and I have no secrets, especially regarding you."

Courtney glanced at Zach again, her eyes narrowing when he raised a brow. "He took me to the spa, and gave me this dress and shoes, but he wouldn't let me go back to the house for a bra and panties."

Law inclined his head, hiding a smile. "You don't need panties or a bra when you're with us, and I picked out the dress this morning. What's the problem?"

"He teased me. He wanted to see if they did a good job waxing me, and then he started caressing me and stopped." Leaning into him, Courtney pressed a hand to his chest. "Last night was so wonderful. You're such a good lover. Why don't we go to your penthouse and make love?"

Law's body tightened when she cuddled closer, his cock jumping at the feel of her warm, soft lips against his jaw. Sliding his hand higher on her thigh and under the hem of her short sundress, he purposely slid his thumb closer to her slit. "You haven't told me why Zach stopped. Did you do something wrong?" He'd purposely hardened his tone, not about to give in to her. Knowing that she needed his strength, he fought his own needs.

"Of course not. I was starting to come, and my legs fell."

"For the second time." Zach's deep drawl, relaxed, but with a sexual tension that Law easily recognized, had Courtney wiggling on his lap again. "Tell Law how you couldn't even do the simplest thing—like holding your legs up so I could explore your slit with my tongue."

"*Simplest?*" Courtney glared at him, her eyes clouded with arousal. "How the hell am I supposed to be able to stay still when I'm coming?"

Zach chuckled softly, clearly enjoying himself as much as Law was. "If you had, you wouldn't be in the condition you are now."

"So how long am I supposed to stay like this?" After throwing a dirty look in Zach's direction, she turned back to Law, wrapping her arms around his neck while rubbing her nipples against his chest. "He told me that if I tried to pleasure myself, I'd pay for it."

Fighting a smile became harder and harder, but Law managed it. "Did he?"

Nodding, Courtney smiled in triumph. "Yes. He did! See? I told you he was mean."

Law reached out and pushed a button on the corner of his desk, locking the office door. "Then you're going to think I'm even meaner." Standing, he held her in front of him, nuzzling her neck as he bent her over his desk, lifting the hem of her dress in the process. "Zach and I need to get your little bottom ready for our cocks, so we bought an assortment of butt plugs for you."

Her gasp made his cock jump, the effort of holding back testing his control. "Butt plugs?"

"Hmm mmm." Law ran his hand over her ass, loving the firm softness against his palm. "We've got to train the muscles in your ass. Although you'll never get entirely used to being filled, we want you to become a little more accustomed to it so it doesn't alarm you as much."

Just the thought of training her ass had his cock leaking moisture. Still leaning over her, he pressed his cock against her hip. "We'll start with the narrowest one and see how you do with that."

Lifting his head when Zach got to his feet, Law straightened, keeping a hand at her back to hold her in place while opening the right hand drawer of his desk. "Can you stay like this, or do you need Zach to hold you down?"

When she gasped and stiffened, Law stilled, sharing a look with his brother.

Caressing her bottom, he bent over her again to search her features for any sign of fear. "What is it, baby? I'm not scaring you, am I? You know I wouldn't hurt you for the world."

"Law?"

Leaning closer, he nuzzled her ear. "Yes, baby?"

"Will you stop if I get scared?"

"We can stop anytime you want. Just remember, though, that if we stop, we stop. I want you to be brave. I want to push your boundaries, and we can't do that if you don't try." He unzipped her dress and slid a hand down her naked back, smiling when she shivered. "We want to give you more pleasure than you could imagine, but in order to do that, we're going to have to take you out of your comfort zone. Baby steps, honey. We won't rush you. We'll explore together."

Zach moved in front of the desk, running a hand over her hair. "Would you feel more comfortable if we had a safe word?"

Courtney blushed and nodded, looking even more adorable.

Zach smiled, his smile filled with pride. "Do you have a preference?"

Shaking her head, she moved into Law's touch, lifting her bottom into the hand he used to caress her.

Law wondered if she had any idea of the untapped sensuality inside her. The passion that seemed to intrigue and frighten her in equal amounts.

Zach nodded and smiled. "Red is your safe word. Okay? If you say no, we won't pay any attention. If you want us to stop, say the word red and we'll stop. We'll go nice and slow."

"Okay."

Law sensed a hesitation that had him leaning closer. "What else? What's wrong, Courtney?"

"Could you please hold me down?"

Law hid a smile, understanding that she wasn't yet ready to participate in her own submission. "You want to be taken."

Her deep blush gave him the answer he'd expected. She turned away to hide her face, something that he would allow her to get away with for now.

Zach smiled, sliding his hands over her back in long, smooth strokes. "She's not ready to give yet, but she will be soon. She's stronger than she thinks." He walked around the desk to stand beside Law, pressing his hand to her back again. "In the meantime, I'll hold her down so we don't have a repeat of what happened in the limo. She's going to have to take what we give her. This time, she doesn't have a choice."

Law smiled at her shiver, her soft cry of pleasure the most exciting and arousing sound he'd ever heard.

Courtney had a submissive streak a mile wide, the need to please and the need for closeness so obvious it nearly broke his heart.

It also renewed his determination to spoil her.

Courtney was a combination of sweet, passionate, strong, and hardheaded—a combination destined to drive him crazy.

He'd never looked forward to tomorrow more.

Lubing a finger, he stepped between her thighs, preventing her from closing against him. His cock leaked moisture, throbbing painfully as he slid his lubed finger into her.

She cried out softly and bucked, clenching on his finger while Zach held her in place. "Oh God! Law!" She kicked her feet as he thrust his finger deeper, her soft little cries spurring him on like no other woman he'd ever dominated.

Even the most experienced submissive had never given him the pleasure Courtney did with every soft cry.

Not taking his eyes from her, he spoke to Zach, knowing that talking about her when she could hear him would excite her more. "She's clenching. Her ass is very tight. I'm gonna need more lube." He slid his finger free and added more lube, not wanting to hurt her. He poised his finger at her opening again, thrilled at her cries of anticipation.

Her breathing became even more ragged, and she appeared to enjoy fighting Zach's hold more than he'd expected.

"No. Don't you dare stick anything in my ass!"

Law smiled, glancing at Zach to see that he grinned from ear to ear. Knowing that she *knew* she could stop him by using her safe word, Law hardened his tone, watching closely for her response. "Quiet. This is mine to fill whenever I want to. Now, be still so I can spread you and Zach and I can get a good look at your tight opening."

As he'd expected, she cried out again and clenched, her slit drenched with her juices. He spread her wide, running a finger over her glistening puckered opening, the strong sense of possessiveness like a fist around his heart.

She was his, and he'd be damned if he'd let her get away.

Seeing that Zach was just as mesmerized by her, Law spread her wide. "Very pretty. It's going to look even more beautiful when it's filled with the plug. It's flat on the end so it won't slip too far into you, and it's tapered so it'll get wider as it goes into you and then narrow sharply."

Bending over her again, he scraped his teeth over her shoulder. "That's so it stays in you until one of us takes it out. Each time you move, it'll move inside you and remind you that you belong to us. This ass belongs to us."

She shivered again, wiggling her ass. "I b–belong to n–no one."

"You're wrong about that." Zach parted her dress as wide as the zipper would allow, running both hands up and down her back. "You're ours, and neither one of us is about to let you go."

Law gripped the narrow plug and slowly began to push it into her, teasing himself and her by withdrawing it slightly several times only to push it a little deeper. "Very good, baby. Damn, you're tight." He had to raise his voice slightly to be heard over her soft cries and moans of pleasure. "It looks like Zach and I are going to have to work on your ass quite a bit this week, aren't we?"

Zach bent to touch his lips to her back. "And work on her ability to focus. It should be a very good week."

Law pressed the plug all the way into her, using his thumb to push the base tightly against her. "Very good, little one. Now, stand up and turn around so I can see how smooth you are."

Helping her stand, he turned her in his arms, smiling when she whimpered and slumped against him. He tilted her face to his, his heart clenching at the trust and desire glimmering in her eyes, while his cock lengthened and thickened at the way she gripped his shirt in her little fists and clung to him.

He felt stronger than ever, filled with a purpose that his life had been lacking.

"Law?"

Holding her close, he ran a hand down her back, moving the straps aside to let her dress puddle at her feet. "Yes, baby. I've got you."

He set her gently on the desk, smiling at her soft cry at the feel of the plug being pushed deeper. He leaned her back toward Zach, who'd already moved to the other side of the desk, his impatience obvious. "That's my girl. Now, let me get a good look at you."

Lowering himself to his leather chair, he kept her thighs parted, looking down at the feast spread before him.

Running his fingertips over her mound, he smiled when Zach lowered his head to take her mouth in a searing kiss that seemed to shock both of them.

Deciding to heighten their pleasure, Law parted her folds and ran his fingers over her clit, his smile widening when she cried out and began to writhe on his desk.

Zach swallowed her cries, one hand in her hair to hold her still for his kiss while the other kneaded her breast, toying with her nipple.

Law pressed a hand to her belly to keep her in place, watching both of them while he manipulated her clit and sent her over.

Slowing his strokes, he let her ride out the pleasure for as long as possible, the sight of her lying naked across his desk an image he doubted he'd ever forget.

He watched Zach gather her close and carry her to the sofa, sitting and settling her on his lap to give her the comfort and care she needed.

Picking up her dress, Law held it against his nose, breathing in the scent of the woman who'd already turned his life upside down.

Zach lifted his head, meeting Law's gaze with a smile. "She's already asleep. I'm going to take her up to the penthouse and tuck her in. Did you have the clothes delivered?"

Law grinned, remembering how much fun he'd had. "She's got a closet full. Shoes and purses to match." His smile fell. Keeping his voice low so as not to wake her, he opened the top drawer of his desk. "Have you talked to Ace?"

"No. Why? Did he dig anything up?"

Law tossed a folder onto his desk. "Her father's in deep financial trouble, and he's desperate. He's an alcoholic now, and he's erratic. He'd do anything to get the property from her. She's the only thing in his way."

"He won't get to her."

"No. We won't let him. Ace has already told all the deputies to watch out for him. His picture's posted in the jailhouse, but the more we can keep her away from Desire, the better."

"Agreed." Zach stared down at her again, his fingers gentle as he pushed the hair back from her face. "Who the hell would have thought we'd ever find the one we've been looking for?" His features hardened. "He won't get anywhere near her. I won't lose her."

"Neither will I. He was kicked out of town before. If he shows up, he'll be kicked out again."

* * * *

Ed Sheldon cursed and tossed his phone aside.

Since Courtney wouldn't answer his calls, he had no choice but to go to her.

He couldn't get to her in Desire. That damned sheriff had made sure that he could never set foot in that town again. He knew how those assholes worked. They probably had his picture in the sheriff's office along with all the others they felt were too unworthy to live in their sanctimonious town.

Assholes.

He picked up the paper again, looking at the picture of the two oilmen walking into the huge skyscraper that housed their oil company and apartment. He'd read the article so many times that he'd almost memorized it.

It went on and on about their diligent efforts to clean up the oil that one of their rigs had spilled—making them out to be heroes instead of careless.

They'd been all over the news, but the picture in the paper had stunned him because it showed them walking on either side of his daughter.

Ungrateful bitch like her mother, she smiled up at Law Tyler as they made their way into the building.

What really threw him was that she was leaning into Law with an intimacy that came through loud and clear while also holding the hand of Zach Tyler.

A whore just like her mother.

Dallas was a big city—a city he knew well. He could get to her there.

She wasn't about to keep him from getting the money he deserved.

He needed it, and he couldn't wait much longer to get it.

Chapter Sixteen

Aware of the stares from other diners, Courtney picked at her salad. "Everyone's wondering which one of you I'm with."

"You're with both of us." Taking her hand, Zach bent toward her and pulled her closer for a lingering kiss. "How does your bottom feel?"

Courtney straightened, biting back a groan when the plug shifted again. "It's driving me crazy, and you know it. How long am I going to have to wear it?"

Law chuckled and reached for her, running a hand over her hair and pulling her close to nuzzle her ear. "We're making progress. At least you understand now that it stays there until one of us takes it out." Straightening again, he eyed her, appearing much more relaxed than he'd been earlier. "You did a lot of whining about it when you were getting dressed. You came real close to getting spanked."

"I don't whine. I'd like to know how you'd feel if someone stuck something up your ass."

Zach raised a brow at that. "How does it feel? No." He shook his head before she could speak. "Not physically."

Courtney thought about it for a minute. "It's difficult to put into words. I'm interested to know how you think it feels. You did it for a reason. What did you hope to accomplish? To make me feel vulnerable? To see if I would do it? What would happen if I took it out?"

Sitting forward, Zach smiled. "Why didn't you?"

Courtney shrugged. "I've asked myself that question many times."

"And what answer did you come up with?"

"I guess because I made a promise. No. That's only part of it." She took a sip of her wine and stared at the flickering candle in the center of the table. "I guess I need to know if I can trust again." She took another sip to ease her dry throat, aware that both men gave her their undivided attention. "The only person I trusted is gone now. When I leave Desire in a year, I need to know that I can move forward, instead of being an emotional cripple."

Zach's brow went up. "Is that how you see yourself?"

Courtney shrugged, surprised that she could talk to them this way. "Sometimes. I have a few friends but none that I can even trust enough to confide in. I haven't even told them about my parents."

Law smiled. "Yet you told us."

Courtney smiled back and took another sip of her wine. "I guess I felt that you were safe. You'll never meet them, and I won't be here forever, so it won't matter."

If she hadn't turned to look at Zach at that moment, she wouldn't have realized that he stiffened. "I wanted you to understand why I couldn't sell the property to you, so you would stop asking me."

Law sat forward, a muscle working in his jaw. "I told you that what's between us has nothing to do with that fucking property."

"I know. It's still there, though, isn't it?" Courtney toyed with the stem of her wine glass, glancing at each of them. "It's how we met. You keep telling Boone to do things to the house as if it's already yours."

* * * *

Zach glanced at Law, his frustration obvious. "Is that how you see what we're doing to the house? What if we're just trying to make it more comfortable for you?"

Law took the glass from her and set it aside, taking one of her hands in his. "Zach and I want to stay with you as often as possible, so the changes are for us, too. The wiring was shot and needed to be changed, and if you think the three of us are going to be able to sleep in one twin bed, you're crazy."

Courtney smiled. "I see your point. You're both kinda big."

"Nothing like a big man to make a girl feel feminine."

Courtney heard the oversweet voice seconds before a woman appeared next to Zach.

Plopping onto his lap, the dark-eyed beauty flicked her nearly black hair back from her face. Her red lips curved in a smile before she pouted at Zach. "I've missed you so much. It's been so long since you called me. You should have let me know that you'd be back in town. If you had, you wouldn't have to sit here with your brother and his date."

Zach sighed and untangled the woman's arms from around his neck. "Hello, Chantal. Things are over between us, or have you forgotten?"

"You weren't really serious about that! You and I were so great together."

"I disagree." With his hands around her waist, he lifted the other woman from his lap and stood. "For your information, this is Courtney, and she belongs to both Law and me."

Law stiffened at the woman's approach, taking Courtney's hand in his, his eyes flat and cold when Chantal spun to him. "Hello, Chantal."

The curvaceous woman lifted her nose in the air, her lips thinning. "Law. I'm surprised you found a woman who could put up with you."

Law smiled at that. "So am I. Now, if you'll excuse us, our dinner is here. Have a nice evening."

Chantal's eyes went wide. She glanced at Courtney, her eyes narrowing as she looked over Courtney's dress. "Nice dress. Good for you. A ten-thousand-dollar dress. Going out with Law, I guess you earned it." After glaring in Law's direction, Chantal flattened her hands on Zach's chest, leaning into him as if for support." Zach, you can't be serious. You're playing a joke on me." She slapped his chest playfully, making Courtney's blood boil. "Imagine—telling me that you and Law are both interested in the same woman." She turned her back to Courtney, blocking her view of Zach.

Her giggle grated on Courtney's nerves. "Zach, why don't you come over later, and we'll take up where we left off."

"No, thank you. Now, if you'll excuse me, I'm having dinner with my woman. It appears that man over there is looking for you. It's not polite to ditch your date to go make plans with another man."

Law pulled Courtney closer while the waiter tried to appear inconspicuous as he set their plates in front of them. "Not exactly a good quality in a woman. Your date looks impatient."

Zach gripped Chantal's shoulders and pushed the other woman away. "Good-bye, Chantal."

* * * *

Law refilled Courtney's wine glass and watched her push food around her plate. "Is something wrong with your dinner, baby?" He glanced at Zach to see that his brother looked furious at Chantal's interruption.

Courtney shrugged. "No. The steak's fine. I guess people are going to talk about us, aren't they?"

"Not in Desire." Zach reached out to touch her arm, his eyes filled with apology. "We love living there, and that's only one of the reasons. Law and I knew a long time ago that nothing would make us happier than sharing a woman. We have to come to Dallas to run the business, but our real home would be there. That's why we want the land. To build the house we've designed to raise our family."

"I'm sure it would be a nice town for you to raise your family in. Some of us weren't so lucky." Courtney seemed to shrink into herself, looking decidedly uncomfortable. Cutting into her steak, she smiled at each of them, her smile so obviously forced it made his blood boil. "Your penthouse is beautiful. It must be very convenient. After working all day, you can just pop in the elevator and be home in a few seconds."

Hating that Chantal's appearance had ruined the mood of the evening, Law vowed to get it back.

The look of sadness in Courtney's eyes knotted his stomach, his heart breaking for the little girl who'd been forced to leave the town she'd grown up in, and for the woman she'd become whose parents hadn't shown her the love she deserved.

A love she so desperately needed.

A love he needed to give her—a love he needed from her in return.

He needed to make her smile again, her unhappiness giving him a sick feeling that surprised him. "I missed you more than I'd expected. While we were here and you were back home, I kept thinking about you being here. When we talked on the phone, I kept thinking about how you would look in my bed."

Pleased that shock and the glimmer of arousal replaced the sadness in her eyes, Law scooped some baked potato, dripping with butter and sour cream, onto his fork and held it to her lips. "Open."

After only a brief hesitation, she parted her lips, allowing him to slide his fork inside.

"Zach fed you your breakfast. Did you like that?"

"Yes. It was a little uncomfortable at first."

"We're going to have to get you used to it. I like feeding you. I'm going to like bathing you even more."

Courtney blinked and reached for her wineglass, taking a sip before turning back to him, her cheeks flushed. "Bathing me?"

Pleased to see that she'd started to become aroused again, he scooped more of the potato. "Of course. It's all part of taking care of you—like shopping for you." He slid the fork into her mouth again, loving the way she responded.

After swallowing, she looked down at her dress. "I can't believe you bought all those clothes. I don't need them. Did this dress really cost ten thousand dollars?"

Law frowned and took a bite of his own steak. "I really have no idea. You need clothes while you're here, Courtney. There's another benefit this weekend, and we want you there with us, and we sure as hell don't want you to be embarrassed about what you're wearing."

Zach grinned. "Besides, we love having out own dress-up doll. We can dress you in whatever we want, and you have no say in it. You have no idea how much fun we're having."

Courtney shook her head and smiled, looking up at Zach through her lashes. "Are you hoping that people finding out that the three of us are in a ménage relationship will make them forget about the oil spill?"

Zach laughed softly. "That would just be a side benefit." His smile fell. "We would never exploit you, Courtney, but we're not hiding you. You're ours, and we want everyone to know it."

She pursed her lips, drawing Law's attention to them. "Have you ever shared a woman before?"

Zach shook his head and cut into his own steak. "Not publicly. In the club—yes—but we've never found a woman that both of us want the way we want you. I've never wanted a woman enough to have for my own, but Law and I have talked about you quite often. Each of us would be happy to have you on our own. Sharing you is more satisfying than either one of us could have ever expected."

Law lifted her hand to his, kissing her trembling fingers. "You're a constant delight to us. We can't keep our hands off of you, but that's only a small part of it." He smiled, anticipation of the night ahead keeping him hard. "You keep squirming. How's that little butt plug feel?"

"Little?"

Zach chuckled softly, leaning close to her. "It's the smallest one Law could find." His gaze lowered to her breasts. "We'll use a larger one before we tuck you in tonight. Each night, we'll use one just a little bigger than the night before."

Pleased at the arousal clouding her eyes, Law was determined to make sure that the closeness would be more than just sexual. "You're ours in ways that you haven't even realized yet. But you'll learn, baby. You'll learn."

Chapter Seventeen

By the time they got back to the penthouse, every inch of Courtney's body tingled with need, their tender seduction knocking down emotional walls with an efficiency that alarmed her.

Zach led her to the sofa, tightening his arm around her when she would have sat down. "No. Not yet." He cupped her face, his thumb and fingers firm on her cheeks as he held her face lifted to his. He brushed his lips over hers, tasting of the cognac he'd had after dinner and warm male. "Law and I are going to explore every inch of you."

"Zach?" Courtney moaned when his mouth covered hers, her pulse tripping when Law closed in behind her and began to slowly unzip her dress.

Zach took her mouth with a slow thoroughness that left her dizzy, and grateful for his hold, she clung to him, wrapping her arms around his neck. Without lifting his head, he reached up to grip her wrists, lowering her hands to her sides again, allowing Law to push her dress from her shoulders to puddle at her feet, and leaving her naked except for her black satin heels.

Zach raised his head, breaking off his kiss to smile down at her. Lifting her hands to his shoulders, he touched his lips to hers again, his voice low and intimate. "Keep your hands there, darlin', while Law explores you."

Courtney gasped at the rush of heat to her slit and nipples, her bottom clenching on the plug and increasing her awareness there. "Why do you say things like that to me? It makes me crazy." She hadn't wanted to admit that, but she couldn't seem to think when either one of them touched her.

Zach trailed his fingertips from her wrists to her shoulders, sending electric currents up and down her arms. "Sometimes we'll tell you what we're going to in order to prepare you for what's coming." His eyes darkened as he trailed his fingertips down her sides and to the outer curve of her breasts. "Sometimes, it'll be to build the anticipation."

Law's lips touched her shoulder. "And sometimes we won't tell you anything all. We'll surprise you and test your ability to adjust. Damn, just the thought of training you excites the hell out of me. A woman we can train as our own."

The longing in his voice washed over her until his words penetrated.

Stiffening, she pushed against Zach's chest, a moan escaping when Law's lips moved lower. "Train me? Oh God."

Law's lips moved over her back, his hands sliding up and down the sides of her body. "We've got so many things to teach you. To show you." His lips slid over her bottom, the scrape of his teeth as he pushed at the plug nearly sending her over. "We've got to teach you to experience pleasure when we fill your ass. We'll show you just how different sensations can sharpen your pleasure. Damn, you're so soft. You taste incredible."

Still holding her face, Zach ran his thumb over her lips while he slid the other down to her breasts. "When we first touched you together, you were jumpy and nervous." His fingers closed over a nipple, the sharp sensation sending currents of pleasure to her clit and ass where Law manipulated the plug. He smiled, a smile of affection and male satisfaction mingled with pride. "Look at you now."

Courtney would never have believed that the feel of a man's lips on the back of her thighs and knees could create such a hunger inside her, but it did.

Lifting one foot and then the other, Law kissed and licked every inch of the backs of her legs and feet, leaving behind a trail of heat and sensation. "Turn her around."

Zach's eyes sharpened, glittering with a possessiveness and erotic intent that stole her breath. "With pleasure. Then I'm taking her."

Law's low chuckle sounded strained, and as Zach turned her, Law gripped her knees. "I know. Spread your legs a little for me, honey." His fingertips traced patterns on her mound, making the sensitive flesh there sizzle with heat. "So soft and pretty."

Zach held her arms above her head and, to Courtney's shock, tied her wrists together with his tie. "There's no reason to panic, darlin'. It's just Law and me."

Having her hands held above her head made her feel even more defenseless, the knowledge that she couldn't cover herself while he explored her more exciting than she would have ever imagined.

Shocking her further, Zach slipped her tied hands behind his neck, leaving his own hands free while keeping hers held high. "You know we wouldn't hurt you for the world. That doesn't mean, though, that we're not going to play with you." He slid his hands to her breasts, teasing the sensitive underside with the tips of his fingers, completely avoiding her nipples. "You're so damned beautiful and soft that we can't stop touching you, and the way you respond only makes us want to touch you more."

Kneeling in front of her, Law lifted his gaze to hers. "You know we're going to keep you bare, right?" He parted her folds, exposing her aching clit. "Very pretty. You're drenched, darling. Your little clit looks red and swollen."

"Yes!" Frustrated that no amount of writhing could get the friction she needed on her nipples, Courtney struggled, the tingling sensation in her nipples driving her crazy. "Touch me, damn it!"

Law's gaze lifted to hers again, his lips twitching when Zach slapped her ass. "Behave yourself."

"I thought men liked a woman to be sexually demanding."

"We know what you need—probably better than you do. We know your nipples are as needy and achy as your clit and that you keep clenching on that plug in your ass and it's driving you crazy."

Zach slid his hands down her belly, making her stomach muscles quiver. "You need attention there, but it's not something you're comfortable with."

"I'm scared. I've heard stories. I've talked to people. It's so intimate. Carnal."

"Are we scaring you?"

"Not yet. A little. I don't know."

Zach scraped his teeth over her shoulder, sending another wave of sharp pleasure to her nipples. "Trust, darlin'. You have your safe word. We'll stop whenever you want—or need—us to. You believe that, don't you?"

She wanted to, but her father had taught her that there were times when a man just couldn't control himself.

Trembling helplessly, she cried out at the slide of Law's tongue over her clit, her knees buckling. "Yes. Oh God!"

Ripples of pleasure raced through her, but Law stopped before she could go over, leaving her dangling on the edge. "No! Please don't stop. Please."

Zach chuckled. "She just can't help herself, can she?" Wrapping his arms around her, he tugged her nipples, sharp tugs that almost sent her over again. With a soft laugh, he untied her hands and released her, steadying her until Law rose and pulled her into his arms. "We're going to have a hell of a lot of fun teaching her some control."

Law's arm around her waist held her in place, his eyes filled with warmth and hunger as he threaded his fingers through her hair. "One day soon, Zach and I are going to take you together—one of us in your pussy and the other in your ass. In the meantime, we're going to get your ass ready to be fucked."

Courtney sucked in a breath, her ass clenching on the plug. "I need to come so bad." The way they talked to her—the way they touched her—gave her a delicious feminine feeling.

She felt safe with them. Warm. Desired. Powerful and yielding at the same time.

They touched her as if they owned her, every caress filled with a possessiveness that should have irritated her but aroused her instead. With every breath, she gave more.

Lifting her hands to his neck, Courtney leaned into Law, watching Zach roll a condom onto his massive cock out of the corner of her eye. "Did you say it that way to scare me?"

Law's lips twitched. "Last night we made love. I was gentle with you. There'll be times when it's not so gentle. It'll be raw. Wild. Hot, sweaty sex. Sometimes the hunger won't allow for tenderness."

"Like now." Wrapping an arm around her waist from behind, Zach lifted her from her feet, running a hand over her ass as he carried her dangling over his arm toward the sofa. He positioned her over the back, spreading her thighs wide. "I want you too damned much to use pretty words. I want my cock inside you. This pussy's mine to take whenever I want to."

He pushed the head of his cock into her, slapping her ass when she wiggled. "Be still. This isn't about you. This is about what I want. I want to fuck this sweet, tight pussy, and you're going to be still while I do it."

Courtney gasped at his deep thrust, grabbing fistfuls of the sofa cushions to steady herself against his fast strokes.

His cock filled her, moving hard and fast inside her, each thrust taking her closer and closer to the edge.

Her inner walls clamped down on him, her toes curling when he gripped the plug and slowly pulled it out several inches before thrusting it back inside her.

Overwhelmed with sensation, she cried out on every harsh breath, struggling to concentrate on staying still. Pleasure consumed every inch of her body, making her tremble, and making it even harder to focus.

Law sat on the floor next to her shoulder, leaning against the sofa. His rough hand gripped her hair and turned her to face him, raising his voice to be heard over her cries. "Zach's enjoying himself. You'd better be still and let him get his pleasure." Slipping a hand under her, he toyed with her breast, closing his fingers over her nipple and tugging lightly.

Zach groaned, a raw, deep sound that added to her arousal. "So fucking good." With another deep groan, he worked the plug out of her and replaced it with his thumb, the sharp sensation nearly sending her over. "I want to feel your ass clenching."

Courtney cried out, the pleasure too intense to fight. With Zach fucking her pussy and his thumb fucking her ass, and Law's attention to her nipple, she didn't have a chance of holding back.

When the walls came down around her, she didn't even care.

Her body jerked as the wave of ecstasy slammed into her, the force of it stealing her breath and sending her world reeling out of focus.

Several sharp slaps landed on her ass while the waves still raced through her, adding to the decadent pleasure.

"I told you to be still!" Zach's slaps intensified the heat, and before she'd even finished coming from her first orgasm, the second slammed into her.

She lost all control of her shaking body, the pleasure taking over and controlling her movements. Tossed in the storm, she fought for something solid to hold on to, realizing through the dizziness that something strong and solid held on to her.

Zach pressed his hand at her lower back while using his thumb to thrust into her ass. "That's a girl. Come again. Yes. Very nice. Fuck, she's tight."

Courtney cried out again when Zach moaned and thrust deep, her pussy clenching on his cock as it pulsed inside her, the thumb in her ass going deeper. "Zach! Yes. Oh God. It feels so good. I can't hold on."

"I've got you." Zach groaned and slid his thumb free. "Damn, woman. You get me riled up."

To her horror, Courtney started crying.

* * * *

Law gathered her close, pulling her free of Zach's cock to gather her onto his lap. "I knew it would happen. That's it, baby. You're okay." Running his hands up and down her back, he held her shaking body pressed to his chest, marveling at her passion.

Lifting his gaze, he met the concern in Zach's. "I knew she would be this way. Her passion's so strong. She finally let go. Go get cleaned up. I've got her." Nothing had ever given him as much pleasure—or satisfied the Dom in him more.

He crooned to her, moving his hands over her nakedness, her cries of surrender spilling onto his chest. "That's my baby. Yes. That's it. Let it all out."

"I c–can't stop. I d–don't know what's happening."

Law nuzzled her neck, breathing in the scent of his woman. "You let yourself go, and we caught you. You're all right, baby. You're very passionate, and you came hard."

Zach smiled as he came back into the room. "You finally trusted us enough to let go." Moving in behind her, he sat cross-legged on the floor and leaned over her, taking her hand in his. "You were magnificent."

Law cupped her breast, sliding his thumb lazily over her nipple. "So incredibly beautiful. I've never seen anything so sexy in my life. Your eyes told me all I needed to know and everything I'd hoped to see."

* * * *

Courtney opened her eyes, smiling up at him. "I've never come so hard. It was scary. I'm still shaking."

"We know." Toying with her fingers, he smiled. "We want you to lose control, and we need for you to trust that we'll be there for you."

His smile made his eyes seem to glow. "You did. You have no idea how much that means to both of us."

Sitting naked on Law's lap, and still trembling from her orgasms, Courtney fought to comprehend what had happened. A little embarrassed, she pushed at his chest. "You don't need to hold me." She started to get up, but Law tightened his arms around her.

"I like holding you." He ran his hands up and down her back. "Besides, you're still a little shaky."

"I'm fine." Confused, Courtney tilted her head back to look up at him, wondering why she still felt so unsteady. "Why do you do this? Is this normal?"

Urging her back against his arm, he ran his hand over her hip, cradling her as he might a child. He and Zach glanced at each other before both men met hers again. "Do what? Is what normal?"

Courtney shrugged, wishing she'd kept her mouth shut. "Nothing." She tried to sit up, needing some time alone, but he tumbled her back, frowning down at her.

"Tell me." Holding her against his chest, Law cupped her jaw, sliding his thumb over her cheek. "What's bothering you, baby?"

Her breath caught at the tenderness in his eyes. "Why are you holding me this way? You did it last night, too."

Law smiled and took her hand in his. "Because we want to take care of you. Part of that is aftercare."

"Aftercare?" Curious, she stared up at him. "What's that?"

"After an orgasm, don't you feel a little shaky? Vulnerable? Weak?"

"Yes."

Zach bent to kiss her shoulder. "As you can see, it'll get more intense as we progress. Your vulnerability will get even stronger, and you'll need time to gather yourself again. We're responsible for taking care of you, and that includes guiding you through the passion and seeing to your care afterward. It's something all three of us need."

Smiling, he slid his arms and stood, lifting her against his chest. "Your bath's ready." Lifting her higher against his chest, he dropped a quick kiss on her lips and smiled. "What did you think I was going to do, just fuck you and walk away?"

Since that had been what had happened after her one and only sexual encounter before she'd met them, that was exactly what she'd believed. Shrugging, she leaned her head against his shoulder, surprised at the change in him.

He'd gone from sexually dominant to warm and loving in just a matter of seconds.

"I guess I didn't really think about it." Surprised at the increased sense of intimacy, she laid a hand on his chest. "You can put me down, you know. I can make my way to the bathroom."

"That's hardly the point, is it?"

To her surprise, he stepped into the tub with her, lowering both of them into the warm water and settling her on his lap. He eased her against his chest, running his hands over her arm and leg. "The kind of relationship Law and I want with you requires a lot more than just sex."

"I know. The Dominance and submission you talked about." She cuddled against him, the combination of his steady caress and the warm water soothing her so much that her eyes drifted closed. "I have to admit that I'm a little nervous about the whips and chains thing. I'm afraid I'm going to be a big disappointment to you."

* * * *

Zach kissed the top of her head, loving the feel of her in his arms. "Dominance and submission can be a lot of things, darlin'. It'll be whatever we make it." Hugging her close, he glanced at Law as he strode into the bathroom wearing only low-riding cotton pants. "We'll see what works for all of us. It's a journey, babe. Law and I will both be watching you closely. We'll take you out of your comfort zone over and over to see how you handle it—like I did tonight."

Lifting her hand from the water, he played with her fingers, satisfied to see that her trembling had eased.

Law lowered himself to the floor beside the massive bathtub. "Something to think about if you disobey us." He slid a hand under the water to stroke Courtney's thigh. "For example, if you do something like going to the club again and trying to keep it from us, we'll have to do something to make sure nothing like that happens again."

Courtney frowned, turning her head to look at him. "I was safe there. All the women I went there with told me over and over how safe I would be."

Law inclined his head. "Which is why we didn't stop you from going. We knew you needed to go to get some answers that you were looking for and that it was the safest way you could do that."

"Why didn't you tell me you were coming home?"

Zach smiled and played with her fingers. "We were going to, but when you didn't tell us about the club, we decided to teach you a lesson." He pressed his lips against her hair, remembering her reaction. "We also thought you might need us."

She blushed and tried to hide her face against his chest. "I overreacted and made a fool of myself, and you were there to see it. I suppose I looked naïve and stupid, huh?"

Zach smiled, his heart softening every moment he spent with her. "Not stupid at all, and you didn't make a fool of yourself."

Law soaped a washcloth and began to wash her legs. "You're a very passionate woman, and you got turned on by what you saw so much that you weren't ready to handle it. You're still afraid that you won't be able to handle what Zach and I want from you, which makes you skittish." Getting to his knees, he slid the cloth over her inner thigh and to her slit. "We're here for you, baby. We'll guide you every step of the way. We'll slow down when you need us to and hold you afterward and help you come down. We're going to teach you just how much pleasure you're capable of experiencing and, in the meantime, show you just how close we can be." His eyes sharpened and held hers. "You can depend on us, Courtney. We're not going to walk away."

Courtney frowned and ran a fingertip over Zach's forearm. "When we were at the club, the women there talked about how close they were to their husbands. Nat said that Jake knows what she's thinking and feeling before she does."

Zach smiled, wondering what she would think if she knew just how much he and Law craved that kind of closeness with her. "I'm not surprised. A Master has to know his sub very intimately. He needs to. He needs to know her limitations and be able to read her moods. You'll find that Law and I will be more attentive to you than you'll expect. We *need* that kind of closeness with you. It's not a game to us, Courtney, but a way of life."

"But when you took those women in the club, you didn't have that?"

Meeting Law's gaze over her head, he winced, wishing he could avoid the subject. "That's right, and that's why those trips to the club became so unsatisfying. We want something more now. We want someone who'll belong to us in every way a woman can belong to a man. It's not just about the sex. It's the everyday things."

"Like buying me clothes and threatening to put a butt plug inside me before I go to bed at night."

Law chuckled. "First of all, that wasn't a threat. It was a warning of what to expect." He ran the cloth over her breasts, smiling down at her. "It's clothes and feeding you and a million other ways of taking care of you." Dropping the cloth, he closed his thumb and forefinger over her nipple, his eyes darkening at her soft cry. "It's making you ours. To spoil. We want to be able to be ourselves with you, and we need that from you. To be yourself."

Zach's cock twitched at the feel of her ass rubbing against it as she writhed on his lap. "Sometimes I don't want to use pretty words. Sometimes I want to fuck you so badly that I ache with it. I want to be able to be honest with you about that."

To his delight, Courtney smiled at that. "When I came out of the club that night, I was so aroused that I wanted you to take me right then and there."

Law's eyes narrowed to slits, his hands moving over her. "And if we'd already been closer, you wouldn't have had to ask. Zach and I could see it. We would have thrown you into the truck and taken you right then and there. We were too damned afraid of scaring you to give you what you needed."

Zach ran a hand over her slick breast. "See how that kind of distance keeps people from getting what they need? We don't just want the sex."

"You want what your brother and your friends have."

Zach nodded. "Exactly. I want that kind of happiness. With you."

Her silence lengthened, but Zach waited her out, pleased that he knew her well enough to know that she had to work something out in her head. Finally, she sighed. "Will you tell me when I do something wrong?" Her voice, that of a lost little girl, had him holding her closer.

"We'll guide you. There'll be times when you're nervous—times when you're downright scared." Zach gathered her against him as tightly as he could without hurting her. "It'll be at those times that we'll need your trust the most, and it's up to us to make sure we have it—and never betray it."

* * * *

Lying between them, Courtney watched Zach spread a liberal amount of lube on the new butt plug he'd just cleaned. "I can't believe I'm letting you do this."

Leaning on his elbow looking down at her, Law raised a brow in that arrogant look that excited her so much. "That's our ass, remember? We can do what we want to do to it." His gaze held hers, the tension in his body telling her how much this meant to him.

Acting on instinct, Courtney laid a hand on his chest, lifting slightly to press her lips against his neck, smiling when he groaned and laid a hand on her waist. "I want to be yours."

Warmed when his hand tightened on her waist, she smiled against his jaw. "Just this. Don't lie to me and say it's something more. I want to get lost in this. I think I need to get lost in this. Don't let me chicken out. I want to experience all of it."

Sliding his hand under her hair to her neck, he leaned back to stare down at her, searching her eyes for something. Apparently pleased with what he saw, he smiled. "I won't lie to you. I'm going to get you so lost in pleasure that you'll never want to get away from me."

"From us." Zach threw back the covers. "On your belly, darlin'. Over this pillow."

With a smile, and Law's help, she got to her knees and draped herself over the pillow Zach had placed in the middle of the bed.

Running a hand down her back, Zach leaned down to look into her eyes. "Spread those thighs, darlin', and be still when I'm putting this in. Absolutely still, do you hear me?"

Caught up in the erotic fantasy, Courtney pouted. "What if I can't be still? It's too invasive. Too intimate. It's hard to be still while you're pushing something into my ass."

"I know, baby. But you're just going to have to do it." Smiling, he ran a hand over her hair. "You want to be good, don't you, baby?"

The way his eyes glittered and his body tensed told her that he'd chosen his words carefully, and that her reaction to them meant a great deal to him.

She couldn't deny that her first instinct was to tell him that she was an adult and had no intention of being *good*, but when she saw the hunger in his eyes, the thought of being good for him and Law excited her.

The idea of challenging him, though, proved impossible to resist. She couldn't allow herself to become pliant and boring.

The sense of freedom she'd found since meeting them gave her the kind of confidence she'd never really possessed.

Shrugging, she wiggled her ass, fighting not to smile. "I'll try, but sometimes I don't want to be good. I'm not a pushover anymore."

Zach smiled, his eyes lit with challenge. "I'd be very disappointed if you were."

From the other side, Law ran a threatening hand over her bottom. "And when you're bad, we're just going to have to do what's necessary to make you good again." His warm breath against her neck sent a shiver of delight down her spine. He lowered his voice to a husky whisper that made her toes curl. "Now, spread those legs and be still, or I'll spank you—and enjoy it."

Hiding a smile, she pouted again, enjoying the game. "You'd really spank me?"

"Yeah, and all the pouting in the world won't change my mind."

Determined to defy him in the near future, Courtney lifted to her elbows, gasping when a hard hand came down on her ass.

Zach caught her wrist when she jerked and reached back to rub the sting away, his eyes dark and filled with a possessiveness that made her heart skip a beat. "Keep those hands where they were. I told you to spread those legs. Now."

Fisting her hands on the pillow, she obeyed him, struck once again by the sense of vulnerability—and the realization that she'd begun to trust them.

A whimper escaped when Zach lifted and spread the cheeks of her ass, the knowledge that he stared down at her puckered opening making it burn. She gasped at the feel of the cold object being pushed slowly into her, her thighs trembling with the effort it took to stay still.

"Oh God. It's too big." Her bottom burned around it, the full stretched feeling making her breathing harsher. Throwing her head back, she leaned into the hand Law threaded through her hair.

Law smiled and bent to touch his lips to hers. "No, it isn't. Zach's being gentle with you, and it's already inside. That plug's just a tiny little thing. When you're ready to have your ass taken, my cock's going to go deeper, and it's sure as hell not gonna just sit inside you like that plug. It's gonna move, baby, and you'll know what it's like to feel taken."

* * * *

Lying in the darkness on his side, Zach held Courtney against him, breathing in the scent of her. He moved his hand slightly over her belly, smiling at the mental image of her heavy with child.

He loved her. He had almost from the beginning. The day they'd met her, he'd known she would change his life, but he hadn't known just how much.

Amused that he was calmer than he'd expected to be, he closed his eyes, loving the feel of warm woman in his arms.

Everything in his life had led to finding Courtney.

It eased something inside him and had him excitedly planning the future.

He and Law had a year with her, and by the time the year was up, and the subject of the property was settled, they could move forward and have the life that he'd dreamed about.

Chapter Eighteen

Law hung up the phone, pushed the paperwork he'd been reading aside, and leaned back in his office chair, staring at the ceiling. Having Courtney in their penthouse gave him a great deal of satisfaction, but he couldn't wait to get the matter of the property settled.

He hated that it stood between them.

"She got back about five minutes ago."

Glancing across to his scowling brother, Law stilled, his stomach knotting. "What's wrong?"

"Thomas said that Courtney's father followed them. He saw him several times today. He was wearing a hat and sunglasses, but Thomas is positive that it was him."

Law shot to his feet. "What happened? Is she all right?"

Zach ran a hand over his hair and blew out a breath. "She's fine. Thomas said she never saw her father, but he did several times. Since Courtney's father never got too close, he didn't confront him. The fact that he followed her here is not a good sign."

"No. It isn't." Dropping back into his chair again, he smiled coldly. "At least he must know now that she's ours and under our protection. We'll have to keep a sharp eye on her at the party tonight."

He sat up, gesturing toward the phone. "That was Ace. Apparently, he found out that Courtney wants to open a flower shop in Desire. She talked to Brenna about it and asked around town to see if there was one." Law smiled and leaned back in his chair. "It looks like Courtney is thinking about staying."

"Thomas said that she went into a lot of flowers shops today." Zach got to his feet, moving around his desk to lean against the front of it. "She didn't touch the money we left on the table for her. Thomas said the only thing she bought was one of those soft blankets that you put over the back of the sofa. A red one." Frowning thoughtfully, he stood again. "Have you noticed how much she likes to have soft things around her, how much she likes color?"

Law sat up, his smile falling. "Now that you mention it, yes. No wonder she likes flowers so much. Hell, I bought her all that black. I thought it would give her confidence, and she looks sexy as hell in it." His lips twitched. "Those damned black garters and stocking get me every time."

Frowning, Zach stared at the ceiling, as if imagining Courtney moving around up there the way Law did. "Did you notice that look of shock she gets each time we hold her? Why the hell is she surprised? We do it all the time." With a curse, he strode to the window. "Something's wrong, and I can't figure it out."

"I've noticed that." And it irritated the hell out of him. "She loves the sex and loves to play more, but she's increasingly uncomfortable with displays of affection. Her eyes light up when she sees us. Jesus, I'll never get tired of that look." Law sat back again, staring at the ceiling. " She's really gotten to me, Zach. More than I'd expected." Cursing, he got to his feet. "Love isn't supposed to tie you up in knots this way, is it?"

Zach turned from the window and frowned. "What are you talking about? I feel great. Courtney's just a little unsure about our motives, but I've come up with a great plan."

"What kind of plan?"

"I'll tell you about it later. I have another plan to take care of first."

Grinning, Zach reached for his phone.

* * * *

Courtney straightened the throw she'd bought over the back of the leather sofa in the living room and stood back, eyeing it critically.

Except for the slash of red, everything in the room seemed to be either white, black, or gray, and she'd wanted to add a little color.

Now she wondered if she'd done the right thing.

If Law or Zach wanted color, they could have gotten it themselves. Her red throw would probably look unsophisticated to them and ruin whatever look they'd been going for.

Seeing movement out of the corner of her eye, she glanced at Thomas, who came out of the kitchen sipping a bottle of water. "I probably should just take that home."

Thomas had taken off his sunglasses when they'd come inside, but it didn't make him appear less scary.

He had a thicker build than either Law or Zach, but he moved in a way that made her think of a coiled spring, ready for action.

His reddish-blond hair had been cut short, his green eyes hard and cold. Almost as tall as her lovers, he had a deadly look about him that probably made him a wonderful bodyguard but also made her nervous.

The stone-faced bodyguard shrugged. "That's up to you. Do you have plans to go out anywhere else today?"

Shaking her head, Courtney went back to the sofa and gathered the throw against her chest. "No. Thank you. I'm sorry I inconvenienced you."

"It's my job. I'll be downstairs. Call if you want to go out again."

Nodding, Courtney watched him go, breathing a sigh of relief when the door closed behind him.

When Law and Zach had introduced him as her bodyguard several days earlier, she'd objected, telling them that she didn't need a bodyguard.

No amount of objecting could sway them, so she'd stayed in the penthouse all week, only going out with Law and Zach, not wanting to explore the city with such a cold, hard man as a companion.

This morning, though, she'd gone stir crazy and needed to go out. She'd mentioned it to Law before he'd left to go to his office on the lower floor, and he'd called Thomas despite her objections.

It was a mistake she wouldn't make again.

When the phone rang, she knew better than to ignore it. She'd done that on her first day here, only to have Law and Zach appear within seconds, thinking that something was wrong.

Laying the throw aside, she went to pick up the receiver. "Hello?"

"Hi, baby. Did you have fun shopping?"

"How did you know I was back?"

"Thomas called."

"Of course he did." Rubbing her forehead, she made her way to the window. "Is he supposed to spy on me?"

"He's not spying on you, damn it! He's supposed to keep you safe."

"I don't need a damned bodyguard!"

"Courtney, the subject's closed. We got a lot of bad publicity from that oil spill."

"But on the news it said that your men caught it in time, and you cleaned it up right away. You still have people out there."

"Yes, we do, and they'll stay out there until every drop is cleaned up, but that's not enough for some people. Plus, have I mentioned the fact that we have more money than we know what to do with? You don't think some crackpot might want to grab you to get Law and me to pay?"

Dropping into a chair, she stared out the window. "I didn't need a bodyguard in Desire."

"In Desire, you've got a whole town full of bodyguards. This isn't negotiable, Courtney. I called you to ask you to come down. Instead, I think I'll come up there."

Courtney winced at the frustration in his tone, and wondered if she'd ever get used to living the kind of life that required a bodyguard.

She hated that she'd put them to even more trouble. She'd always done her best to take care of herself, and being thrown into a world where someone else took care of her was harder to get used to than she'd expected.

She'd never been needy, and they wanted her to need them.

She just wondered how long it would take for them to get tired of it.

She'd gone out today because she'd been restless, the realization that she'd begun to fall in love with both Law and Zach hitting her hard. She needed some time alone to think.

She'd been afraid that she would fall hard for them but hadn't counted on it happening so soon.

Or for the fall to be so hard.

They worked steadily to smash every barrier she tried to hide behind, their need for closeness and trust not to be denied.

In a year, she'd be a basket case.

She'd leave town with her heart torn to shreds, and couldn't blame anyone but herself.

She'd gone into this thing hoping to get some of her confidence back and to fight the loneliness that had been a major part of her life ever since she could remember.

The instinctive need to distance herself from them proved harder every day, but the way they held her and looked at her gave her a warm feeling that proved impossible to resist.

They made her feel loved. Adored. Cherished.

And she'd begun to believe it.

Unable to fight it, she'd found herself drawn deeper each day into their world, each step drawing her in closer.

Each day, she wanted—needed—them more.

They still inserted the butt plug into her ass each night, the awareness they'd created there driving her crazy.

They hadn't taken her there yet, and although they were forceful and arrogant in the bedroom, neither one of them had been hard or rough with her.

They hadn't whipped her. They hadn't used the nipple clips Law had told her about.

She sensed that something held them back.

She could only think of two things that would have.

Either they feared scaring her off before the year was over because they were afraid it would jeopardize their chances of getting the property, or they no longer wanted her in that way.

Depressed, she'd gone out to think and had only worked herself into a worse mood.

Stiffening when the door opened, she watched Zach come into the room, closing the door behind him. "Contrary to popular belief, I don't need a babysitter, Zach."

Zach's eyes narrowed, his steps never slowing. "Are we talking about Thomas?"

"Partly. He makes me uncomfortable. He's too mean looking. Too quiet."

Zach smiled. "He's not there to be your companion, Courtney. He's there for your protection. He's supposed to be watching out for dangers not having a conversation with you."

Courtney shrugged and got to her feet, hating that he made her feel stupid. "Did you come up to make sure I got home all right—or were you concerned that I might have spent all that money you left on the table?"

It still infuriated her that they'd done it. Pointing toward the kitchen, she began pacing. "It's in there on the table where you left it."

She started past Zach again, yelping when he snagged her around the waist and yanked her against him. "Put me down, you oaf!"

"Oaf?" Zach carried her to the large sofa and dropped into it, settling her on his lap before she could escape. Leaning her back over his arm—a habit that always made her feel protected and feminine, while allowing him to see her face clearly, Zach frowned down at her. "Talk to me. What's wrong?"

Panicking at the wave of longing and the need to curl into him, Courtney fought his hold. Pushing out of his arms, she gained her balance and leapt to her feet. "Nothing's wrong! Nothing! How dare you leave money for me like I'm a whore?"

Zach frowned and got to his feet, moving toward her. "We left you money to go shopping. We wanted you to buy something nice for yourself or buy some of the things you want for the house." He took a step each time she did, moving closer. Reaching out a hand, he frowned when she avoided him. "You trusted us enough to leave Desire with nothing except your purse. It isn't fair to make you stay here all day, especially while we're still dealing with the oil spill. We just wanted you to have a little spending money when you went out. There are a lot of nice shops downtown. I specifically told you to come home with a dress that you could model for me. You disobeyed me."

"A *little* spending money? You left a hell of a lot more than a little spending money." She barely managed to avoid him when he reached for her again and knew it was only a matter of time before he stopped letting her get away. "Stop it. Just stop it!"

Zach paused, his eyes filled with concern. "Stop what, darlin'? What am I doing that's upsetting you so much?"

"Stop being so nice to me, damn it!"

* * * *

Stunned by her outburst, Zach paused, searching her features. Alarmed at the tears shimmering in her eyes, he reached for her again, not letting her get away. Wrapping his arms around her, he fought back a wave of panic and settled with her on the sofa again.

"Okay. I'm obviously missing something." When she tried to get up, he tightened his hold. "Don't bother. You're not getting up until I get to the bottom of this."

He slapped her ass once, relieved when she stopped struggling. "Now talk."

"We're supposed to be having an affair—a temporary affair. I told you I'd sell the property to you when the year's over. Stop trying to make me fall in love with you."

Zach stilled, automatically tightening his hold when she would have struggled. With his heart in his throat, he held her close so she didn't see the smile he just couldn't hide.

She was falling in love with them.

Running a hand up and down her back, he fought to keep his tone sober. "I didn't realize what I was doing. I'm sorry."

"You know that I can't stay in Desire."

"Maybe you'll change your mind."

"I can't. I told you there's too many bad memories."

He kissed her hair, smiling again when she snuggled closer. "We haven't really had a chance to replace them with good ones, have we?"

"I thought you were going to make me submit to you."

She submitted a little more each day, and he found it adorable that she didn't even realize it.

It seemed, however, that the intimacy had gotten to her.

Careful not to let his relief and amusement creep into his voice, he leaned back to look down at her, keeping his expression cool. "You will submit to us. You have been, or have you forgotten that you had to wear a butt plug every night when you went to bed?"

She blushed, looking so adorable that he wanted to laugh and hug her close again, but he knew she needed something else from him now. "I promised that I would sell the property to you. I'm sure you've got a slew of fancy lawyers around here somewhere. Couldn't one of them write up a contract that I can sign?"

Zach kept his expression closed. "Of course, but there's no need for that."

A flare of panic came and went in her eyes. "Why not?"

Zach allowed a small smile. "Because I no longer intend to buy that property from you."

Her eyes went wide. "You don't?"

"Nope. You can keep it. Now, it's out of the equation." He ran a finger down her arm. "Unless, of course, you need the money."

Shrugging, she sat up. "For what?"

"Maybe your flower shop? The one you plan to open in Desire?"

Her eyes narrowed. "How did you know about that?"

Sliding a hand over her belly, he imagined her carrying their child. "I try to know everything about you. You didn't tell me, though."

With a sigh, she relaxed against him. "I don't know what I'm going to do exactly."

Loving the way she cuddled against him, he moved his hand up and down her back in the way he knew settled her. "You're going to do what you planned. You're going to open one in Desire. We need a flower shop there."

Straightening, she looked up at him through her lashes. "I already told you that I can't stay. Besides, I don't have the money to start the kind that I want. I looked around to see if there was one that I could work in."

Zach pulled her back. "Nope. Closest one is in Tulsa. I don't want you travelling back and forth every day."

Sitting up again, she glared at him. "This is my decision."

Pride in her stubbornness had him fighting a smile. "No. It isn't. You gave yourself to us for the year, and I'm not letting you out of it."

"You can't do that!"

Zach shrugged and rubbed her back again. "We have an agreement." He slid his hand up her shirt, unfastening the front closure of her bra and pushing the edges aside. Cupping her breast, he ran his palm back and forth over her nipple as he leaned her back over his arm. "Face it, baby. We own you for the next eleven and a half months."

Zach feared he'd gone too far until he saw the flare of heat in her eyes. He whipped her shirt over her head and tossed it aside before doing the same with her bra. "We've gone easy on you because of all you've been through, but you're getting an attitude. If I don't nip this in the bud now, you're going to think you can keep getting away with it."

Zach recognized her need to challenge him and understood that she needed the security of knowing that not only could he handle her and her moods but that she could also count on him to keep his word.

She also had a submissive streak, one that her passionate nature wouldn't allow her to ignore.

Her hand tightened on his shirt, something he doubted she even realized, her nipple tight against his palm. "What are you going to do?"

The breathlessness in her voice made his cock swell even more, the hunger in her eyes as she leaned into his touch stoking his dominant nature in ways that no other woman had done before.

Her sweet femininity gave him a feeling of power and heightened his sense of masculinity, filling him with satisfaction and a completeness that he'd never known before.

Each day it grew stronger.

So did his love for her.

Keeping his expression cold, he reached for the fastening of her jeans. "You know damned well what I'm going to do. It's what you've been asking for with those eyes ever since I walked into the room."

Gripping his wrist, she leaned into him, her lips warm and soft on his jaw, strengthening the sense of power and love flowing through his veins. Pressing her breasts against his chest, she scraped her teeth over his jaw.

"You're not thinking about spanking me, are you?"

"No. Thinking's pretty much over. I'm gonna do it. You're deliberately baiting me to see how far you can go. Well, darlin', that invisible leash around your neck is pulled tight. You've reached the end of it."

Aware that Law came through the door, Zach slid Courtney's jeans to her knees, knowing it would make her bottom feel even more exposed. He turned her over, meeting Law's gaze. "You're just in time."

"So I see." Law raised a brow in question, his lips twitching when Zach shook his head and ran a hand over Courtney's ass.

Unable to resist pressing his fingers into the firm, smooth cheeks of Courtney's ass, Zach sighed. "She's in a mood, one that I'm about to take care of." Knowing she couldn't see his face, he allowed a smile at her soft moan and shiver. "She needs an attitude adjustment."

Law came forward, his eyes dark with emotion and hunger, not stopping until he knelt at her side—a deliberate move to increase her sense of defenselessness. Running his hand over her ass, he smiled at her moan. "I think she's ready to have two cocks at once. I'll get the lube."

* * * *

Courtney gasped, her bottom clenching. "You don't need to do this."

"I think I do. You need this, and so do I." Zach's tone brooked no argument, his hand coming down hard on her bottom.

Courtney squealed, the sting much more intense than the pain.

Shocked by the feeling of belonging and the trust that allowed her to be so vulnerable, Courtney wiggled on his lap, gasping at the heat his slap created in her bottom and her slit.

Zach rubbed her bottom, massaging the heat in, his hand firm on her back. "You're not getting away." Reaching under her, he tugged a nipple, sending another rush of heat to her clit. "There's only one way to stop this. You know your safe word. You gonna use it, or are you brave enough to take what you earned?"

Gritting her teeth, Courtney pressed her thighs together, amazed at the effects of his erotic spanking. "I'm not using it."

"Good girl." Law's deep voice washed over her skin, his words giving her a thrill that she would never admit to. "I'm going to lube your ass so, when your spanking's over, we can both fuck you. Then we're going shopping. This time you're going to buy what we tell you to." Gripping her bottom, he lifted and spread her cheeks, plunging a lube-coated finger inside.

Fisting her hands on the gleaming tile floor, Courtney cried out, and instinctively tried to tighten her bottom cheeks against Law's decadent invasion. "Oh God. Are you really going to take me there?" Shivering at the way he thrust into her, as if he owned her ass, Courtney gulped in air at the thrill of erotic delight.

Having something in her ass always overwhelmed her, the wickedness of it sending her senses soaring.

Zach closed his fingers on her nipple, bending over her and giving her a sense of security that stuck her as odd in her present position. "Maybe we should gag you."

"I'm gonna gag her with my cock." Law withdrew his finger with a quick movement that left her gasping and her ass clenching at emptiness.

Courtney moaned at the feel of his naked body against hers as he moved to kneel in front of her.

"Open." Zach's hand came down on her ass again, not as hard as it had the first time but with enough heat to have her writhing again.

The way they gave her their undivided attention made her feel so sexy, and yet so adored.

She shook everywhere, every erogenous zone screaming for attention.

Their dominance excited her.

Their confidence excited her.

Loving them scared the hell out of her.

With a gentle but firm hand, Law lifted her head. "I want to feel your mouth on my cock." He pressed at her jaw, forcing her mouth open and, with no warning, shoved the head of his cock inside. "Suck. You want it nice and hard when I shove it up that tight ass, don't you?"

She'd wanted rough. She'd needed it.

The effect it had on her was so completely different than she'd expected that she found herself floundering.

Another slap landed on her ass, her lubed bottom clenching at the heat. The thought of being taken in both openings overwhelmed her so much that she didn't even struggle while Zach spanked her.

Hunger had her sucking greedily at Law's cock, the taste of warm male—the man she loved—intoxicating.

Her senses reeled as Law moved slightly, and seconds later, his lubed finger thrust into her ass again.

Zach held her cheeks parted wide, the heat of his hands almost unbearable against her hot skin.

She whimpered around Law's cock, earning another slap.

"Quiet. You deserve this, and you know it. I won't put up with any attitude from you, my little sub. You're going to learn to behave yourself and do what you're told. Keep sucking Law's cock. He's gotta get quite a bit of lube in that ass to get it ready for his cock."

His icy tone and sexual demands pulled her into their private world so fast her head spun. "I don't give a damn how much you whimper."

As soon as Law withdrew his finger, Zach's hand came down on her ass again. "You're going to learn to obey us, aren't you, little one? Spread those legs."

Courtney rushed to obey him, gasping when he spanked her slit, setting her clit on fire. Jerking, she lost her grip on Law's cock, gasping as she pressed her thighs closed against the heat. "Ooohh!"

Zach slapped her ass again. "I fucking don't believe you!"

Without warning, he stood and threw her over his shoulder, slapping her ass as he strode into the bedroom. "You want it, baby. You got it."

He set her on her feet with a speed that left her dizzy. Holding her waist, he steadied her while Law moved in behind her. "Looks like you've gotten yourself into quite a bit of trouble, Courtney. If you want to use your safe word, now's the time."

Some demon inside her refused to quit, and as she watched Zach go to the closet and come back with a small whip, she lifted her chin, unable to look away from the menacing strip of leather. "I'm not using it."

"Good." Law smiled coldly. "We'll see how long you can hold out."

Courtney couldn't take her eyes off the whip, the long handle and flat, round piece of leather on the end fascinating her. Scaring her.

Thrilling her.

"Spread your legs."

Before she realized what he was doing, Law had fastened cuffs on her ankles. When she couldn't close her legs, she looked down, stunned to see that each cuff was attached to a bar that made it impossible to close her legs.

Zach dropped the whip on the bed and caught her wrists, her pitiful efforts to pull away making him laugh. "You're not getting away now, darlin'. Since you can't keep those thighs spread, we'll keep them spread for you."

They lifted her to the bed and tied her wrists to the headboard with an ease that stunned her.

Fighting to get free, she remembered the struggles of the woman at the auction and how much the struggle had excited her.

Shocked to realize it had the same effect on her, Courtney moaned, her breath catching when Law wrapped a hand around the bar and lifted it, effectively exposing her entire slit.

Zach smiled, running the tip of the whip over her slit. "Nipple first. Or clit?"

Courtney couldn't believe this was happening. She shook helplessly, even more aroused than she was the night at the club.

Zach smiled, sliding the tip of the whip into her pussy. "I see you've just realized what's in store for you. Are you sure you don't want to use your safe word?"

Aware that both men watched her closely, she looked at their eyes—really looked—warmed to see that both men looked for a sign of fear from her.

She trusted them not to hurt her, more than she'd ever realized.

The need to challenge them simmered hot, and with a hunger unlike any she'd ever known, she slowly shook her head. "Not a chance in hell."

The relief and lust in their eyes told her she'd made the right decision.

Alarmed at the positon she'd found herself in, she knew that after this, she'd have her answers.

She'd either fall apart or prove that she could be what they needed.

Law smiled, running his hand over the back of her thigh. "Nipples first. I want them nice and sensitive for tonight. She has no idea what's in store for her."

Holding her breath, Courtney watched Zach move slowly to the side of the bed, her nipples beaded tight with anticipation.

The first strike stunned her, and it was a few seconds before the pain hit her.

She felt it everywhere.

The sharp pain seemed to awaken every erogenous zone in her body like never before, the pain dimming almost immediately and leaving behind a heat and sharp sensation that had her fighting her bonds. The need to cover her nipples drove her wild, but with her hands tied above her head, she was defenseless.

Law rubbed the heat in with the palm of his hand, drawing a moan from her. "Very good, little sub. One more and then we'll give our attention to the other one."

Flames of desire licked at her and then began to consume her. Her clit, pussy, and ass screamed for attention, and the next strike to her nipple made the heat even hotter.

She didn't know she could feel so intensely. Didn't know the heat could get this hot.

She didn't know that the men she loved could make her feel as though she was the most adored, desired woman on earth.

The looks in their eyes spoke volumes, the heat in them—the pride—had her close to coming.

She wanted to be everything to them. She could take this because she knew they needed to give it to her. She could take this because the pleasure was like no other.

With them, she felt special and as if she truly belonged, which intoxicated her as much as the pleasure.

As Zach moved around to the other side of the bed, her left nipple ached with anticipation.

Her entire body was on fire.

Arching, she lifted to him, needing the heat—the flash of pain—more than she needed her next breath.

She wanted it hot. Hard. Rough.

She wanted every bit of their passion.

She wanted them to take her with a hunger they'd never had for any other woman.

Zach touched the tip of the whip to her nipple. "Do you want this, little sub?"

Nodding, Courtney twisted frantically, struggling to close her legs against the sharp awareness in her clit. "Yes! Yes, damn you!"

With a glint in his eyes, Zach brought the whip down on her nipple with a sharp snap of his wrist, his eyes narrowing and burning with hunger at her cry. "One more and then two to your clit."

She didn't know if she could stand it.

Her clit felt huge, throbbing with every beat of her heart. The heat from his earlier slap there still lingered, and she didn't know how she could stand the sharp pain of the whip there.

Something must have shown on her face because Law lowered himself to the bed next to her, his firm grip on the bar lifting her legs even higher. "Scared of that whip on your clit, aren't you?" He bent to take a throbbing nipple into his mouth, sucking hard and ignoring her cries as the heat grew, the sizzles of raging need like jagged ribbons of electricity straight to her clit.

Lifting his head, he smiled down at her. "Your clit'll be sensitive for days. Every time one of us touches you there, you'll be ready to come. And because we know you'll be sore there, we'll rub a cool cream on you there before we go to the party tonight. You'll be aroused for hours, darling."

The thought of that had her squirming again, her breath catching when she saw that Zach had moved to stand between her legs. She looked up at him just as he struck her clit.

Her scream echoed off the walls, the heat so intense that the warning tingling sensation began, the realization that she'd started to come stunning her.

Zach smiled. "She started to come. Damn, Law. We sure as hell picked the right woman. I don't want to hit her clit again. I don't want her to come until we're both inside her."

Law grinned and rose. "Take the bar. Give the whip to me."

Courtney shook harder, rocking her hips and whimpering, the need for release making her violent. No matter how much she tried, she couldn't close her legs or get any friction against her clit.

Need threatened to drive her mad.

Law moved to stand at the foot of the bed, his gaze on her slit. "Since she still has another strike coming, and since I'm the one who's going to take her ass, guess where the next strike is going. Baby, you can pump your hips all night, but fucking air isn't going to give you the release you need."

Courtney struggled, the hunger making it impossible to remain still. Her bottom clenched, the thought of the whip coming down there increasing the sharp awareness around her puckered opening that made her hungry to have his cock inside her.

Law raised the whip slightly. "Of course, I still have to put more lube into her tight ass before I can fuck it."

Courtney jolted when the whip came down, the need to rub the stinging heat unbearable.

Her bottom hole clenched over and over, but the heat remained.

Zach's eyes narrowed, glittering with need and emotion. "You're so fucking incredible. My cock's throbbing so fucking hard that I can't go easy."

Courtney couldn't stop rocking her hips, so close to coming that tears stung her eyes. "Don't you dare go easy."

Law squeezed more lube onto his finger, his eyes hard and cold. "Not a chance." He thrust his finger into her and began fucking her ass with it, not giving her any time to adjust. He withdrew just as quickly as he'd entered her, only to squeeze more lube onto his fingers and thrust into her again, this time with two fingers.

Crying out at the burning sensation, she rocked her hips to take him faster.

"Like having your ass fucked, don't you, baby?"

Zach's voice had become so harsh that it sounded as if he'd swallowed glass. "Good thing because it's going to be fucked well— and often." After rolling on a condom, Zach lifted her and lay back on the bed and, sliding his powerful thighs between her and the bar, effectively held her in place with her legs spread wide.

With her wrists secured to the headboard, her breasts pressed against Zach's chest, every movement intensifying the heat from the whip.

Zach's hands firmed on her hips, pulling him against him as Law rolled on a condom behind her. "Very nice. I like having you draped over me and restrained. That bar is keeping your legs spread wide just the way we like them." He moved her on him, the friction against her swollen clit eliciting a cry from her. He smiled. "Ready to come, aren't you, little sub? Not yet. First, your Masters are going to fuck you."

Courtney moaned, her breath catching when she felt the head of Law's cock against her tingling puckered opening. "God. It's so hot. It burns. OhGodohGodohGod. It's going into me."

Shocked, she found herself trying to pull away from him. "It's too hot. Too big. Too different."

Law's deep chuckle sounded as if it had been ripped from his soul. "I told you my cock would feel nothing like those little butt plugs. It's hungry for you, not like those pieces of rubber. Don't try to pull away from me. Stick that ass out and take it like a big girl."

Zach fisted a hand in her hair and pressed at her lower back, forcing her to stick her ass out. "You're getting fucked in that ass, baby. And it's going to be tight as hell with both of us inside you."

Courtney held her breath, the feel of Law's cock pushing its way inside her ass like nothing she could have imagined. With Zach's cock filling her pussy, the too-full, stretched sensation made it difficult to catch her breath.

Heat. Lust. Fire.

"It's so much. Too intimate. Too wicked. Oh God. It's so sexual."

Need stuck its talons in her and wouldn't let go.

Unable to move, she groaned when they did, setting up a rhythm that quickly had her racing toward the edge.

Zach plunged deep, lifted her from his cock several inches as Law thrust, each stroke forcing her ass to accept more of his cock.

They moved faster with each stroke. Harder. Their groans and hands rougher and more erotic as they plunged their cocks into her.

Clenching on both of them, she found herself lost in a world of sensation she never wanted to leave.

Her cries mingled with their groans as they fucked her hard and deep, the constant friction against the inner walls of her pussy and ass so erotic and decadent.

They made her theirs more with every thrust, their words of praise and encouragement raining all around her.

Zach groaned, his teeth clenched. "So fucking good."

Law pressed his hand to her back, his cock going so deep she would swear she could feel it in her stomach. "All ours. Our. Little. Fucking. Sub. Ours. Our woman."

With a groan and a curse, Law thrust deep, the feel of his cock pulsing inside her sending her over in a rush.

A kaleidoscope of colors burst behind her eyes, the intense wave of pleasure hitting her so hard that she couldn't breathe.

It swept through her over and over, and if not for Law's and Zach's holds, she would have panicked.

Every nerve in her body seemed to explode with ecstasy, the pleasure so intense she lost control of her body.

Heat exploded everywhere, her body jerking with the pleasure.

She cried out over and over, her voice becoming hoarse and weak as the all-consuming sensations held her in their grip, refusing to let go.

Heat. Pleasure. Burning. A wash of tingling that wouldn't end.

It wouldn't stop, and even when the pleasure began to subside, her body wouldn't obey her.

It felt as if her soul had been ripped from her, the vulnerability of losing herself so intense that she began to shake again. Tears filled her eyes, but she didn't have the energy to cry.

She felt as if she'd been stripped bare, her body no longer her own.

Zach cursed and pumped harder, faster, and, with a loud groan, pounded into her several times in rapid succession before his hands tightened, holding her to him as he found his own release.

Slumping against him, she whimpered, totally spent.

Law's warm lips moved over her back. "Such a good girl. So precious to me." His hands moved against her ankles, removing the cuffs. "Easy, baby. We've got you."

Zach reached up to release her wrists, gathering her close. "Go get cleaned up. I've got her."

Still deep inside her, he rolled to his side, pulling the sheet over her rapidly cooling body, holding the back of her head to press her against his neck.

"You'll be all right in just a minute, darlin'. I've got you. I won't let go."

Courtney nodded, wishing she had the energy to hold him, too. She loved the solid feel of him against her body, the warmth that he wrapped her in.

Drowsy, replete, weak, she slumped in Zach's hold.

They stayed that way for several minutes, and she'd just started to fall asleep when Law came back.

Slipping between the sheets behind her, he bent to kiss her shoulder as he ran a damp cloth down her body and to her slit. "Be still, baby. It's nice and warm. I just want to clean you up a little before you go to sleep."

"Don't wanna."

Law chuckled, his breath warm against her ear. "You'll feel better. That's a girl."

Zach held her leg up to spread them. "Easy. She's gotta be sensitive."

"I know she is, Zach. I am being easy with her. Now, let's roll her to her belly so I can clean her ass."

"No."

Law chuckled and sat up, spreading the cheeks of her bottom and wiping her clean. "No doesn't work with me, remember? Just relax. I'm almost done. There. Don't you feel better?"

He handed the washcloth to Zach, who bent to touch his lips to hers. "I'll be right back, baby."

The bed dipped as he rose, but Courtney didn't have the energy to open her eyes.

Law cuddled her close, his firm caress settling her. "Go to sleep, love. I'm right here, and Zach'll be back in a minute."

"Law?"

"Yes, baby?"

"Were you satisfied?"

"Absolutely. And so were you. You goaded Zach into that on purpose, didn't you?"

Courtney didn't feel up to talking about it. She knew she would only sound silly. "Maybe. Will you stay with me?"

"Dynamite couldn't move me."

* * * *

It took several minutes for her to stop shaking and a few more before her breathing evened out. By that time, Zach had slid into bed on the other side of her.

Holding her against him, Law sighed. "She wouldn't say it."

Lying on his side, Zach took her hand in his, playing with her fingers. "She's scared. Let me tell you what happened when I came up here."

Law listened, his heart pounding by the time Zach finished. "So you really think she loves us?"

"Yeah." Zach yawned and closed his eyes, still holding on to Courtney's hand. "She damned near said it and then used her temper to hide her fear. She's scared of loving us. When I told her that we no longer wanted to buy the property, she panicked, especially when I told her that we'd take it out of the equation. She's been hanging on to the idea that all we wanted was the property for so long that, now that it's gone, she's reeling."

Law's chest swelled. "We've got to get her centered again. I want her to have a chance to think. The papers are ready."

"Good. Once she sees those, she'll know for sure that we really love her."

* * * *

Damn it.

He stepped back against another office building and looked across the street to the tall building that housed Tyler Oil.

He hadn't been able to get near her.

The man walking with her all day had turned toward him each time he'd gotten close, and despite the mirrored sunglasses hiding his eyes, the warning in his look had been unmistakable.

The Tyler brothers must have hired a bodyguard to keep everyone away from his daughter so they could make sure they got that property.

There had to be oil on it.

There had to be. Oil had been found all over town.

They wouldn't be willing to pay so much for it if there wasn't oil on it.

It would be his.

He'd earned it.

He'd put up with those assholes in Desire for years and had to walk away with nothing.

He'd get his share and had no problem using his ungrateful brat to do it.

Chapter Nineteen

Courtney leaned closer to Zach, keeping her voice at a whisper. "This is embarrassing."

Zach lifted another of the vibrators on display, studying it without looking at her. "Maybe you'll remember that the next time we leave money for you, with explicit instructions to buy yourself something nice and to get a few things for your house."

Amused at the way they'd boxed her in, she glared at him, fighting not to smile. "I did buy something for my house. The red throw."

"I thought you bought it for the penthouse."

Courtney shrugged. "I did, but I changed my mind."

Standing on the other side of her, Law looked away from the vibrator he held and wrapped an arm around her waist. "Why?"

"I just did."

"Again, why?"

Forcing a smile, she glanced at him. "If you'd wanted color in your penthouse, you would have made sure you had it." Shrugging, she turned away. "It just doesn't seem to fit in with the rest of the penthouse. It looks out of place."

Law's eyes narrowed and sharpened. "Sometimes you don't know exactly what you want until you see it. Once you do, you can't imagine being without it. I want the throw, Courtney. It brightens the penthouse the way you brighten our lives. It adds color to the penthouse the way you've added color to our lives. It's not out of place. It enhances."

Smiling, he reached out to touch her cheek. "It's the first thing I see when I walk in there. It's a bright spot in a colorless room, just like you're the bright spot in our lives."

Amused and incredibly touched, Courtney laughed. "You're not trying to tell me your lives are colorless, are you?"

To her surprise, he didn't smile back. "We didn't think so until you came into it and showed us just how much we were missing."

"I really wish I could believe that."

Zach ran a hand down her back. "It surprised us, too. Let's finish our shopping. I'm looking forward to getting you ready for the party."

Shifting restlessly, Courtney kept sneaking glances at the wall of adult toys. She didn't have a clue what some of them would be used for, but Law and Zach looked pretty knowledgeable.

"You look like you know what you're doing."

"I do." Law pulled her closer, bending to brush his lips over hers. "You didn't seem to mind when I was fucking your ass."

"Or when you're coming." Zach ran hand over her ass and handed her the vibrator he'd been inspecting. "We're getting this one."

"Please don't make me go up there and pay for it."

Law's brow went up. "How will you learn your lesson if we don't make you pay for disobeying us?"

Her face burned at the thought of going to the register to purchase such a thing. "Please!"

Folding his arms across his chest, Law pursed his lips. "Since I can't let you get away with disobeying us, it'll cost you."

"Anything!"

"You have to wear what we give you to wear tonight for the party. Nothing more. Nothing less."

"Deal!" She'd gladly wear any one of the beautiful dresses they'd bought for her.

Once out on the street, she went eagerly into Zach's waiting arms. "I can't believe you made me go in there."

"Your eyes were so wide I was afraid they were going to fall out."

Courtney giggled. "I should have known you'd notice. I didn't know what half of the stuff in there was."

Law came out just in time to hear her, smiling when Zach threw his head back and laughed.

Glancing at the bag, she smiled up at him. "Thank you."

His lips twitched as he raised an arrogant brow again. "You're welcome. Just remember your promise. We're going to hold you to it. Let's go back to the penthouse and get you ready for the party. The hairdresser should be waiting for you. I want your hair up tonight."

Pushing her hair aside, he nuzzled her neck, sending threads of tingling sensation through her. "I have a particular fondness for this spot right here."

* * * *

Patting her hair, she eyed her reflection critically.

The intricate updo suited her, and she'd taken a light hand with the assortment of makeup they'd ordered for her.

She couldn't have afforded the designer brand, and she'd bet that what they'd bought would have cost her several months' salary.

Satisfied with her appearance, she opened the bathroom door, anxious to see the dress they'd picked out for her to wear tonight.

Dressed only in her robe, she paused just inside the bedroom they now shared, smiling at the sight of Law and Zach wearing what she suspected were designer tuxedos. "You both look so sexy. I suppose you're going to know a lot of women there."

Law turned from the mirror where he straightened his tie. "We will. None of them can hold a candle to you." His eyes glimmered with approval. "I like your hair that way. You look beautiful. Did you find everything you needed?"

Courtney smiled and shook her head. "That's more makeup than I could use in a lifetime. In case you haven't noticed, I seldom wear more than lip gloss and mascara."

Law smiled. "I noticed. We thought having it would build your confidence for tonight. I know you're nervous."

Zach came out of the closet, removing a dress from its hangar. "Lose the robe. It's time to get dressed."

She eyed the royal blue gown, running her fingers over the smooth material. "It's not black."

Law grinned. "Almost every other woman there will be wearing black. You won't."

Long-sleeved, the gown had a slit up each side and a plunging neckline. A very plunging neckline. "I don't remember seeing this one in the closet earlier."

Zach smiled. "I had it in mine. It's one of the things we put aside for later."

Courtney frowned. "I don't understand."

Zach laid the dress on the bed. "We've been trying to go slow with you."

"Afraid you might scare me off?" She smiled at that, her body still humming from their earlier lovemaking.

"Not anymore."

Laughing softly, she stared toward the dresser for a bra and pair of panties, more relaxed with them than she'd ever been.

Law stepped in front of her before she reached her destination. "No. No panties and no bra. You can't wear them with that dress anyway."

Wondering at the tension emanating from them, she went to the bed and lifted the dress. Seeing that she had to step into it, she did, surprised when Zach closed in behind her, zipping the dress to her waist, leaving the bodice hanging.

Law knelt at her feet, sliding a hand up her calf. "Lift your foot, babe, so I can slip on your shoes."

Zach kept her steady, holding her against his chest and cupping her breasts as she slipped on the satin high-heeled sandals. Closing his fingers over her nipples, he pressed his lips against her neck. "Hmm. With your hair up, I can get to this spot easier."

Tilting her head to the side, Courtney closed her eyes and moaned at the delicious sensation. "How do you and Law always seem to find that spot?"

Zach's chuckle vibrated against her neck. "We told you that we'd learn your body and that soon we would know it as intimately as we know our own. We've only just gotten started."

"God help me."

Law straightened and, even though she wore high heels, he towered over her. "There's no help for you tonight, my love."

Smiling, Courtney reached for the bodice, but Law clicked his tongue, holding out a hand to stop her.

He reached into his pocket, his gaze holding hers. "There's a little something else that you have to wear with the dress."

Courtney's breath caught when she saw the strand of what appeared to be diamonds. "Oh. My. God. Are those real diamonds?"

Panicked, she pushed back against Zach's hard body, but he didn't budge. "I don't want any diamonds. Take those back."

Zach rolled her nipples between his thumbs and forefingers, his lips warm on her shoulder. "Nope. We had this specially made for you. Jake Langley owns the jewelry store in Desire and makes special orders for a lot of people in town." Sliding his hands lower, he cupped the underside of her breasts. "This was made just for you."

It looked too short to be a necklace, but Zach held it out and closed the distance between them, holding the sides parted as if he intended to put it around her neck.

She held her breath, pushing back against Zach. A moan escaped when Law touched the backs of his fingers over her nipples.

Law smiled. "This goes on your nipples, baby. They're not tight, and won't be painful, but it'll create an awareness there that should drive you—and us—crazy all night. I'm going to make it just tight enough to make sure it doesn't come off."

She couldn't believe the things they did to her. Their eroticism continuously surprised her, their attention to her and her pleasure always amazing. "What? You want me to wear these in public?"

Zach took her hands in his, holding them at her sides. "Yes. You're going to wear them to the party, actually a benefit, and there's no way you can take them off without us knowing about it."

Law placed the loop over her beaded nipple, using a small wheel on the side to tighten it. "We have some others for you, too, but I like these for tonight."

Courtney gasped at the feel of the loop tightening on her nipple, fisting her hands at her sides and dropping her head back against Zach's chest, caught up in the warm rush of need.

Zach chuckled and kissed her hair. "She likes them, and so do I. The thought of playing with them has me hard already."

Law adjusted the second loop over her other nipple, eyeing them critically before tightening each a little more. "I don't want them to come off."

She gasped again when he released them, feeling the weight of the stone tugging at her nipples for the first time. "Oh, God! It's like you're pinching my nipples.

Law tapped the chain, sending it swinging. "And each time you move, it'll send the chain swinging, like little tugs to your nipples. It'll help you remember just who you belong to."

Courtney moaned and smiled at him. "Like I could ever forget. Do you plan to do this kind of thing to me often?"

Zach released her hands and lifted the bodice of her dress. "Absolutely. You'll never know what to expect, darlin'." He fastened the top of the dress at the nape of her neck. Tracing his fingertips over her shoulders, he kissed her shoulder. "You look stunning."

Law took a step back, eyeing her critically. "Beautiful. To an untrained eye, it'll look like part of the dress."

Staring into her eyes, he tugged lightly at the chain, sending it swaying, his lips twitching when she gasped. "It seems to be tight enough."

Zach turned her in his arms and deftly slid pierced earrings into her earlobes and fastened them. Once finished, he stepped back, his gaze raking over her. "Beautiful. This is one party I wish we could skip. I can't wait to make good use of that vibrator when we get home. Have you ever used a vibrator or had one used on you before?"

Shaking her head, Courtney went to the mirror, her jaw dropping when she saw the diamond earrings glittering against her neck. "These are diamonds, too. Damn it. Look, I'm not one of those women who fuck you for your money."

Law's brow went up, his expression all arrogance. "If you were, you sure as hell wouldn't be wearing them."

* * * *

Aware of the scrutiny directed toward Courtney, Law held her closer and danced toward the large terrace. "I like the feel of you in my arms. Zach's watching you, wishing you were in his arms again."

She glanced around the room and sighed. "Everyone's staring at me."

Lifting his gaze, he zeroed in on another group of people who kept staring at Courtney—past girlfriends and colleagues—his fury rising.

His satisfaction when they noticed his attention and looked away came from the knowledge that he had a few choice words for each of them the next time he saw them.

Smiling coldly when he saw Zach striding angrily toward the group, he pulled Courtney closer, taking her hand in his as they reached the terrace. "They're stunned by your beauty."

"Bullshit. These women are gorgeous, and they're all looking at you like they want to take a bite out of your fantastic ass."

Grinning, Law led her to a corner, backing her into it. "I'm glad you like my ass, baby, because I have a particular fondness for yours." Smiling at her gasp, he bent to touch his lips to hers while tugging at the chain attached to her nipples. "Especially being inside that tight ass. Just thinking about it makes me hard. Thinking about fucking your pussy makes me hard. Thinking about everything about you makes me hard."

Delighted with her blush, barely visible in the dim light, he smiled again and took her hand in his again, leading her to the lush garden.

She looked up at him, her steps not quite steady. "I'm surprised there isn't a line of women following us out here to kill me so they can have you alone in the dark."

"I think Zach and I made it pretty clear that the only woman we're interested in is you."

Lowering himself to one of the stone benches, he settled her on his lap, amused at himself. He'd done exactly what he and Zach had teased Ace about ever since he and Hope had gotten together.

Having Courtney on his lap filled a need inside him, especially when she leaned into him so trustingly.

With a hand beneath her chin, he lifted her face to his. "You know, of course, that I'm in love with you." Amused that it seemed to take several long seconds for his words to penetrate, he tightened his hold when she gasped and tried to jump from his lap.

Courtney's eyes went wide, the dim light from the surrounding lamps enabling him to see her expression clearly. "You promised not to say things like that!"

His stomach clenched at the panic that flashed in her eyes then turned to knots when sadness replaced it. "I agreed not to lie to you about how I feel. I'm not, and I sure as hell never told a woman I loved her before. But, knowing you, I should have expected to have it thrown back in my face."

If possible, she stiffened even more. "What does that mean?"

Law sighed, running a hand up and down her back, hoping to ease some of the tension in her little body. "It means, my love, that you're waiting for us to skip out on you the way your mother and father did. The only person you ever trusted is gone now, and you're afraid to let anyone else in. Too bad. I'm going to keep pushing my way in until I wear you out and you have no choice but to accept what I feel for you."

"We're supposed to be having an affair!"

Aware that Zach approached from his right, Law tugged at the chain and wrapped a hand around the back of her neck to pull her closer, nibbling at her full bottom lip. "We are, darling. We're having a wonderful love affair."

"It's not supposed to be a love affair. It's supposed to be about sex." She wiggled and tried to get up again, but Law tightened his grip, not about to let her go until she understood what she meant to him.

Her eyes shone with unshed tears, breaking his heart. "I don't fit in here, and I can't stay in Desire. Besides, you don't know me well enough to love me."

"I know all I need to know. This isn't something I take lightly, Courtney. I know what I feel."

Zach sat on the bench next to him, running a hand over Courtney's thigh. "Since it seems there's going to be an argument about whether we love you or not, you might as well know that I'm in love with you, too. It seems as good a time as any to get it all out in the open."

Shaking her head, she tensed again. "You can't love me."

Zach smiled, his brows going up. "Really? Interesting, because we do."

"I don't fit in here."

Law rubbed her back, his hand on her hip firming when she tried to jump up again. "You will. You fit with us, and that's all that matters. If you don't want to come to Dallas with us, you can stay in Desire."

"I told you that there's nothing but bad memories for me there."

"That's not true. You have a lot of memories about your mother, and you told me yourself how the people in Desire tried to help you. You were just a little girl then. Don't tell me that you don't have a good memory of that time we spent in the park."

Her blush delighted him. Shrugging, she stared in the distance. "I do." She bent her head, chewing on her lip in that way she did whenever she was working herself up to something.

Law glanced at Zach and waited.

Finally, she lifted her head. "Why don't you take me to your playroom? Is it because you don't think I can handle it?"

Law grinned, sharing a look with Zach. "Because we don't have one."

She blinked at that. "Why not?"

Zach leaned forward, taking her hand in his. "Because the only place we've ever been able to give in to that particular need is when we're in Desire, and we go to the club."

"Oh." She chewed her lip again. "What if I can't give you what you need?"

Law smiled, the memory of her earlier response emblazoned in his mind. "You do. Beautifully." Gripping her chin, he smiled. "Look at me." Lifting her face to his, he angled her face toward the light so he could see her clearly. "You're not getting away from us, especially since I have a feeling that you love us as much as we love you."

Courtney gasped and tried to get away. "Bullshit. Let go of me. I want to go home."

Law stilled. "Where?"

"Desire! I want to go back home."

The knots from his stomach loosened. "So you do think of Desire as home. Interesting."

"Shut up and leave me alone."

Zach lifted her against him. "Oh, no. Neither one of us is about to leave you alone. You're getting yourself all worked up again. You want to go home. We'll go home."

Courtney blinked. "You'd leave the party just to take me home?"

"It seems there's very little we wouldn't do for you." Law dug his phone out of his pocket to send a text to the driver. "Bernard will meet us out front."

* * * *

They'd be back soon. A few days.

He'd heard the men working on the house say that they had to hurry to finish before they got back.

His daughter wouldn't give him what he needed, so he had no choice but to get it himself.

She'd grown up to be just like her mother. Neither one of them had ever understood him.

Easy Street was just a roll of the dice away, but neither one of them understood that.

He'd had bad luck his entire life.

He was due some good luck, and the house that old biddy owned was the answer.

He had to admit that the old gal had been smart.

She'd held out, not accepting any offers for years, and had finally worked them up to a million dollars.

If they were willing to pay that much, there had to be oil there.

He would make them pay even more.

Chapter Twenty

Zach held her close on his lap, idly playing with the chain attached to her nipples. "You get your way with us a little too easily."

Need clawed at her, giving her the bravery she needed. Unclasping the top of her dress, she let it fall, arching to thrust her breasts out in the way she knew excited them so much. Hiding a smile at the stunned look on Zach's face, she pouted and lowered her head to look up at him through her lashes. "I guess you're gonna make me pay for that by letting you have your way with me."

Zach recovered quickly, his eyes narrowing. "That's only fair, don't you think?" He removed one shoe and then the other, his hands firm as he massaged her feet.

Courtney let out a pitiful sigh while shaking with anticipation. "Yes. I guess I've been a little demanding. It's only fair that you make me pay for it."

"I'm glad you see it." Law reached for her, his gaze steady as he tightened the loops on her nipples, the increased pressure drawing a moan from her. "Behave. It's just a little tighter. Keep your hands behind your back and kneel in front of Zach."

Her heart pounded furiously, thrilled that they'd understood her, giving her what she needed without hesitation. She attempted to appear reluctant as she obeyed him, her pulse tripping when she saw Zach unfastening his trousers.

Zach's hand slid over her hair, pulling her closer. "Open your mouth, Courtney."

The hum of the limo seemed to vibrate the chain, sending wave after wave of need through her. Pulled forward, she reached for

Zach's thighs to balance herself, gasping again when Law moved to the seat behind her, lifted her dress, and smacked her bare ass.

"Keep those hands behind your back. I want my payment in full, so you'll do exactly as you're told."

His icy tone washed over her, the power in his voice and his hands fulfilling her wildest fantasies.

Gulping, she closed her mouth over Zach's cock, acutely aware that her ass and breasts were exposed.

It felt so naughty, increasing her arousal until her juices began to drip down her thighs. Spurred by need, she began sucking Zach's cock, crying out around it when Law smacked her ass again.

"No one told you to suck. Just close your mouth around his cock and hold it there. Now, spread those thighs." A hard slap to her inner thigh made the heat even hotter.

Her clit felt swollen and heavy, throbbing so badly she couldn't stop whimpering.

Zach's hands firmed, moving her up and down on his cock. "Whenever you're told to kneel, we expect those thighs to be spread wide."

One hand left her hair, and seconds later, she felt a strong tug at her nipples.

Zach growled in his throat. "We want your breasts, your pussy, clit, and ass available at all times. You'll rarely be allowed to wear a bra or panties, and never when you're alone with us. You'll sleep naked and between us every night. You'll do what we tell you to do, no matter how much it embarrasses you. You're ours. Every part of you, and we won't be denied what belongs to us."

Each word aroused her more. The thought of being an object for such compelling men proved more exciting than she'd ever thought possible.

A hand at her back forced her to arch it, pushing her ass higher, the tenderness in his firm touch unmistakable.

Law kept his hand there as he slid his fingers over her slit. "You're soaking wet, darling. You look forward to being used, don't you? Stop wiggling. You're to remain perfectly still."

A hard slap landed directly on her clit, and before she could stop herself, she jumped, pulling herself from Zach's cock and rising to her knees, closing her legs against the incredible sensation. Biting her lip to hold back her cries, she squeezed her eyes closed, her breathing ragged.

Immediately aware that she'd made a mistake, she opened her eyes again and rushed to get back into position, bending and putting her hands behind her back as she took Zach's cock into her mouth again.

Law's hands closed on her hips, his firm caress filled with a possessiveness that she loved. "It looks like she needs some discipline already."

He wrapped an arm around her waist and, with a strength that excited her, draped her across his lap. "Be quiet, unless you want Bernard to hear your screams."

Pressing her lips closed, she tightened every muscle in her body in anticipation, but it didn't do any good. She jolted at the first slap and struggled to remain quiet, but instead of pausing, Law kept spanking her.

Although the slaps weren't hard, they were hot, stinging her bottom until it felt as if it was on fire.

Struggling against his hold, she cried out when the slaps kept coming, each one in a different spot so she couldn't anticipate where the next would land.

By the time he finished, she was breathless and her entire ass and thighs burned.

To make matters worse, he kept her there, rubbing the heat in.

"When you're being spanked for punishment, most of the time you'll have something in your ass. We're going to have to get some ginger. That'll keep you from clenching. A hot ass seems to be the only way to get your attention."

"Ginger?" Courtney moaned again at the tug to her nipples.

Zach leaned forward and dragged her back toward him. "Lick my cock. Slowly."

She couldn't believe how much she wanted to defy him and earn another spanking, but the taste of Zach's cock and the way his hands tightened in her hair told her how excited he'd become.

She loved that she could have such an effect on him, and planned to take full advantage of it.

Flattening her tongue, she began to lick his cock from the base to the head, thrilling at the way it jumped and thickened. Another moan escaped when Law adjusted her dress again, draping it over her back to leave her bottom exposed.

Running his hand over her heated skin, he sighed. "When we get back to Desire, we're going to have to get some ginger. She's going to be squirming all over the place when we push that piece of ginger in her ass. We should probably tie her up first."

Zach chuckled, a low, menacing sound that sent another surge of heat through her. "Ace always keeps plenty on hand."

Courtney's curiosity couldn't stand any more. "Why are you going to put ginger inside me?"

Several more slaps landed on her ass, not hard enough to hurt, but enough to make it even hotter. "It burns!" The intense heat travelled to her slit, making her clit feel huge, the tingling warning her that she could come at any moment.

Her pussy and ass clenched, their talk exciting her even more—something she suspected they knew very well.

Law bent over her from behind, the heat of his body through his clothes enough to make her bottom burn so hot she couldn't stay still, the need for more overwhelming.

"Quiet. A piece of carved ginger up your fine ass will burn if you clench on it. Hmm." He tugged at the chain again, her whimper of need making his cock jump against her ass. "Every time you clench, it'll burn even more. By the time I'm finished, I have a feeling you'll be willing to do anything to get me to rub some cooling ointment inside you." Sitting back on his heels, he ran his hands over her bottom cheeks. "Yep. You'll be on your knees, holding your ass cheeks spread wide and begging me to give you some relief."

Just the thought of it made her even hotter. Without thinking, she took the head of Zach's cock into her mouth and began to suck greedily, thrilled with the groans pouring out of him.

With a curse, he pulled her from his cock. "Damn it! I didn't tell you to do that. You're the most undisciplined submissive I've ever seen!"

The reminder of all the submissives he and Law had had in the past had her stomach clenching. Determined to wipe all of those other women out of their minds, she smiled up at Zach, barely able to make out his features in the low light. "I guess you'll have to train me."

Even in the low light, the flash of heat in his eyes made them appear to glow. Leaning forward, he cupped her cheek. "Yes, darlin'. I guess we will. Our own little submissive trained just for us."

Law straightened the bodice of her dress and clasped it again. "We're almost at the airport. Behave yourself."

Because she was barefoot, Zach carried her to the airplane and straight to the back, flinging open a door to a bedroom.

* * * *

Zach settled Courtney on her feet next to the bed, running his fingertips down her back, delighted at her shiver.

Her arousal and daring surprised him. Delighted him. Thrilled him.

As he and Law led her deeper into the world of Dominance and submission, she seemed to glow from within.

She reveled in it.

Remembering how aroused she'd become at the auction, he circled her, eyeing her as a perspective bidder would eye a submissive at auction as he unclasped her dress. "Lift your arms above your head."

Pausing in front of her as she did, he hid a smile at the excitement in her eyes as her dress puddled at her feet.

Watching that excitement grow as he tugged at the chain, he bit back a groan when his cock jumped again.

Loving her had to be the most exciting thing in his life.

Her gasp made his cock jump again. "What are—"

"Quiet." Watching her eyes, he noted the flare of apprehension and the heightened desire. He knew it would add to her excitement but that he and Law would have to watch her carefully to make sure that they didn't overwhelm her.

Tugging the chain again, he let his gaze rake over her. "You aren't always going to know what we're going to do to you. You'll have to learn to adjust."

He continued to circle her, his cock pounding at the sight of her red ass. He knew how hot it would be and, running his hand over it, knew that they would keep it hot. The knowledge that he would be fucking her fine ass nearly made him come in his pants, something he would never have believed possible.

"Your ass is red, darlin'. It's probably cooling down by now."

"No. It isn't."

"I think you're lying to me. Spread your legs wider." He circled to face her again, lifting her chin to stare into her eyes. "I need to decide if I'm going to buy you or not. I need to inspect you."

Her eyes went wide when he ran a finger over each nipple.

Aware that Law stood back, watching her with his arms crossed, Zach hid a smile.

Law eyed her coldly. "Thrust those breasts out. He wants to see what he's getting."

Courtney's moan nearly undid Zach.

Eyeing her as he would piece of merchandise, Zach reached up to pinch her nipple, delighting in her pleasure-filled cry. "Pretty."

Circling her, he ran the tips of his fingers over the warm cheeks of her bottom, smiling at her shiver. "She's been spanked. Does she misbehave often?"

Law's lips twitched. "All the time. She needs a strong hand and a lot of training."

Zach met Law's gaze and smiled before kneeling behind her. Grinning at the amount of moisture coating her inner thighs, he was purposely rough as he parted her ass cheeks. "Has her ass been broken in?"

"Yes."

Delighting when she shivered again, Zach stood, determined to fulfill that particular fantasy. "I'll have to check for myself, of course."

Law opened a drawer. "Her dildo and the new vibrator are here. Help yourself."

Hiding a smile, Zach pretended to ignore Courtney's moan. "I will. Do you have lube?"

"Of course."

Zach accepted the items from Law and tossed them onto the bed behind her. "I want to see her clit."

Law took a step toward Courtney, his arms crossed again, his expression cold and unforgiving. "You heard him. Spread your folds and show him that clit."

* * * *

Shaking, Courtney lowered her arms, her eyes on Law as she reached down and parted her folds.

Drawn into her wildest fantasy, Courtney realized that they no longer took but had made her a participant in her own submission.

Another step, one that she'd feared she couldn't take.

Her exposed clit felt huge, the air moving over it almost more than she could stand.

To her amazement, Zach knelt in front of her, eyeing her clit as though studying it.

Her knees shook as he reached out and touched a finger to it, the sensation so sharp she cried out and jolted.

In two steps, Law was behind her, slapping her ass and reigniting the heat. "Be still."

Zach sighed as though disappointed, but his eyes glittered with hunger. "She's very undisciplined."

"She's still worth a high price."

Zach shook his head. "I don't know. Would you hand me the dildo, please?" Without warning, he plunged a finger into her pussy. "She's soaking wet. She does like being played with, but does she like being filled? Fucked?"

"Absolutely."

"I'll see for myself." Zach didn't even glance up at her as he poised the dildo at her pussy entrance, but Law stood next to her, his eyes never leaving hers.

"Be still, little sub. Your new buyer wants to see how well your pussy takes being fucked. Don't move and be very quiet. Do this for me. Don't embarrass me by crying out or trying to get away. Spread your legs wider. A little more. That's it. Concentrate on keeping your balance. Your new Master isn't through with you yet."

Remembering the woman on the stage, and her Master's words for her, Courtney nodded, the strength in Law's eyes helping her to settle enough to go on.

Her orgasm remained just out of reach, and she didn't want to come and bring the fantasy to a halt before they'd finished.

She'd never felt so desired. So wanted. So needy.

How could she ever walk away from this?

She belonged to them for as long as they wanted her and would give them everything they needed.

Locking her knees, she nodded again, her love for them overwhelming her.

Zach seemed to know when she was ready because, as soon as she'd settled some, he began to push the dildo into her.

Biting her lip to hold back her cries, she struggled to remain still as he slowly filled her and began to fuck her with it. She was so close to coming that she panicked, knowing she couldn't hold back much longer.

Her hands shook, and holding her folds parted became more and more difficult, the brush of Zach's fingers against her clit as he fucked her with the dildo nearly sending her over.

She wanted to lean into Law, but she knew she wasn't permitted to move. Looking up at him, she blinked back tears of frustration. "I'm gonna come. Please."

Law's eyes narrowed, becoming icy and cold in a heartbeat. "Don't you dare! He's not through with you yet. Don't you dare embarrass me that way."

Caught up in the fantasy, Courtney nodded again, crying out when the dildo began to vibrate. Alarmed, she closed her eyes, fighting not to come. "I can't. I can't. I can't stop it."

A heartbeat before she went over, Zach pulled the dildo from her and stood, eyeing her coldly. "She really is undisciplined. Does she think this is for her?"

Law slapped her ass. "I apologize. I haven't owned her for very long. Her passions sometimes get the upper hand."

Shaking his head, Zach moved in behind her, making Courtney shake even harder. "You said her ass is broken in?"

"Barely."

"I'm an ass man, and if I buy her, her ass is going to be filled and fucked often. I need to see if she can take it."

Gripping Courtney's chin, Law turned her face to his, the warning in his dark eyes unmistakable. "She'll take it. She'll take whatever you do to her. She won't move, and she sure as hell won't come."

Oh God!

He was going to do it!

The tingling sensation started in her clit, and panicking, she took several deep breaths, somehow pushing it back.

"Bend her over."

Law retrieved a chair from the other side of the room and placed it in front of her. "Hands flat on the seat of that chair. Knees locked."

Grateful for his help, Courtney bent and pressed her hands on the seat of the chair, needing it to balance herself. Acutely aware that her position left her ass vulnerable, she curled her toes into the soft carpet, squeezing her eyes tight against what she knew came next.

"I need to inspect her ass first."

"Be my guest."

Oh God!

Even though she'd braced for it, the thrust of Zach's finger, coated with cold lube, left her gasping.

"She's tight." Zach's voice, cold and deep, sent a shiver through her, a shiver that combined with the shivers running up and down her spine as he pushed against the inner walls of her ass as though testing their resilience. "Very nice. Has she ever had a vibrating dildo in her ass?"

"No. We haven't gotten that far yet."

The sound of the dildo being turned on had Courtney shaking even harder.

"Well, she'll be fucked with one now. I don't want her to move."

Law slapped her ass several times, heating it and making her puckered opening tingle. "Stay still. Do you need me to hold you?"

Courtney knew she'd never make it on her own, and the fantasy of being restrained excited her even more. "Yes. Please. I'm gonna come."

Law sighed, but his hands shook as they moved over her ass. "We'd better move to the bed." With a strong arm around her waist, he lifted her, draping her over his lap at the edge of the bed, leaving her legs dangling.

Pressing her face against the covers to muffle her cries, she fisted her hands in the bedding, gasping when Zach stepped between her legs to keep them wide while Law held her down, pulling her ass cheeks wide.

"She's ready."

The feel of the vibrating dildo against her puckered opening had Courtney kicking her legs, but nothing could stop it from going into her.

Muffling her screams of pleasure into the thick bedding, she felt the dildo being pushed relentlessly into her ass, forcing the tight ring of muscle to burn and give way.

Almost immediately, Zach began fucking her with it, the sensation so intense and carnal that she came almost at once.

But he didn't stop.

Her ass clamped down on the dildo as she came, making her feel even fuller and intensifying the vibrations against the inner walls of her bottom.

Nothing had ever felt so naughty. So decadent.

Nothing had ever made every nerve ending in her body explode with pleasure over and over until she could no longer fight it.

Her screams into the bedding became hoarser and more ragged, the tingling sensations in her ass and clit making her brain go numb.

She couldn't kick any longer, her body worn out as the sparks of pleasure kept erupting.

She came over and over, one orgasm barely releasing her from its grip before she found herself caught up in another.

At that moment they owned her. Body and soul.

They could do whatever they wanted to do to her, and she would give them whatever they wanted.

With a moan of surrender, she slumped, her body and mind giving in to them.

* * * *

Law heard her moan, felt the way her body slumped, and knew she finally belonged to them. "She surrendered."

Zach's eyes seemed to glow, the pleasure in them sharp. "She did." Easing the dildo from her, he turned it off and tossed it aside, reaching for the vibrator they'd bought earlier that day. "Turn her over."

Law smiled. "Don't you think she's had enough?"

Zach grinned. "One more. This time, we'll both watch her face and see her surrender."

Courtney moaned as they flipped her but didn't open her eyes. A shiver went through her when Law parted her folds again, but she didn't lift a hand to stop him.

"Courtney?"

"Hmm."

"One more and then you can sleep."

She whimpered but made no move to stop them.

To his delight, she lifted her arms above her head and gripped the bedspread in her tiny fists. "Whatever you want. I'm yours."

Zach grinned. "We're going to have to do this to her more often." With a flick of his thumb, he turned on the vibrator, earning another moan from the woman they both loved. Touching it to her clit, Zach watched her face, his eyes shining with love for her as she went over again with a long whimper. "That's my good girl."

Law sucked in a breath as the Dominant inside him broke completely free.

She was his. Theirs. Completely.

Plans for her future had already been put in motion.

She was his woman—and, soon, his wife.

Chapter Twenty-One

Law carried his sleeping woman into the bedroom that had been remodeled, smiling at her moan at being disturbed. "It's okay, baby. We're home."

When Zach pulled the covers back, Law lowered her to the center of the king-sized bed and began to undress her.

Zach grinned and tossed her dress aside. "I don't think we're gonna be having any conversations with her tonight."

Law stripped out of his own clothes and tossed them aside. "Tomorrow's soon enough. I'm beat. We'll talk to her in the morning."

Zach threw his own clothes toward a chair. "It's a good thing we had the limo bring us home. I saw Ace's truck in the driveway. He's having a rare night off, so I'm glad we didn't bother him to pick us up at the airport."

"Hmm. Yeah. We'll let him know we're home in the morning."

Pleasantly tired, and looking forward to proposing to Courtney in the morning, Law checked her again to make sure she slept soundly before allowing himself to drift off to sleep—only to wake minutes later to the smell of smoke.

"What the fuck?" He threw the covers aside just as Zach leapt from the bed.

Grabbing his trousers, Law rushed to the door and flung it open, his heart pounding nearly out of his chest when he was confronted by a wall of flames. Slamming it shut, he whipped around to his brother, trying to keep the panic out of his voice when he saw that Courtney woke up. "Zach, we're trapped in here. I'm gonna try the window."

Coughing, he hurriedly stepped into his pants and raced for the window, throwing it open. The sight that met him scared him to death.

Fire leapt from all around the house, but he could see no other way out. "We've gotta go out through this."

Turning, he saw that Courtney sat huddled in the bed, staring at him wide-eyed while Zach, who'd already thrown on his pants, came out of the bathroom with a wet sheet, which he hurriedly wrapped around Courtney.

Lifting her high against his chest, Zach strode toward him as Law ripped the burning curtains from the window. "Let's get the hell out of here."

A siren blared in the distance, but Law knew that he couldn't wait. "This old house is going up fast. Son of a bitch." Relieved to see Ace outside, frantically spraying a hose, Law turned. "Ace is here." Turning, he yelled out the window. "Ace!"

Ace turned, his eyes going wide in horror when he saw them. Running toward them with the hose, he sprayed all around the window, fighting the flames. "Get the hell out of there! The whole house is going."

Law turned. "I'm going out. Ace is spraying the hose over here. We've got to get out before this thing collapses. Hand her to me as soon as I'm out."

Law didn't have the time to comfort Courtney, but he shot her a smile of reassurance before climbing out the window.

The cold water from the hose drenched him almost immediately, and without hesitation, he turned back, taking Courtney from Zach's arms. Turning again, he raced past Ace. "Get Zach the fuck out of there."

* * * *

Sitting on Ace's porch with Courtney in his lap, Zach watched the firemen put out the last of the fire.

Hope touched his shoulder again as she had over a dozen times in the last half-hour. "Thank God you're all all right."

Zach took her hand in his, looking up to see that she'd started crying again. "We're fine, honey. Why don't you sit down?"

She'd been a bustle of activity, getting blankets and getting Courtney dressed in some of her clothes. She'd handed out bottles of water and kept touching them as if to reassure herself that they were still there. "I can't believe this. Thank God Ace went over with that hose. I don't know how he knew about the fire. We were sound asleep."

Ace, who stood in the yard, grim-faced as he watched all the activity, turned to give his wife the smile she needed. "I keep telling you people that nothing goes on in my town that I don't know about. Now, sit down before you fall down."

He turned to Zach. "The paramedics are here. I want you all checked out."

"We're fine. We'll get Courtney checked out."

Ace's jaw clenched. "I said *all* of you. You'll let them look you over if I have to hold you down for them to do it." His gaze shifted to Hope. "I told *you* to sit down."

Law moved his chair closer, running his hand over Courtney's leg as he looked up at their sister-in-law. "Ace is really rattled. Sit down, honey. I haven't seen him like this often, but he'll be a bear for days. He walked right into those flames with nothing but that little hose. Christ, I'm glad he was there."

Zach lifted Courtney's hand to his lips, pleased that she'd finally stopped shaking. "I can't believe he didn't get burned."

Hope snorted. "No flame would dare."

Increasingly nervous at Courtney's continued silence, Zach bent to whisper to her. "Are you okay, baby? You're too quiet."

"I'm fine. The house is gone." Her lower lip trembled. "I'm just glad Aunt Sally wasn't alive to see it."

Zach looked up to see Rafe Delgatto striding toward Ace, holding the arm of an older man, who appeared to be in handcuffs. "What the hell?"

Courtney stiffened.

Zach had never been quite sure how his brother did it, but Ace shifted his stance, somehow appearing larger and more menacing—a threat to the man in handcuffs and a protective wall between him and the others.

Rafe glanced at the porch. "We called the fire company as soon as we saw the flames. Saw this man leaving the scene. He smells like gas and has empty gas canisters in his car." He met Zach's gaze. "Is she okay?"

Courtney jumped from his lap, taking several hurried steps back toward the front door.

"Dad?"

Stunned, Zach gaped at her, the fear in her eyes and in her voice infuriating him. "That's your father?"

Ace nodded, turning slightly. "Yes. I recognize him from the picture I have of him hanging in the station. Keep her up there."

* * * *

Courtney stood frozen, staring at the man who'd terrified her for most of her life.

With Law and Zach at her side, she didn't fear him nearly as much.

She felt everyone's eyes on her as she shook off Law's and Zach's hold, moving away from them to the porch steps. She couldn't take her eyes from her father, and holding the railing, she made her way down to him on legs that shook.

Still struggling to come to terms with the fact that he'd actually burned her house down, almost killing her, Law and Zach, she watched his eyes as she approached him.

Aware of Law, Zach, and Ace close behind her, she stopped several feet from her father and waited until he looked at her.

Curiously numb, she shook her head, drawing on her lovers' strength to confront her father. "Why?"

Her father tried to lunge closer, but Rafe held firm. "Because it should have been *mine*! Because you weren't going to give me any of the money from it. I earned it. Not you. What have you ever done for it but spread your legs for those two?"

Ignoring the insult, she held her arm out when Law and Zach started toward her father. "You hate me that much? You hate me so much that you would have killed me for it?"

Shaking his head, her father blinked back tears. "No. I didn't know you were here. I swear. I wouldn't have hurt you. I heard them talking when they were working on the house. You weren't supposed to be back yet."

Blinking back the tears, he smiled, an evil smile that sent a chill up her spine. "Now you can't live here. You won't collect."

Courtney smiled back, the hands on her back and shoulders giving her the strength she needed. "Neither will you."

Law stepped forward. "She'll live here. Tomorrow, we'll get a trailer and she can live in it *on* the property until she fulfills her obligations to the will."

Her father snarled. "You really want that property, don't you?" He turned to Courtney, his eyes frantic. "They're only using you! Can't you see that, you dumb bitch!"

With a growl, Zach lunged at her father, but Ace nudged him hard, his eyes cold as they met Rafe's.

"Get him out of here. Book him. Arson and three counts of attempted murder."

Courtney watched the deputy lead her father away, the lump in her throat threatening to choke her.

Law led her back to the porch and handed her a bottle of water before settling her on his lap. "Drink this. Just lean on me. Everything's going to be fine."

Sipping the water, Courtney stiffened when one car and truck after another pulled into the driveway and yard of Ace's house. "What in the world? Who—"

Law pulled her against him, kissing her forehead. "Friends. Neighbors. We stick together here."

Courtney knew some of the people who'd arrived and was quickly introduced to others.

Jesse Tyler and her husbands, two of the biggest men Courtney had ever seen, Clay and Rio, arrived.

Gracie and her three husbands came from the diner, handing out coffee and sandwiches.

Marshall, Joseph, and Carter Garrison were introduced as the new deputies. Marshall smiled. "We've already met, haven't we?"

Courtney nodded, meeting Zach's and Law's questioning looks. "He was with Ace at the park that day."

Hunter and Remington Ross, she recognized from the club. After checking to make sure she was okay, they joined Ace.

When the paramedics arrived, it seemed that everyone there had to check to make sure none of them had any injuries.

Ethan Sullivan and Brandon Weston arrived with more blankets, food, and an offer to stay at their hotel.

She met Lucas Hart, Devlin Monroe, and Caleb Ward from Desire Securities, who had a long conversation with Law and Zach.

Of course, Boone, Chase, Sloane, Cole, and Brett arrived.

The women gathered on the porch while the men hovered in the yard, all deep in conversation.

Chase stared at the now burned house and shook his head before turning to her. "You didn't even get to enjoy the remodel."

Courtney blinked, accepting another cup of coffee. "You did more work?"

Zach grinned and shook his head. "She was sound asleep when we got here. She didn't see a thing."

By mutual consent, everyone cleared out about an hour later, leaving Courtney, Law, Zach, Ace, and Hope alone on the front porch of Ace and Hope's house.

Sitting on Zach's lap, Courtney stared toward the remaining ashes. "I can't believe that it's gone. I wonder what's going to happen now."

Law rose from his chair, reaching into his pocket as he shared a look with Zach over her head.

Zach's lips touched her cheek. "What's going to happen now is that you're going to marry us."

Courtney gasped when Law pulled a small box out of his pocket and opened it, revealing a huge square-cut diamond ring. Tears blurred her vision, and her mouth opened and closed several times, but nothing came out.

Law knelt in front of her, removing the ring from the box and taking her hand in his. "Will you marry us?"

Holding her breath, Courtney looked into his eyes, amazed at the love she saw shining there. She turned to look at Zach, seeing the same love in his expectant look.

"You really want to marry me?"

Zach smiled. "We really do. Say yes."

"But I don't even know if I'm going to inherit the property now."

Law tugged her hand. "It doesn't matter. We don't care about the property. You're what we care about."

Courtney nodded, love for both of them bubbling inside her. "Yes."

Hope gasped. "I think I'm gonna cry."

Minutes later, after congratulations and hugging, Ace and Hope went inside, leaving Law, Zach, and Courtney alone on the porch.

"I'm glad the house is gone."

Law pulled her closer, running a hand up and down her back. "You are? Why?"

"Most of the bad memories I have of this town came from there. I want to start fresh."

Zach, who'd pulled her legs onto his lap, rubbed her knee. "We'll make good memories now. We'll start fresh."

Courtney sighed and leaned back against Law's arm. "I love you, you know? Both of you. I love you so much that it hurts sometimes."

The tension Courtney hadn't been aware of in Law's body eased.

"It's about time you said it."

Zach grinned. "I knew it that day at the penthouse. You wanted the pleasure but not the affection. I knew that day that it was because you were scared because you'd realized that you loved us."

Happier than she'd ever thought possible, Courtney giggled. "You're way too observant. I'll never be able to keep any secrets from you, will I?"

Law smiled and bent to take her lips with his. "Nope. Not a chance because your husbands are going to be watching you like hawks."

Epilogue

Courtney giggled, holding on to the hands of the men she'd married that morning. "Why do I have to wear a blindfold? I thought we were going to go see the lawyer before we left for Florida. Where are we going?"

Zach chuckled. "You sure have a lot of questions. You have to wear a blindfold because we have a surprise for you. We *are* going to see the lawyer because we know how much it's been eating at you now that you've seen the plans for the house."

Law lifted her hand to his lips. "We're going to fly to Florida right after, and as for where we're going—right here."

Pulled to a stop, Courtney shifted restlessly. "Okay. Where's my surprise?"

Hands at the back of her head pulled the blindfold loose, and when she opened her eyes, she saw Law stick it into his pocket.

Grinning, he bent to kiss her. "We'll need that later."

Zach turned her, both men stilling on either side of her.

Courtney stared in disbelief, turning to look around the adjoining buildings to make sure she wasn't mistaken. "This building—this is where my father's ice cream shop was. It looks so different."

Law hugged her, watching her closely. "It is. Same spot, but we had the other torn down. Every piece of wood, every nail has been replaced. It's for your flower shop."

Courtney gasped. "What? My own flower shop?" She started crying and found she couldn't stop. "I can't believe this!" She looked at each of them, wondering if she'd ever get used to being married to such two amazing men. "You did this for me?"

Zach grinned and hugged her. "I'm sure as hell not gonna run a flower shop. You have to pick out the sign, though. We had no idea what you wanted to call it."

Courtney smiled through her tears, so touched that she trembled. "How about *Bloom of Desire?*"

Law smiled indulgently. "Sounds perfect."

Zach nodded. "Great for a flower shop, but it's a little tranquil compared to what we've been through."

Courtney laughed, as she knew he'd meant her to, easing the tension. "That would be X-rated, Zach."

Law dug a key out of his pocket and handed it to her. "And something with a hell of a lot more heat. Come on. Let's go inside so you can look around, but you're not getting started until we get home from our honeymoon."

* * * *

Courtney looked up from the letter, staring at Mr. Franks in disbelief. "I don't understand. Are you sure this is right?"

Sitting back in his chair, the lawyer glanced at Law and Zach sitting on either side of her, meeting their frowns with a smile. "It's right. You read it yourself. The property's yours."

Law squeezed her hand. "Read it, baby."

Courtney nodded and had to wipe away tears and swallow the lump in her throat before she could begin. "It's a letter from my aunt."

Zach ran a hand over her hair. "Read it, honey."

Courtney cleared her throat again and began to read.

My dearest Courtney,

If you're reading this letter, then you've done just what I wanted you to do.

You've fallen in love.

That's the greatest gift I could have ever given to you, and I want you to treasure that love as much as I've treasured my love for your uncle.

I hope you understand now why I wanted so much for you to live in Desire.

I wanted you to have the kind of love I had, the kind of love that means something more than with most people.

Now you'll be part of a town that will protect you and part of a loving family that will make you happy all the rest of your days.

Take advantage of every minute with your lover. You never know how much time you have, so make every minute count.

I love you so much, Courtney, but now you've found the love that can only be found between a man and a woman.

The property is yours, of course. It always was. I just wanted you to have the chance to have what I had.

Love—the most important thing in the world.

Love,
Aunt Sally

Courtney choked several times as she read it, and when she finished, she cried so hard that she threw herself into Zach's waiting arms.

Running his hands up and down her back, Zach blew out a breath. "What a hell of a woman."

Lifting her head, she smiled through her tears. "She was. God, I miss her."

Law pulled her against him and stood, shaking the lawyer's hand. "Thank you."

Mr. Franks smiled and inclined his head. "A pleasure. Take good care of her. She's just like her aunt, and women like that are hard to find."

Law touched his lips to Courtney's temple, his hand tightening possessively at her waist. "We know. We've spent a lifetime looking for her."

THE END

WWW.LEAHBROOKE.NET

ABOUT THE AUTHOR

When Leah Brooke's not writing, she's spending time with family, friends and her furry babies.

For all titles by Leah Brooke, please visit
www.bookstrand.com/leah-brooke

Siren Publishing, Inc.
www.SirenPublishing.com

Lightning Source UK Ltd.
Milton Keynes UK
UKOW06f0813120217
294173UK00015B/413/P